Edge of

Ridiculous

Anne Coffer

LeeLoo Publishing / Texas

LeeLoo Publishing™
http://leeloopub.com/

First Print Edition, 2017

ISBN-10: 0998884301
ISBN-13: 978-0998884301

I dedicate this book to my husband, Ben.

CONTENTS

ACKNOWLEDGMENTS

Where to begin? First, my parents and grandparents. When I wanted to be a paleontologist, they bought me books on dinosaurs. When I wanted to be an Egyptologist, they took me to museums. When I said I wanted to be an astronaut, they taped episodes of NOVA. (By now you can tell how totally cool I was.) No matter what I've wanted to be, I'm proud to say my family has never told me I couldn't. Whether it was realistic or not. Thank you for always encouraging my dorky and creative spirit.

I want to thank my husband for being a strong support during my trials of doubt. My best friends Rebecca and Marquel for being the driving forces behind my creativity and courage. I seriously couldn't do anything without you guys in my daily life.

My mentors and fellow writers of the Write Right Critique Group in Lubbock, Texas, thank you. (Here's looking at you Mary Andrews!)

And the staff of Denny's on 50th and Slide in Lubbock, Texas, because I said I would say hi.
So, hi!

1. Bob…I mean, Asrieth.

It's May 23rd, 2008.

I check my watch. *2:37. Need to leave in three minutes.* I stand behind Rachael, my sister-in-law, to watch her fill out my online dating profile. She fills in female, 29, and single. I roll my eyes. She licks her lips as she uploads a picture of me from last Christmas. Probably because it was the last time I didn't wear my work uniform or sweats. Not to mention I'm about fifteen pounds heavier. Next she lets the world know I'm 5 feet 5 inches and an Aries. I study her with critical eyes and narrow them as she fills out my body type.

"Can't you lie a little?" I ask. "I don't think anyone expects you to be honest there."

She pauses and glances over her shoulder to me, as if she's forgotten I'm here.

"What?"

I shake my head, "Never mind."

"You're average. There's nothing wrong with that." She fills in my eye and hair color next. Brown and brown.

Oh I'm average all right. Don't forget to mention one boob is bigger than the other while you're at it. "You know, I don't think I'm ready for this."

She shakes her head and continues. No tattoos. No pets. Hobbies…

She spares me a glance for prompting.

"Reading. Movies. I don't know."

Rachael nods and embellishes. *I wish I was half as interesting as she makes me sound.* Favorite food. Favorite color. Favorite everything. Don't smoke. I work for a major retail chain. Some college. I live alone in Lubbock. I identify as Christian: Other. Only speak English. One sibling: a younger brother. My entire life conglomerates into a single page on the internet.

I glance at my watch again. *2:41. I'm going to be late.*

"Okay!" Rachael stretches in my computer chair, clasping her hands. "What do you want in a mate?"

"Phillip."

She nods, unsure of how to respond. "You agreed to do this…"

I know she's only trying to help and so I keep my irritation to a minimum.

"After you both badgered me about it—"

"You said after your birthday and it's been almost two months."

"I know." I glance at my watch again. "I have to go. I'm going to be late. Can we just save our progress and finish later?"

She's not satisfied, but nods. "All right. Call me tomorrow?"

"Sure."

"You know what they say about West Texas," my coworker begins. "If you don't like the weather, wait two hours and it'll change."

I snort and cast my eyes back downward to the stack of $20 bills I lost count of to begin again, adding them in intervals of five. The manager twirls his keys as he resumes locking up the sliding doors at the front of the building. My coworker continues counting his register next to mine and we remain in silence as numbers fly through our dull brains.

I finish first and close the till.

As I fantasize about the delectable TV dinner and sweatpants waiting for me at home, I take a moment to watch the other drones of the closing shift walk in and out of isles stacked with electronics. The DVDs are straight and CDs in order. Prime and ready for a careless customer to rifle through them tomorrow. Computer monitors are dark and cold, a stark contrast to the bright glimpse of what they offer the retinas of customers throughout the day with their aquarium screensavers. When the loops of movies and games and advertisements are shut off and the TVs powered down, the store is eerie. I prop myself against the counter and wait for the manager to collect my till.

He's in a hurry tonight and we aren't long.

I head out to my car, small purse slung over my shoulder and keys in hand. It's nearly midnight and the loop is quiet. My Ford Focus is dark and cold as I slide into it. I blink a moment. Sometimes my motions are automatic and I don't recall my actions. Such as un-locking the door or throwing my purse over to the passenger seat.

I sigh and turn on the engine.

It's May. It should be warmer than this. It hit the low

90s today and now I wish I brought a jacket to work. The engine warms and I turn the AC over to the heater. I chafe my arms and fantasies of pizza by-products coupled with ranch and the internet call to me. I close my eyes. They're so heavy.

Driving down the loop late at night mesmerizes. When you don't have traffic to focus on, you lose yourself in the rhythm of yellow lights passing by. I note my exit and signal to slow down and wonder why it's so difficult a task for people. Signaling.

Down the off-ramp and in the beam of headlights a man waves. I slam on my brakes, jerking the wheel, veering my Focus to the left embankment. The front of my car clips down and the grass and dirt halt it. My air bag deploys and I slam back against the seat. I can only lie still a moment.

Can I breathe? God, my nose hurts. And my neck. *Hope neither is broken.*

I wave away the haze of powder and punch at the inflated bag protruding from my steering wheel.

"Ass hat," I spit, then stroke it. "Sorry, thanks for saving me."

Talking to inanimate objects is a habit of mine since I'm not often talking to animate ones except in the context of work; and those don't count. *Maybe Rachael should have included that tidbit in my profile.*

I open the door and fall out of my seat onto the soft damp grass to cough, breathing fresh cold air, and shiver. Oil and steam leaking from my engine are dominant aromas. I bury my face towards the ground and have regrets the moment I breathe in. The man who waved me down stands over me.

"Hi," his eyes are wide and light. I can't tell the color in the yellow glow of the streetlights.

"Hi." I wipe my mouth with the back of my hand as I study him. He's tall and broad-shouldered. His blonde hair is cropped.

He's hot.

"Are you all right?" he squats down next to me and reaches out to my face.

I smack his arm away, "Yes. What about you?"

"You didn't hit me."

"I mean flagging me down in the middle of the road like an idiot." I lay back, resting my forearm over my eyes, "Oh my God my head hurts."

"Oh, that."

Honk! Honk! Honk!

I move my arm. He's still close to me.

"So what's going on? What's your name?" I ask. *I need it for insurance purposes. Of course. Right. Definitely need his contact information. For insurance. Of course.*

"…Bob?" He smiles.

"That is so fake."

"Hey," he looks around. Behind him a line of cars stop on the ramp. "Where am I anyway?"

I grimace and sit up, "Quaker and the loop."

"Long name," he narrows his eyes. "Is there an abbreviation? I've never been here before."

I laugh, "It's the street. You don't know what city we're in?" He straightens up to stand over me. I'm not sure if he's actually tall or appears to be from my current position.

He doesn't answer me. The closest car pulls over to the side to allow the others to pass by in the big ass hurry Lubbock drivers are always in. The driver's side door opens and an old man bends down into the car. The dome light of the white Cadillac is on and he debates with his wife. She's on a Blackberry with shaky, unsure hands.

I study Bob, "You really don't know?"

"I don't," he frowns.

"You have amnesia?" I rub my neck. *It hurts so bad.*

"Not exactly."

I roll my eyes, "You're lost?"

"I can't really explain."

The old man shuts the door leaving his wife in the dark. The unnatural glow of the phone lights up her wrinkled face. He makes his way towards us on uneasy footing.

"So what can you explain?" I ask. I hold up my hand to silence any reply, "Never mind." *I can't expect much from a man who waved me down via dumbassery.* "Lubbock. You're in Lubbock, Texas."

"Is Texas the country?"

"Some people seem to think so."

He shifts from foot to foot, opening and closing his mouth several times. I know he wants to say something and so I wait for it. *I still need to exchange numbers with him. For insurance, of course.*

I study him. Aside from tall, handsome, and in the dark, his clothes don't fit. The pants are too short and shirt too tight in the shoulders.

Bob twirls on his heel as the old man walks up. His breathing labors and I fear he'll fall over.

"Are you all right young lady?"

I smile, "Yes, I think so. Thanks."

"My wife's calling 911." He sizes up the stranger next to him, "What happened?"

Bob opens his mouth and hesitates.

"Sorry." He turns tail and runs.

"Hey! Hey!" I try to stand and my head spins. I tumble around the grassy embankment. The old man tells me to stay put, but anger drives me onward toward the stranger. He grows smaller and darker in the distance until he disappears. Leaving me with a wrecked car and hiked insurance rate.

Bastard.

I'm. So. Mad.

The stranger is indeed good at what he is, being strange and nowhere to be found. I have only a sore neck to show for injury, which is lucky, but arguing with the insurance company for two days about the repairs on my car isn't. My poor little Focus is a parked wreck in my driveway and the outcome of arguing where to get it repaired. At least they towed it to my house. I have enough of a headache without dealing with the man who caused the entire incident missing. The old couple who helped me out came through as witnesses for the accident report, but it doesn't help to track him down and pay for damages.

"I swear if I find that worthless piece of sh—" I purse my lips. I'm still on the phone with a police officer. *I need to at least pretend I'm an adult.* He gives me his sympathies and informs me they will be in touch if they find any leads. I thank him and shut my flip phone.

It's a hot day. The window unit of the house I rent from Mrs. Morgan chugs away as I sprawl on the couch.

Knock! Knock! Knock!

I jump. My eyes are heavy. *I must have dozed.* I set my phone down on the coffee table and peel off of my fake leather couch to pad across the worn wooden floors of the living room. I hesitate when the knocking resumes with urgency to a steady pounding. Sneaking up to peer through the peephole, I stare a moment. The thick glass distorts the image of the last person I expect to see. I open the door.

"You have some nerve—"

Bob pushes against the door knocking me off balance. I flail back to regain it. He shuts the door and leans against it. He's taller than I recall. Over a head above me. His blonde tresses are light against his tan skin. A blue flannel shirt that's seen better days stretches tight over his torso with jeans cut off at the knee.

I quirk my face. *He's wearing jorts.*

His dark eyes scan the room before resting on me. I blush under his scrutiny and realize this is the first time he sees me clearly. He takes a step forward.

I blink. *I thought his eyes were blue for some reason. No matter. Intruder!*

I ball my hand into a fist and put all of my weight behind a punch to his strong, handsome, attractive jaw. He sprawls back and trips over his own feet, tumbling onto the wooden floor in front of the door. I turn to grab the bat propped in the corner for this type of occasion, and as I whirl back around he's sitting up and rubbing his jaw. He glares at me, but doesn't move. I stand over him holding the bat up in the air.

"What do you think you're doing, *Bob*?"

"Okay. I know this looks bad—"

"Bad? *Bad*? Who in the hell *are* you? Get out of my house! I'm calling the cops!" I waver. A swimming force hits my head as though a tsunami rocks my brain around my skull. Calmness overcomes me. I'm weak in the knees. This sensation alarms me. I chalk it up to adrenaline, but it bothers me all the same. My heart thuds as I watch him close his eyes and take a deep breath. I hope my neighbor and landlord, Mrs. Morgan, saw him.

My eyes shoot to the picture window in the front of the house. Sirens blare down the road. I cock my brow and smile as they increase in volume. Bob tenses. The picture window is next to the front door, and so he leans over to look out. Neither of us can see beyond the thick, gauzy white curtains.

I really like those curtains. Such a great price too.

I snap back to the present and my smile fades as the sirens pass us by. They quiet as the cars drive further away. This time he smirks, and I don't like it.

"What's your name?" he asks.

"None of your business."

"I'll tell you mine," he offers.

"Oh, you mean it's not Bob?" *Sarcasm on full power.*

"No. My name is Asrieth."

"I think I prefer Bob. At least I can pronounce it." I lower my aching arms. My muscles burn as I rest the end of the bat to the floor. *I need to work out.*

"Bob is fine too."

"Quit distracting me from the fact that you're in my house as an intruder." I grip the bat, raising it again. My arms tremble. He smiles at me. "Seriously, you're freaking me out."

He pushes off the floor and stands straight. I peer up at him and wonder how many times I can pummel him before he takes me out.

"I know this is strange, but I'm asking you for a favor," he puts his hands up in surrender.

I don't buy it.

"I think I did enough when I didn't run you over. And crashed my car in doing so. And how in the *hell* did you find me?"

"That was a happy accident. I was...taking a stroll

when I saw your car. I recognized it."

"A nice little stroll from the cops?"

"That is not what's important here."

"What is?" I wonder if I can make the fifteen foot dash to my cellphone lying on the coffee table behind me before he catches me.

"I've no intention of hurting you. I need you to hear me out. If you help me, I'll definitely make it worth your while."

This sounds better, but I can't be sure.

"I don't know you or anything about you except that maybe you're crazy and or on some kind of heavy drugs."

He chuckles.

My eyes widen, "Yeah, that *really* isn't convincing me you're sane."

He nods and steps back towards the picture window. My eyes flicker to his hands as he shoves them into his pockets.

Jorts. I keep a straight face.

"What can I do?" he asks. "To convince you that I'm not what you think I am." He glances at the bat I'm wielding with shaky arms. "Except let you beat the shit out of me. I'm not willing to do that. In fact, I don't think a sane person would."

"Fair enough," I lower the bat. My arms are on fire. "But I *will* do it if you try something. Just know I'm capable!"

He rubs the red spot on his jaw, "I don't doubt that. So, what's your name? Seriously."

"I don't know if I want to tell you that."

"If you don't I'll make one up."

"Well, if you do please be creative this time."

"Okay. George."

"George? That's not even the right sex," I raise the bat. *Oh the buuuurrrrn.* His hands shoot back into the air.

"It isn't? Well, I like it. It suits you. George," he grins.

I have a funny feeling he doesn't find me all that threatening.

I raise my brow. My fingers loosen on the bat and I lower it, resting the blunt tip on the wood floor.

He seems…nice enough. Strange, weird, attractiiiiive, but not a creeper. He relaxes and lowers his hands. I find myself leaning on the bat like a walking stick. *When did I do that?* My barriers, the very alert system meant to keep me alive, lower.

I sigh, "Okay. Fine. What's your story?"

"Can I have a seat? I've been running—er, strolling for a while."

"Sure. Whatever." I'm too tired to hold up the bat as he saunters past me into the living room.

He plops onto the couch. Bob sinks into the cushions and lays his head back, mouth open, eyes closed. I glance to the window and remain in my spot.

"Well, go on."

"I'm looking for someone," his eyes shoot to my cellphone, then back to me. "And I'm not familiar with this area. If you can help me find him, I'll make it worth your while."

"Yeah, you said that. You're not into some illegal stuff are you? The mob or gangs or something? Cause if that's the case you can forget it."

"No. I'm only searching for someone. I have his first and last name. I know he's here. I just need to talk to him for a few minutes."

"About what?" I ask.

"You won't believe me."

11

"Probably. How did you end up on the road?"

He sighs and rubs his grimy face with his dirty hands. I cringe at the pores that must be suffocating beneath. I fight the compulsion to wash my face.

"You won't believe that either."

"So basically, and correct me if I'm wrong, you've told me nothing and expect me to help you find some random guy who you may or may not gut? You can't possibly expect me to help you. And why ask me anyway?"

His black brows furrow and he stares down at my stained coffee table.

I knew I shouldn't have gotten it in white. Wait, he's not a natural blonde.

"You asked me if I was okay. You seem like a decent person."

I disappoint myself. I should have a harder heart. He seems so sad sitting there staring at...*is that a coffee stain? I don't drink coffee!*

I don't take my eyes off the stain, "You don't know anyone?"

He shakes his head, "I don't."

I moan. *Damn my moral compass and compassion ...plus, he's hot.* I roll my eyes at my own shallow inclinations. *For all I know he's playing me. Like those guys at the mall selling lotion and bath salts with their charm.*

"I'm sorry, but until I know more I just...can't."

He glances up at me and nods, "I can understand. I suppose if a random man popped into my world—"

Wait. What?

"Wait, what? Your world?" *Did I hear that right?*

"City. Town. Road?" He smiles, forcing it. "Not world. That's silly."

"Oh no. I know what I heard. And no one says silly

anymore." I see what's going on. *He's either from another planet or absolutely crazy. No wonder he doesn't want to tell me. My eyes shift up as I ponder. He knows that sounded crazy. And don't crazy people not realize they're crazy? Isn't that what makes them crazy?*

Thoughts roll over in my mind while he watches me. *Now I'm the one who seems off their rocker. God knows what face I make while deep in thought.* I glance over to a small bookshelf next to the couch. Fantasy titles dominate the paperbacks and my heart flutters as I read through familiar titles. Little five by eight treasures of my heart.

"Oh, what the hell," I catch myself saying. I open my mouth and frown. I am compelled. I can't control what's coming out of my mouth as I—"Tell me everything. I won't turn you in. If nothing else it'll make an interesting story." My fingers trace my lips, trying to stop them from their involuntary movement. *I need chap stick.* I purse my lips together, resisting as I continue, "But if I declare you crazy you have to promise to leave me alone."

He cocks his head to the side and smirks, considering me.

"I'm sure you'll think me crazy. So I can't promise. You're the only person who's given me the time of day. I won't let you go so easy." His smile is charming, but the words preceding tinge it with creepiness.

"That's really not helping," I roll my eyes. "Just tell me already."

He pats the couch cushion next to him. I remain where I am. He frowns and leans forward, resting his elbows on his knees.

"Now that someone is willing to listen I hardly know where to begin." He pauses long enough for awkward silence. "Okay. I'm from Werdofium."

I suppress a giggle. *It sounds like weirdo. Fitting.*

His eyes narrow. I didn't suppress it *that* well.

"Anyway," he continues. "It's not a place you can find here. On Earth. It's another dimension or planet. Or both. We're not sure yet."

I nod.

"I came here through a portal. I'm looking for someone who escaped to this plane."

"Escaped?"

"Yeah."

"Is he a bad guy?"

"You could say that."

"And here I thought you were going to tell me there's a chosen one you need to take back to save you all."

He smiles, "No. It doesn't work like that. He escaped. I need to take him back to carry out his sentence. If I don't I face serious consequences."

I nod, "And, so, you're the police?"

"Not even close," he chuckles and shakes his head.

I cock my brow, "So more like a bounty hunter?"

He nods.

"You seem familiar with our language. Clothes. Even some customs."

"Ah. This isn't my first time here. To this plane. Lubbock, yes. Earth? No."

"And exactly how many planes have you been to?"

"My own and this one. Others exist, but I've no need to visit them."

He sounds reasonable. Assuming this is true.

"Well, if you're familiar with everything, how come you can't find the guy?"

"Oh that. Stupid really. I forgot my reading

glasses."

I guffaw, "Seriously?"

"Yes. Seriously," he points to the metal band at his neck. I notice his lips are off from his voice.

I jump back. *He's dubbed!* I've been watching his eyes the whole time.

"This is my translator to speak," he gestures to small metal loops cuffed to his ear cartilage, "And this is to understand. I forgot the glasses, so I can't read. I just have a name and city."

I blink. "That makes…sense. You need me to help you find the house? You can't search for or even read the address….street signs. Anything." *The marvel of literacy. How crippling it must be for those who can't read.*

He nods, "Exactly."

"And what about making it worth my while?"

"Oh. Yeah…" He rubs the back of his neck, "I haven't figured that part out yet. You're the first person who's even listened to me."

I roll my eyes, "Why don't you go back to weirdo town and get the glasses?"

"The portal's closed. When I met you the other night I just arrived. It won't open again until I've found him and I have a month, so…if you can find it in your kind, loving heart—"

I snort.

"—to let me stay here with you too."

"I'm hardly a charity."

He pouts.

Faker.

"You probably still think I'm crazy—"

"You are correct sir!"

"—but if you help me find Rinkai…well. You'll see."

"Rinkai equals bad guy, right?"

"Indeed."

"How does finding him prove your case?"

"Once I have him a portal will open. I won't have to wait. The sooner you help me find him the sooner I can be gone."

"So you have the ability to leave now?"

He puts up his hand, "I do, but only once. And I can't go back without him."

I glance down to his lips as he speaks. They still don't match the words. If I paid attention instead of staring into his dreamy eyes I'd notice sooner...*Dreamy eyes?* I scold myself and shake my head, trying to clear the constant vertigo that arrives with him.

I glance to the wall opposite the picture window. The dying rays of sunlight cast an orange glow over the numerous pictures I spent hours hanging. *They're still crooked.* At this point getting rid of him seems reward enough. *Even if he's pretty to look at.* Calling the cops will get me the same result. Vertigo flushes my brain and I lean on the bat. I have no control over what I say next.

"Okay. You can spend the night here."

I can't fight this dire feeling. This *need* to help him. Something is wrong. I am a rational individual, but a little voice deep in my mind wants adventure. As Rachael said, *I am very average. I dropped out of college to do what? Join the glamorous life of retail? Here is a handsome man asking for my help. How can I refuse him?*

The thoughts are in my head, but they are not my own.

2. Monster On The Mound

It's May 27th.

I glance at my watch. *3:57.* Three minutes and I can leave. I drum my fingers on the counter. It's a slow Tuesday afternoon and I'm anxious to return home. Hoping to find all of my items and windows intact. When I woke up this morning and rushed to get ready for work, all thoughts of Bob were gone and my motions automatic. I slept better than I had in years and still ran late. The lump of blankets on the couch went unnoticed and I didn't remember my house guest until driving to work.

I glance at a family approaching. Two grandparents and a small child. I smile as the indulgent grandmother gets her grandson a piece of candy. They buy the treat and are out the door. My coworker shakes his head and leans on the counter.

"What?" I ask.

He sighs and crosses his arms. He faces me, "I read about something today."

"Congratulations?"

"It depresses me. That's all."

"How?"

He smiles, but it's bitter, "It was an article about how all human deeds are influenced by the basic drive of selfishness. Even the good ones we think are selfless."

"What?" I can't help but to think of my recent charity to Bob.

"In the end we do good deeds to feel better about ourselves. Or to make others approve of our actions and I can't…find anything to argue against that."

"What about that grandma? She just wanted to make the boy happy."

"That's what made me think about it. It's a nice gesture, but it gives her pleasure to make him happy."

I nod.

"Every nice thing I've ever done for anyone in the end made me happy," he continues. "Anything I do for my kids or wife. It makes me happy to make them happy. I feel good. Even if I end up doing something I don't want to. Taking out the garbage for my wife pleases her and it makes me happy."

"I see." I notice the time and begin the process of clocking out, "I see why that depresses you."

"It ruins those moments knowing my own selfish drive is what makes them happen."

I bend down to pick up my purse and keys from beneath the counter.

"I can think of worse things that make a person happy. At least it's the well being of others that makes you happy and not their suffering. Your selfishness still benefits others. So feel better about that," I smile.

He nods, "See you tomorrow."

I slip out the side door before I'm caught by a clueless customer and get into my rental car. It's a Focus newer than mine. I turn the key and roll down the windows to let out the hot air built up from its time in the sun. I'm apprehensive to return home. I think of my own selfish reasons for helping Bob. *I want adventure. I want excitement. Maybe even a little romance.* I shake my head. I already gave romance a chance and the let down was life changing.

I turn the heater over to AC and flip open my phone to find another missed call from Rachael. I can't explain to her a total stranger is staying in my house. The man who caused my wreck no less. I'll continue to avoid her until this mess gets worked out. *Or until I have a con-vincing reason for harboring him. I still don't understand it myself.*

I find him out in the backyard exercising. As much as I want to witness what glistening muscles must be beneath the ill-fitting flannel shirt, his sweat seeps through the taught fabric. He perks up as I open the back door. I grip my purse and keys, eager to find if he's a figment of my desperate imagination, then drop my purse to the floor by the back door and walk outside, keeping hold of my keys.

"I think we need to find you something to wear."

He glances down at himself, "Why?"

I tick my head back towards the house, "I think I have something."

"All right."

He follows me inside to my bedroom. I take a deep breath and kneel in front of my dresser, wrapping my fingers around the nobs of the bottom drawer. *Phillip's drawer.* Bob stands behind me patiently. *He needs a shower.* I bite the inside of my cheek and pull the drawer open.

Over the clothes I know lay beneath is a layer of newspaper articles about Phillip's disappearance and death. I haven't opened the drawer in months and pain and regret and sadness overwhelm me. Tears blur my vision and I take a deep breath. Bob kneels on the floor next to me, his eyes rest on my face. He glances to the clippings of paper. His brows furrow.

"Are you all right?"

I nod and press my lips together. If I speak I will cry. Instead, I gather clippings into a pile and lay them on the carpet next to me. Hot tears slide down my cheeks and I ignore them as I rifle through Phillip's old clothes. I find a Marvel t-shirt and camouflage shorts and dig out some clean boxers and a pair of flip-flops. I pile them together and place the shoes on top to offer them to Bob.

His brows furrow as he takes them. He sits next to me not taking his eyes from mine.

I swallow and find my voice, "They're my boy-friend's. This is…was his overnight drawer." I still can't think of Phillip in past tense.

Bob nods. He glances down to the newspaper clippings. I pick them up and replace them in the drawer before closing it.

"Thank you. I'll take care of them," he says.

I nod and wipe my face. I stand up, my knees aching, and point to the bathroom.

"Now take a shower. You stink."

He smiles and gets to his feet, "Yes ma'am."

"You know how it all works?"

He pokes his head into the bathroom. I approach and turn on the switch.

He nods, "Similar to home. I think I've got it." He closes the door and water runs through pipes in the wall.

I go through the house to the back door and retrieve my purse. I pull out my cellphone and check the phone log to call Rachael.

"Hey," she sounds irritated. "About time you called me back."

"Yeah. Sorry."

"So when do you want me to come over?"

I bite my lip, "I don't want you to."

"Why not?"

"I know your intentions are good, but I'm not ready. I'm really not. I can't think of Phillip without…" On cue my breathing grows erratic, "Without getting worked up. I don't want to do that to anyone. It's unfair to the other person." *Assuming there will ever be another person.*

"You won't get over him if you—"

"Well it's my decision. Okay? It's my decision. I get to decide when I'm done grieving. Not you, not Anthony, not anyone."

The pause feels like years.

"Okay. You're right."

"Thank you." I take a deep breath, "Thank you. I'm sorry. I opened Phillip's drawer and I'm just not ready."

"I understand. Look, I need to go give junior a bath. I'll call you later, okay? We'll go to a movie or something."

"Okay."

"Just you and me, okay?"

I smile, "Okay. I'll talk to you later."

"Bye."

I shut my phone. My chest tightens. My face

crumples. I glance to the bathroom door and hold my breath to listen for running water. The shower's still on. I allow myself to sob. I wipe my red face. *I'm such a traitor to find Bob attractive and want to help him.* I'm glad he's here and all I can think about is my betrayal to Phillip for thinking so.

It's 5:37 and we sit down at my computer, Bob pulling a chair in from the dining room. Phillip's clothes are still a size or two too small, but they fit better than the others. I boot up the screen and type in my pass-word. Bob holds a scrap of paper withdrawn from the dirty pockets of his jorts. I bring up Google and he hands it to me.

J. Smith. I sigh.

"Is this all you have?"

He shrugs, "Yeah."

I gesture with the paper, "This is a very common name."

"It is?" He cocks his head to the side.

I'm irritated, but it's not his fault. *With a name like Asrieth I'm sure Smith is a weird name.* The white pages yield forty matches. I quirk my lips and glance at him. He watches my every move with a glower.

"Well, it's not as bad as I thought, but forty is still a large number. How are we going to do this?"

"How do you find where people live?" he asks.

"Hmm." The site I'm using gives me addresses if I pay for premium membership. Instead, I go to the website of the local phone book. Now there are over three-hundred results. "Pppppp."

"What's wrong?"

"This is going to be difficult. There's over three hundred possibilities and not all of them have a listed address."

He nods, "We have to try."

"Yeah. Yeah," I roll my eyes. "How are you gonna find this guy anyway? What if they don't open the door?"

"Ah. Easy. I can sense him."

I cock my brow, "Oh, well that's simple then, isn't it?"

He narrows his eyes, "Yes. You're giving me that face."

"What face?"

"The one where you don't believe me."

"I don't know why I shouldn't. I'm about to drive you to three hundred houses and hope for the best."

We're unsuccessful. *Surprise!* I pull eighty addresses from the phonebook to start with and we're on number seventeen. The sun sets and I study a paper map, trying to determine where the next address on the list is. Lubbock is a grid, so it's easy enough to find. I turn on the engine and put the gear in reverse. Bob stiffens in his seat. He does not like car rides.

I hand him the map and put the car into drive once we're on the residential street. He crumples it in his grip.

"You want to just go home?"

He shakes his head, "No. The sooner I find him the better."

"All right."

Other than the unpleasantness of the car ride itself, he scowls in worry.

"I'm sure we'll find him," I say.

"Yeah."

In the backseat sits the box of candy I bought to give unsuspecting homeowners the guise we're raising money for charity. It's a viable way to get them to open their doors. For those who buy some, I feel guilty. *I'll really donate their money to charity after this.*

We drive down the residential road in silence. Children play in front yards with their neighbors while adults relax on front porches with glasses of sun tea in their hands. Careful to watch the road, I glimpse the gathered groups enjoying this May evening.

I wish I had friends.

We try three more addresses to no avail and decide to go home. Twenty is a good number to start and I have work in the morning.

It's June 10th, 10:38 pm, and I pull into the drive-way in my new car.

Well, newer at least.

I wait for the garage door to open and pull in to turn off the headlights before killing the engine. Another missed call from Rachael blinks its notification on my phone. I'm in a bad mood. The closing shift always makes me grumpy. I fist the top of fast food bags and juggle them with drinks and my purse as I close the car door with my butt and moan. I forgot to close the garage door. I'm eager to get inside since I'm an hour behind. The last time I came home this late, Bob worried. He feared Rinkai got me and I don't want another episode.

The garage door hums down and I stumble inside. The glow of the muted TV lights up the living room. My eyes dart around for movement and find none. Bob's not on the couch in his usual spot. I worry and set down the food on the coffee table, shoving his lunch plate aside, and sit on the couch. On the coffee table's scratched surface sits a scribbled note.

"I be back," I read aloud with a smile.

In the two weeks he stayed with me I taught him the alphabet and important words. Just in case. And even though the phone is a strange concept, he learned the TV and remote in two days.

Sometimes he goes to the park down the street. I glance at my watch. *11:02.* I get up and grab the food on the coffee table before I pick up his drink and walk into the kitchen. On the way I spot the pile of gold ribbons he accumulated on my dining room table.

He's difficult to keep from Rachael. She's the only person in my life who knows something's off, but suspecting it's a new boyfriend, she hasn't said anything to me. I think she hopes one day I'll introduce her. *Fat chance.*

I'm still not sure if Rinkai or Werdofium are real, but I also don't care. I enjoy the company. *If Bob's crazy he's a harmless crazy.* He only does little things, like having me buy all of the gold ribbon I can find, but those little things don't hurt anyone. When I ask him about his world he's vague and changes the subject. I don't know if it's a gap in his insanity or a terrible place. Neither is an appetizing reason.

I sigh. *I don't blame him for living in a fantasy world.*

I pick out my dinner and leave his in the bag to set in the microwave and place his drink in the fridge. I take my food back to the couch and flip through the channels.

I start awake.

The TV's still on, but now a late night infomercial overtakes the programming. I roll my eyes. *Yes. I know I need to lose weight. I don't need you to remind me. Asshole.* I turn off the TV and look around. I glimpse my watch. *3:36.*

Now I worry. This is Bob's longest excursion from the house without me.

I hoist myself off the couch and decide it's time to go looking for him. As I change in my room I try to think back to my drive home. *Did I see him outside the corner store? No. Where did he go?* I toss my work clothes onto the floor and slip on jeans and a t-shirt and hoodie before pulling my hair into a loose ponytail, making my way to the shoe pile next to the garage door. My eyes dart between flip-flops and sneakers. *Adventure shoes? Yes.* I slip on my low-top Converse and knock over the bat I kept out in case Bob did turn out to be something bad. I pick it up and carry it with me before grabbing my purse and keys.

The summer air is hot and sticky.

I roll the windows down in my car so I can call out for Bob while I cruise around the neighborhood. A couple miraculously walking at this time of morning offer to help me find my dog. I politely decline.

Bob and I don't have a plan for him getting lost. He doesn't wander far from home.

I turn onto the next street and find the park. Maxey's parking lot is empty, but the lights over the baseball diamond for Little League are on. I glance at the clock in the dash. *4:55. There's no way a game is going right now.* Other than not knowing what time of year baseball happens, I do know this isn't right. I park and kill the engine, then glance over to my bat in the floorboard leaning against the passenger seat. I sigh. Bob isn't anywhere by the community center…*but I better go check the field.*

It hits me.

A feeling. More than a simple feeling. The molecules in my body will me forward towards the diamond. My chest heaves. It's oppressive. *If I don't leave the car it's going to fall into a giant crack that opens up beneath! I need to hurry!* I grab the bat and keys and eject myself from the car. I stumble away and whirl to face it. I blink, expecting the earth to open up and swallow it.

I wait.

Of course nothing happens. The doom disappears. I shake my head and pocket the keys and grip my bat. The spell of panic resides. I take deep breaths and approach the car. My feet still need to run away. My heart still pounds in my chest, but nothing happens. I lock the car door and close it and breathe outward, puckering my lips.

As anxious as I am about going to the diamond, I'm happy to leave Doom Car for a few minutes.

My sneakers crunch over the pebbles in the parking lot as I approach the community center. I pass and on the other side is the baseball field. I stop once it comes into view and squint as I'm not sure if what I see is real.

In the middle of the diamond, on the other side of the chain link fence, a little boy in a baseball uniform shuffles on the pitching mound. Equally weird, Bob stands on home plate. They lock in a stare.

"George, come here," Bob doesn't take his eyes off the boy.

My feet slide along the ground as an invisible tug drags me forward until I reach the fence. A force pushes me against the chain link fence and relents. I stick the toes of my Converse in the holes and climb over. I lose my footing on the way down and fall. Millions of invisible strings grip me and drag me towards Bob, forcing me to my feet, my head swimming, as an existential crisis approaches. I blink rapidly and without any will of my own, I'm next to Bob. He holds out his hand and I give him mine. He pulls me behind him and my feet plant to the ground. I gasp trying to regain control of my own body and glance down. I still grip my bat. *Somehow.*

The boy isn't over nine. His gold and black Little League jersey is clean, but fresh grass stains mar his white pants. He holds a baseball mitt in his left hand.

I squint and the boy blurs, but only the boy. The rest of the world is crystal clear as always.

"What the hell?"

I blink.

Underneath the shadow of the boy's baseball cap stretches a giant grin. It extends up to his eyes in a lipless smile engulfing most of his face. There's no nose, only small black eyes set back in dark leathery skin.

My heart jumps and I lose my voice.

Bob tenses and I gladly let him shield me from the…*thing.* I can't identify him as a little boy anymore. I point like a simpleton and put my hand to my mouth.

The thing cocks its head to the side. I can't tell if it's watching me or Bob. *I really hope Bob.*

"Hello, young lady," when it speaks the voice distorts and disembodies. It comes from everywhere but its mouth.

It's in my head! It resurfaces from my nightmares as

a child. The grinding grumbling I swear comes from the monsters in my closet or under my bed. My fingers grip Bob's shirt. *Saying I'm afraid is an understatement. I'm terrified.* The world spins around me and I find myself burying my face against Bob's back. He reaches back to rest his hand on my hip.

"The joys of puppet kind," Bob mumbles. "They don't use their mouths to communicate. Just to eat."

I dare a peek, "Rinkai?"

"Yes."

An elongated dark green tongue covered in warts slides between extensive sharp teeth as Rinkai opens his mouth wide. The teeth are long enough they push backward into his mouth when it shuts. As he opens up again, the teeth appear to grow until they are all I see under that little baseball cap.

"I think I'm gonna be sick."

The voice of the creature, the puppet kind, hovers in my mind as it speaks, "Are you sure it's me you need to be afraid of? I'm not the one who's put a spell on you."

"Bullshit," Bob replies.

A cold sweat drenches my body as I continue to fight the urge to run. Amidst the terror I catch Rinkai's point.

"Wait, you put a spell on me? You son of a bitch! No wonder I can't resist helping you. That is so not something I normally do."

"George! This isn't the time."

"By all means, Asrieth, this is the perfect time," little deft fingers crawl up my spine as Rinkai speaks. "Dearest Asrieth. One day the rift will open and magic will flow through into this realm. Soon we can use its full potential, but even now your charm spells that work so well at home have an effect in this realm." The tongue slithers down to the ground, lying on the white plate of the pitcher's mound, "Though, not as strong, but just wait."

"What?" Bob raises his hands in front of himself, palms facing Rinkai. "What do you mean?"

"A natural rift opens."

I shiver and stay behind Bob, "Can we please leave?"

I don't want to be here. I want to run and run and never look back. I don't know what's holding me here. An anchor weighs down my feet and so I stay in place. My face twists as I stomp.

"Asrieth, let her go. She has nothing to do with this," Rinkai's tongue flops around in the dirt at his feet.

Bob cocks his brow, "I know. She came here. I didn't ask her here."

"Is that concern I hear? For an Earthian?"

Bob answers with a growl and tightens his hands into fists.

"Let go. Give up your charms. Let her make up her own mind."

The invisible anchor keeping me next to Bob disappears. I'm free. I shake my head and lean against him. My brain goes for a swim down the Nile.

"There! George, you need to go," Bob speaks over his shoulder to me, but he keeps his eyes on Rinkai. "Run. Now."

"Yes, George, leave. Before this gets nasty," fabric tears and I peek past Bob.

That was a mistake.

My stomach lurches as the limbs of Rinkai extend to unnatural stick thin lengths. His uniform stretches to mere rags hanging off of his lanky body. His arms are longer than his legs; his dark leathery skin now covers all of his body. The creature's long clawed fingers flick the baseball cap off. I follow the cap's journey to the ground before raking my eyes up the length of the nine foot tall thing. On top of his head are a few thick grey hairs. Its black eyes are shining in the bright lights of the field. His tongue is the length of his body and no longer drags the ground. It slides into his mouth like a noodle before ejecting out again. Saliva drips and spews making the ground at his feet darken with moisture. A low guttural moan vibrates with his true voice. My ears ring and I drop the bat to cover them until it stops.

"Fuck," Bob whispers.

Eff this noise!

My feet find their inner bunny and I dash away. I make a jump towards the fence and climb over it in a scramble. Rinkai's laughter floats in my head as I fall on the other side. I'm not in the best shape of my life, but adrenaline doesn't let the wind catch up yet. A block away my legs still pump strong and the lights of the field shut off. I dig my heels into the manicured lawn I'm cutting across and stop to turn around to the darkness of the park.

The wind catches me and I wheeze. The lights of the parking lot are still on and I spot my car. I consider going back to drive home, but something tells me not to. The invisible string that pulled me toward Bob pushes me away from the park. It tells me to keep going.

Seems like a good idea to me.

I know it's Bob. *I hope.* I bite my lip against the pain of the stitch in my side and dart further down the street. I know something out of this world happens behind me, and despite my constant wish for adventure and fairy tales…*this isn't what I had in mind.*

31

I commit my first trespassing transgression and duck into a back yard. I can't run any longer. The neglected wooden fence has a perfect opening for me to crawl into and I'm careful to peek around, hoping not to get caught by the people who live here. Or a monster. *Neither is good.*

A streetlight nearby lights my way, but still casts shadows for me to crawl into and hide. I spot a small storage shed tucked into the corner of the yard and sneak into the space between the shed and the fence. I crouch down, trying not to think of what creepy crawlies call this place home, but the creepy crawly at the park is menacing. Dangerous.

I can survive a spider bite.

I sit back onto the dirt and lower my head between my knees to catch my breath, curling my arms around my legs, facing down into my lap.

Is this really happening? Bob isn't crazy. He isn't crazy. Or we're both crazy. Is that contagious?

Now I reconsider introducing him to Rachael or even Mrs. Morgan to ensure he's not a figment of my imagination. I told my landlord he was a visiting cousin in case she saw him, but if she did she hasn't said anything.

I lift my head to rest my eyes on my forearm and rub my eyelids against the soft cotton of my hoodie sleeve. *Good thing I wore adventure gear after all.* My feet throb. Sweat drenches my skin and hair sticks against my face and neck. I sit up straight and relax my legs to retie my ponytail. It fell loose during what I'll now dub *The Great Run of 2008.*

I look over to the dark house and glance down at my watch. *5:28.* Faint coloration of sunlight fills the horizon. I sit and wonder if it's safe to go back after dawn. *It's not safe to stay in this random backyard for much longer.* The feeling of being followed passes and I catch my haggard breath.

I wait, stretching my legs and shifting to keep my limbs from falling asleep. My throat grows sore in the cooler night air. I swallow and the first light comes on in the house. *Time to go.*

I crawl out from the space by the shed to crouch through a hole in the fence to the alley. I blink, studying the corridor. *I don't recognize anything.* I'm sure I crossed Indiana Avenue, but other than that, no clue. I walk to Indiana and cross, brushing dirt and cobwebs off my clothes. There's no traffic in the early morning hours.

Now I have an idea of where I am and lumber on towards Maxey Park pulling my hood up and shoving my hands into my pockets, keeping my gaze on the sidewalk while strolling past houses. People are out in their robes collecting newspapers. I concentrate on the cracks of the sidewalk and know I shouldn't step on them. *Lest I break my mother's back.* I reconsider stepping on them.

I don't want to go back. I'm afraid of what I will, or won't, find.

I may find the manipulative, and yet still dashing, Bob dead in a pool of his own blood. *If he has blood.* Or a pile of Rinkai. *Or there's no sign of anyone and I've completely lost it and made everything up. How hard did I hit my head in the wreck? My two choices are ending up in a padded cell or things like Rinkai really exist in the world.* I shiver and my mind wanders to the monster.

If Rinkai wore a disguise, what does Bob really look like? I shudder. I can see why Bob calls Rinkai "puppet kind". He's dangly and wooden like Pinocchio's cousin on steroids. *I hope Bob looks more like a Calvin Klein kind.*

I grow angry as I think of Bob charming me. It explains a few things. A lot of things. He's nice but, it's not enough.

I pull on the strings of my hoodie to tighten it around my face, destroying my peripheral vision.

The unlit lights of the baseball field come into view before I reach the park. I slow my pace and listen for any unusual noise. Early morning presents itself. A songbird sings in the trees and a horn honks in the traffic nearby, building up with the morning rush. I avoid the ballpark completely and walk around the outer edge to the parking lot. I'm relieved the ground didn't swallow it up in the night.

I'm so tired.

I reach into my jeans pocket for the keys. They're not here.

"Shit," I turn my pockets inside out. I search the loose pockets of my hoodie. Check my bra. "Shit. Shit. Shit!" *I must have dropped them somewhere…*

I glimpse the baseball diamond lightening with the rising sun and take a deep breath and approach with caution. My breaths grow erratic as I squint and slow. I cock my brow and quirk my head.

"Nothing," I whisper. I shake my head and blink. The diamond is empty. No signs of any struggle or fight. Not even signs of recent activity. A glint in the orange glow of the rising sun catches my eye. I approach the chain link fence and spot my tangle of keys in the dirt at the base. I reach my hand through the hole in the fence with some maneuvering and retrieve them. I stand up, keys in hand, and study the diamond again.

Nothing. Exhaustion weighs me down. I break down and cup my hand over my mouth. *Did I make it all up? Is he even real?* I look around as a car pulls into the small parking lot. A jogger gets out and stretches for his early morning run. I glance back to the diamond before resolving to head home. I ignore the jogger's friendly wave as I unlock the door and slump into the driver's seat.

On the drive home I consider talking to the therapist Rachael recommended when Phillip first went missing. *Perhaps it's time I saw someone.* I consider the repercussions of my lapse of sanity and who I should tell. I'm on autopilot as I press the button and watch the garage door lumber upward. Searching the darkness, I blink and squint.

Did I see something move?

I take a deep breath. *I've been hallucinating for over two weeks. Of course I did.*

My car creeps forward into its spot and I kill the engine, pressing the garage door remote. It closes behind me and for a moment, in the darkness, I'm all right. I feel relief. I open the door and dinging reminds me to grab the keys. The dome light shuts off when I close the door. The hairs on the back of my neck prickle outside of the protective shell of my vehicle. My breathing quickens of its own accord. I stumble to the door leading to the house, tripping over the broom propped up next to it, and let myself in. I shut the door behind me and lean against it.

The TV turns on.

I step away from the door into the living room. Relief washes over me before terror seizes any reaction.

Rinkai sits on my couch with the large remote in his small hands. His small, childlike hands.

3. Much Ado About Puppet Kind

As I sat on the couch and read my favorite novels I wished those adventures would happen to me. The tales of love and tragedy. Action and danger. I willed the books to open up, glow with some awesome purple color, and suck me in. *How wonderful that would be,* I'd think. One adventure after another.

It's easy to believe in unicorns and fairies and handsome knights, but in the back of my mind I never think with those beautiful things come the nightmares. The kind of monsters when at the end of the book, or chapter, or night, I'm thankful aren't really here.

But no matter how many times I blink, Rinkai remains on the couch.

My initial reaction is to grab my bat and pummel him. I realize a couple of things. The first being I left my bat in the car. The second is Rinkai looks like a normal little boy. I remain frozen in the doorway. He seems totally human. Sandy blonde hair, blue eyes, and no creepy grin. His clothes are still torn from his trans-formation. Mud and blue stuff smear him head to toe.

He's the poster boy for *Lord of the Flies*.

I swallow.

He lifts the remote and turns the TV off. Silence fills the room. He appears harmless enough, but knowing what lies beneath his innocent façade makes me shiver. He's also in my house.

My fortress of solitude has been penetrated by a puppet on drugs.

"Relax," his voice is soft. It comes from his mouth as opposed to inside my head. He sounds like a real child.

I scowl, "Why are you here?"

I cross the living room to the kitchen as casually as possible. I'm trying to remember if I own any butcher knives. I turn the corner and hide out of sight.

"George, you've no idea what's going on. I'm the good guy. What do you really know about Asrieth?"

I open the silverware drawer as slow and quiet as possible. *Dammit.* Nothing but butter knives. *I'm such a bad Texan. Not one steak knife.*

"I know enough," I reply.

"You know nothing."

For a little kid he sounds menacing.

"I know that when he finished he was gonna leave me alone. He hasn't hurt me and I can't ask for more than that. I guess." I close the drawer in silence and search for anything useful.

"You're not angry that he charmed you? Not angry that he shamelessly used you for weeks? Duping you into helping him?"

I bite my lip, "I'm irritated. I don't think angry's the right word." *I'm just elated he's real. Unless this is a hallucination too.* I narrow my eyes and poke my head out. Rinkai remains still on the couch, watching me with his black eyes. "And he didn't get my couch so damn dirty."

The puppet smiles, "I'm glad you're relaxing." He hesitates, "I understand my appearance can be unsettling to your kind. Is that why you assume I'm bad?"

Rinkai's eyes grow bigger and his mouth stretches beyond normalcy. I'm not sure he's aware of it. I duck back into the kitchen. My heart thumps in my chest.

"Uh, well, Bob said you were bad," I struggle to keep my voice level in my rising panic. "He said he needed to take you back."

"That's a matter of perspective. Don't you think?"

"I don't know." *I don't care either.*

"Sir Frances Drake was a villain to the Spanish and a hero to the English. Isn't it a matter of perspective?"

Frowning, I try to recall history class as I grab a big metal spatula I have for cookouts. It's unused.

"So does that make me English or Spanish?"

"It makes you Vietnamese."

"That has nothing to do with—"

"Exactly."

I frown. *He has a point.*

"Well, you made me…Spanish by invading my home."

"It doesn't matter. I'm passing time until Asrieth's arrival."

My eyes burn from exhaustion. I keep holding my breath to listen for any sounds of Rinkai's movement. My knuckles are white around the metal spatula. *I spent all night running from this asshole just to find him waiting for me at home.*

"How did you know where I live?" I ask. *Do I really want to know? Yes. To prevent something like this from repeating itself. Idiot. Idiot. Idiot.*

"I followed you."

Color drains from my face. My heart skips a beat, "From the park?"

"Where else?" Rinkai's soft voice rolls over gravel as it deepens.

"What happened?" I swallow the growing lump in my throat to keep him talking. I need to know where he is.

"It was fun to watch you stumble around in the dark," he's closer to the kitchen.

I back up to the window overlooking the backyard.

"We are creatures of the night, Asrieth and I," he continues. "You could suppose he's not as ambitious as I and others are, but it's there. The darkness is in him."

He's next to the kitchen door, but out of sight. I turn and drop the spatula to open the window. I unlock it and the pane rises. I kick out the screen and turn as Rinkai rounds the corner. I freeze.

The cracking of bones and stretching of his leather skin reverberates into the kitchen. He fills the doorway with his lanky frame. In the light of day it's worse. I stumble back and fumble through the window opening. His tongue shoots out and wraps around my ankle, halting my advance to the outside. My torso hangs past the sill as my legs are kept inside by his strength. I collide with the wall and the wind knocks out of me. My back bounces off of the siding of my house. I blink and kick with my free foot. Instead he uses his tongue to thrash me against the house, again, and again, and again.

I shield the back of my head. Each time it's difficult to raise my arms in defense. His breath fogs the glass as he watches me struggle against him. I cough and struggle for air as he repeats his violence against me. My vision blurs as he pulls me against the wall under the window. Worse than the bruising is the lack of air. *I'm going to suffocate.* His tongue slides from my ankle and I roll onto the soft grass. I can't focus my eyes on the puffy clouds in the morning sky. I cough and gasp for breath, crawling.

The wet tongue slides around my waist and up my spine, straightening me out in front of the window as Rinkai lifts me to my wavering feet.

He presses his face against the glass and his voice dominates my thoughts, "So fleshy and plump. What a delicacy."

Is he calling me fat?

"You are definitely the bad guy," I wheeze.

My eyes shoot open. I'm angry. *Fight or flight.* My hands shoot forward and grab the window trim, yanking it down with force onto his tongue. He howls and tightens his grip around my waist.

I continue to slam the window down over him, taking advantage of the springs in the frame.

"I haven't been to Tokyo!" Slam! "I want to write a New York Times best seller!" Slam! "I haven't swum with the dolphins yet!" Slam!

The puppet's grip slackens and I fall to the ground and scramble back. As quickly as my adrenaline came, it's gone. Exhaustion overwhelms me and I crawl for the back gate. Behind me glass shatters and wood splinters to land on the grass. Bony fingers wrap around my ankle and yank. I yelp and roll onto my back to look up as Rinkai pulls me towards him.

He towers over me, having blown a hole through the wall of my kitchen. His tooth-filled grin leers down at me. The long tongue flops at his feet.

"George!"

Past Rinkai in the gaping hole of the house Bob

stands. He dashes from the kitchen to the backyard carrying yards of gold ribbon. Rinkai's head spins in a circle to follow him. I cry out in relief as the puppet's grip tightens on my ankle.

Bob blurs. He dodges Rinkai's free hand with surprising dexterity and maneuvers the ribbon to bind the puppet's arms and legs. My eyes flutter as a faint golden trail follows Bob. Rinkai thrashes at the ribbon, grinding the bones of my ankle. I suck in my breath, but my eyes glue to Bob. He hastens and the ribbon covers most of Rinkai's leathery skin. Bob chants in guttural tones and the ribbon's golden light intensifies. Bob tears off the last strip and licks the tip. He yells and strikes Rinkai across the face with it. To my surprise it impacts with force and sticks to Rinkai's skin.

The puppet freezes. His grip on my ankle remains. I sit up and pull on his bony fingers to free myself to no avail. A gust of wind picks up and my hair whips around as I struggle with the leathery hand. At first I think a storm blows in and search the sky. It's clear. Instead of clouds and rain, thousands of silver beads reflect in the morning sunlight falling towards us. They concentrate together as they form a curtain of quick-silver hanging in the air inches above the grass in an oval. Its mirrored surface reflects the image of Bob grabbing hold of Rinkai. Edges of the suspending mirror ripple as I gape. It towers over Bob. There's room enough for a car to drive through.

"What in the hell?"

Bob yanks the frozen puppet towards the portal. I jolt with the movement, Rinkai's grip dragging me with him. I sit up and pull. I dig my elbows and free foot into the grass to resist. Panic rises and I yell for Bob.

"Help me!" The wind rushing past deafens my

cries.

He faces the mirror and reaches toward it. His hand disappears into the silver liquid. It ripples.

I claw the grass and dirt shoves beneath my nails. I think of the creatures on the other side. The worst of my imagination surfaces. There are hundreds, if not thousands, of other puppets on the other side.

Bob tugs and I lurch forward. I wriggle and pull and kick and claw to try to free myself. We approach the portal. My shirt rolls up my back as he drags me. Small rocks and damp grass slide along my sensitive skin. Bob steps through the portal, his hand around Rinkai's other wrist, and disappears. I'm a few feet away, but we go faster. The wind roars past, increasing in speed the closer we get. Now most of Rinkai disappears into the quicksilver.

I'm next.

"No. No. No!" I lean back and dig my elbows, heels, anything into the soft earth. I search for something to anchor myself and find nothing within reach. *I don't want to go to Bob's vague and terrifying world.*

I watch my own horrified expression in the mirror. My feet slide through. I expect it to be like water, but instead my lower extremities simply feel gone. Like they don't exist. Not even the pressure of Rinkai's grip registers.

The gate to my backyard breaks open. Mrs. Morgan, in her pajamas, runs to me. Her teenage daughter hovers by the gate and stares at the portal consuming the lower half of my body.

My landlord yells and grips my forearms as I reach out for her. *Thank God.* Her acrylic nails bite into my skin. She digs her bare feet into the ground and pulls with her slight frame.

Courtney, her daughter, comes to her senses and joins us. They each take an arm. Sudden force lurches me into the portal, out of their grasp. I hold my breath as I submerge into the quicksilver.

The pressure of Rinkai's grip on my ankle returns. Air whips around me and I take a deep breath looking around. Black and purple mist a veiled starry sky. *I've never seen anything so beautiful.* I can only gape before a bright flash envelopes me. Dozens of black feathers swirl within my vision.

Now darkness.

Air raises hell around me. *I'm flying—or falling really fast!* The air is warm with a tinge of copper taste. I smell blood, but still can't see. A splash below warns me seconds before I dive into liquid. Rinkai's frozen grip drags me down. I choke on the water in surprise and pinch my nostrils shut. My lungs burn.

Something grabs the shoulder of my hoodie and yanks me upward. The water swooshes with the force of someone swimming next to me and we break the surface. I gasp and heave for precious oxygen. I flail to tread water. Below Rinkai anchors me.

Helpful hands grip me by the collar of my shirt and hold my head above the surface. Droplets of water splash me when someone, or something, dives into the water close by. The water swirls in currents below and Rinkai's grip loosens and I'm free. I kick my feet in ecstasy. I blink searching for shapes in the darkness. Rocky ground comes up beneath my hands and knees and I crawl onto the hard shore. I roll over and lay on my back. The hands let me go.

I sit up.

"Wait," my voice echoes and bounces around the cavern walls.

My protest reverberates around the room. I search blindly around the pebbles and find a smooth flat rock. I rest my head in my arms over it. My scalp tingles, then the back of my neck, as hundreds of legs crawl over my skin. I scream and sit up, flinging whatever it is away. I feel shame as I start to cry.

"Where am I? What's going on?"

A man speaks. I assume. I don't understand a word he says. For all I know he's conducting controlled moaning. *I suppose that's all talking really is anyway.* I curl my legs inward and hug them. The room is warm, but the layer of water dripping down my body cools it. I rub my eyes and darkness remains in my vision. I'm exhausted. I can't think. Or move. I'm glad I didn't drown or explode in the portal...*but to what end? To sit in a cave with creepy crawlies? To sit in perpetual darkness?*

I sob into my arms and shiver. Again small tingles up my back. I reach around to fling it away, but instead of something small and manageable, I can wrap my hand around it. The dozens of legs kick and two pincers penetrate my shoulder before I crawl away. The pain sears as it travels down my back and through my shoulders. The legs cling to me, then yank away. Fingers hover over the wound on my shoulder. I slap at them, still blind, and crawl forward towards the water. The effort mixing with panic and hyperventilation is too much.

I lose consciousness.

Pain in my shoulder rouses me.

I lay on my stomach and the pressure of a bandage keeps my eyes closed. A hand moves my hair to the side and tips of fingers press the bite on my back. I suck in my breath and jerk away. My hands reach for the bandage.

"George! Stop it."

I repress a cry at Bob's familiar voice. *I'm not abandoned.* A motor runs close by in the warm room. Quiet. I'm laid out on a plush surface. Probably a bed. My hands run along the soft sheets beneath me. *It's satin.* Bob's weight dips the mattress to my right and he moves my hair again as I relax onto my stomach. My shirt lifts up to my neck, but I don't care. I'm still tired.

"I'm trying to patch you up."

His fingers dig into the open wound and I grit my teeth.

"What bit me?"

"Mertyl," he answers.

Liquid drips into the holes of the bite and a soothing effect coats them. My skin tingles as it knits itself together in rapid healing.

"I see. Who's—" Stinging shocks my system as the soothing medicine wears off. "Mertyl!" I grip the sheets.

"My pet."

"Are you being vague on purpose?"

"Absolutely."

"What is it? Your pet *what*?"

He hesitates and his warm fingers spread a cream over my shoulder. The sting subsides.

"Centipede is what you'd call her."

I lift my head as far as I can.

"It's not close by is it?"

"Um…she's not close…"

"What?"

"Or on the bed or anything."

"What?!"

He holds me down when I try to sit up.

I can hear his smile as he speaks, "She's my baby. She's not as bad as some of the other things crawling around here."

"What can *possibly* be worse than a giant fucking centipede?"

"You'll see."

He lets me sit up on my haunches, "I don't think I want to."

Bob stands and the redistribution of weight knocks me off balance. I flail and try not to move. I don't want another run in with Mertyl. Once still, I pull down my shirt and reach beneath the collar. There are two rough patches of skin.

"It'll scar no doubt."

"Chicks dig scars," I reply.

He chuckles. His weight dips the mattress down again as he sits in front of me. I balance and his hands steady my shoulders.

"Okay," he begins. "I think I should prepare you for a couple of things before I take this bandage off."

"Why is it on in the first place?"

"The magic blinded you in the portal. It's temporary and common for people to experience the first time."

"Wait. There are other people from my realm here?" I ask.

"Yes. They come here for one reason or another."

I huff, "Like being dragged here against their will?"

He answers with silence. The weight in front of me lifts off the bed. Heavy booted feet on a hard surface walk away.

"Bob. Come back. Tell me what happened."

"No," he sighs. "You're right to be mad at me. I *did*

drag you back here. It wasn't intentional, but you were stuck to Rinkai. I had him bound and I couldn't undo it to set you free and risk losing him. The fact of the matter is if I came back without Rinkai…well. I couldn't do that."

I bite my lip.

"If I came back without him I was dead for sure. Or close to it. Worse than death maybe, but taking you with me means a higher chance of survival for both of us. I couldn't waste my portal, George. So yes, you should be angry because I'm selfish. And I'm not sorry. I did what I had to do."

"If that's your line of thinking then how are my chances of survival here much higher?" *I'm angrier about the fact that he's not sorry. I can deal with being here—on accident. I can't deal with his callousness.*

The footsteps stop pacing.

Why am I surprised? It's not like I really know him. He charmed me to do what he wanted before. There's no real reason for him to care about me. I give him credit for not letting me die of his stupid pet's bite.

"Thanks for taking care of me then," I say.

The footsteps come back and the bed sinks under his weight.

"It's the least I can do. Sorry about Mertyl. She loved on you, but doesn't respond well when you react violently."

"Fair enough, but she has to understand she's creepy as hell."

"Not to me."

He reaches behind me and fingers the knot of my bandage loose.

"So, the things to warn you about. There is a giant centipede curled up on the bed."

I nod.

"And I'm sure you've figured out that I don't look like I did in your realm."

"I wondered. Just please, please tell me if you're scary."

He pauses before unwrapping the layers of bandage.

"I'm sure I can be. I know I can, but I am similar to humans. So it shouldn't be too bad. Mertyl will probably scare you more than I will."

"There aren't any dead bodies piled in the corner or anything?" I ask.

"No. That's just unsanitary."

The bandage falls off, but I keep my eyes closed. I squeeze them shut when the shield of the gauze releases.

"I'm scared," I cup my hands over my eyes.

His callused fingers close over my wrists and pulls them away, "It's not that bad."

I crack open my eyes and keep them in a squint to adjust. I cup my hands to my brows to protect my wide pupils from light as I open them further. I stare down at my lap and concentrate on the denim of my grass-stained jeans. Past them are black satin sheets.

"These are some pimpin' sheets."

The bed shakes as he laughs, "You like them? I got them from your realm."

"Yeah, they're comfy. I have some red ones myself."

"I know."

"Oh yeah." *He did live with me for a little bit.*

I keep my eyes down. My vision adjusts, but I'm afraid. I wonder what kind of place we're in. *Is there blood on the walls? Skulls hanging from the ceiling? Giant centipede on the bed? Oh yeah, there is that.*

I'm afraid to see him above all.

He shifts and a hand comes into my view. It's large and pale tinged with blue. Black veins are visible on the underside of his wrist and protrude from beneath a leather gauntlet buckled to his forearm. Razor sharp black nails jut from his fingertips. I laugh as his hand waves back and forth.

"Can you see yet?"

I drop my hands and look him in the eye.

4. Welcome To Werdofium!

I blush and suppress a smile as I study Bob.

His frame is large, bigger than in my realm. He must be close to seven feet in height. His skin is pale white with a tinge of blue and tattoos cover his bare torso. I can't help but to admire how absolutely sculpted he is with broad shoulders atop a lean physique. Leather straps cross his chest and black leather hilts of swords stick out upward from his shoulders. Black metal armbraces with silver studs are strapped with buckles to his forearms. He wears pants of thick black leather and his boots are similar with hard steel covering the toes. His unruly white hair falls into his black eyes bordered with thick black lashes and topped with dark brows.

He's a Goth Calvin Klein kind. I resist the urge to cling to his thigh to pose for a book cover while he holds a sword in the air.

"Close enough!"

"What?" he asks.

"Nothing," I clear my throat. "That's a lot of leather."

"Mertyl is hardly the only ankle biter around here," he ticks his head.

I glance over my shoulder. Curled up in the corner, as promised, is Mertyl. She's further away than I imagined, as the bed is huge. I gape at the sheer size and glance back to Bob. *It makes sense. He's a big guy.* I'm guessing Mertyl herself is close to six feet in length, but it's hard to tell.

I shiver and scan the room.

Lavish black, red, and silver decorum cover the large rectangular room. The walls are a dull grey stone and the floors are a smooth dark slate. Set in the wall to my left are black wooden double doors, the silver handles firmly latched. Through their small panes of frosted glass red light glows, layering the room in a bloody red hue. The motor I heard earlier is a small engine tucked under a black desk set in the cattycorner across the room. Next to the desk a carved door of black wood with an ornate handle of onyx polished to a shine remains closed. To my right another wooden door stands ajar and beyond is what must be a bathroom.

"So, I'm gonna assume we're in your room, area, place."

"That is correct madam."

"Well, this is better than I expected," I say.

"What were you expecting?"

I glance away with a small smile. *Not for you to look this good.*

"I can't say," I answer.

"Right. We have to figure out what to do." He stands and paces in front of the bed. It springs back up without his weight on the edge.

I continue to survey his room. On the desk are several items familiar to me. A few magazines and books, a white Christmas ornament, and lots of gum. He follows my gaze to the desk and smiles. It's wolfish. I frown when I notice his sharp teeth. They're pearly white and come to a perfect point.

His smile disappears, "They're natural."

"It's fine," I offer. "I just need to get used to them."

He smiles again keeping his teeth hidden, but they gleam as he speaks, "I'm glad you can overlook it."

"Now that's ridiculous. Your shining personality can make me overlook anything."

"Bullshit. You don't know me that well."

I shrug, "True."

"That'll change."

"Why?"

He sits on the bed beside me. It dips down. He seems restless.

"Bob," I lean towards him. "You *are* going to take me back. Right?"

"I would like to…," he rubs the back of his neck.

"You'd like to?" I scoot off the bed and stumble to the desk. I grip its worn edge and lean against it. My head swims. I turn to face Bob who remains sitting on the bed, "What does that mean?"

He cocks his brow, "What do you think?"

I close my eyes to allow my head to clear. When my feet are firm on the stone floor I cross my arms and stare across the room. I'm numb to the news. Nothing else sinks in. I comprehend only confusion as to why nothing can go my way.

"What?"

Bob frowns at his booted feet, "I can't make a portal."

"What? You made the one that brought us here!"

His eyes draw up to mine, "I'm sorry." He masks

his face in neutrality.

I clear my throat, "I'm stuck here forever?"

"Well, not forever."

As reality sinks in, pressure presses down on me. *I'm going to crack.*

"Okay, Bob, if you don't want me to freak out right now and start bawling like a little girl, I need you to at least tell me why you can't send me home. And please, please tell me you're not just being an asshole about it."

"I promise it's not like that."

"How do I know that? Like you happily said earlier, I don't know you well." *Crack.* "You charmed and manipulated me like a puppet for your personal use. I know I'm not some mystical being and magical and pretty or smart, or, or—"

"—nice—"

"Shut up!" I march up to him and stick my index finger in his face. "Shut. Up. I fed you and housed you and did everything I could to help you."

"Because I manipulated you, right? Isn't that it?" His black brows furrow and he stands. I crane my neck to look up as he continues, "It wasn't out of the kindness of your heart. You just made that crystal clear."

I moan and turn. I rub my hands over my face and leave them pressing against my eyes. *I will not cry.* I walk towards the door and drag my palms down my cheeks. Tears blur my vision.

A hand rests on my shoulder, "I'm sorry."

"Me too," I face him. He lowers his hand and offers a small smile.

"Don't be such a wuss."

I sock him in the gut, "You ruined the moment." I shake my hand. I cause pain to myself instead of him. I nurse my hand and offer my best angry face.

He quirks his brow and folds his arms. I find myself laughing.

Over the next hour he explains everything I need to know.

We can't make a portal because there are rare components involved that go into the making of one. The most important, and rare, is Ertaiu.

"Erataee," I say.

He shakes his head, "Ertaiu."

I shrug.

"In addition to the ingredients, we need a summoner. They're the only ones who know how to apply the ingredients and incantations correctly. They study for decades."

"I don't understand. How did you make the one in my yard?"

"I didn't technically make it. A summoner, to put it in simple terms, bottled one for me. Which takes great skill as well. So I only had one bottle. All I did was throw it and recite a short spell."

"So it's a long, expensive, complicated, and stupid process. Spell?"

"However you want to look at it. It's a little bit of science and magic. I only had the bottle because I was there on official business. It's impossible for me to access either the ingredients or a competent summoner for my own use."

I nod.

"If the opportunity presents itself," he continues. "I'll take you home."

I smile and nod.

He quirks his lips and sighs, "In the meantime I think I should prepare you for what's outside this room."

"Okay," I swallow. *Not sure I'm going to like this.*

"When someone from your realm has been here a while the magic properties in the air begin to…" he pauses. *For dramatic affect I assume.* "Mutate."

My eyes widen, "Mutate?"

"Yes. Not all of them are bad. Everyone's different."

I wave my hand to stop him, "No. I don't want to know."

He nods.

"Something else…"

I moan, "What else can there possibly be?"

"Because of the mutations there's a market for….well for lack of a better word, fresh, Earthians."

"Fresh?" My heart skips a beat, "Like meat?"

He nods, "Slavery. And there are slavers who specialize in the capture and selling of Earthians. If someone does not claim you, you are considered up for grabs. So to speak."

I nod and watch his uncomfortable expression, "So…"

"Yes. I claimed you on our arrival."

"Well isn't that lovely."

"What would you have me do? You have no rights here. I do."

"It's fine. I don't care. As long as you don't expect me to be your actual slave," I say.

"Never crossed my mind."

For some reason I believe him.

"Anything else?" I ask.

He quirks his lips and searches the room.

"Ah, yes," he says.

I brace myself.

"We need to get you translators."

"Oh." *That's not too bad.* "Why?"

"I can't keep wearing mine. I'll continue in English when I need to speak Werdonic. You need a hearing and speaking translator. English isn't the official language anymore."

I nod, "Okay. That makes sense."

"The Witch insists on only Werdonic in her empire."

I blink, "Witch?"

"Our leader. Avoid her."

I nod with wide eyes, "Does she eat children or something?"

"Nah," he shakes his head. "She's a recluse, but she lives here in the palace and runs Mythreale."

"Mythreale? Which is…"

"The country we're in."

I cock my head to the side, "And we're in a palace?"

He nods.

Okay, that's awesome. I glance to the double doors with frosted glass. "And that's outside? Why is the sky red?"

Bob points to the motor, "That's what the machine is for. It filtrates the air."

"From what?" I cover my mouth and nose.

"Sometimes we use blood in our magic. It gets into the air. The remnants of spells linger and over time can be absorbed through air filters like the one I have. The blood has magical properties to it. It takes some getting used to if you're not from here. Think of it as magic steam or humidity."

I gape, my tightening hand muffles me, "That. Is. Disgusting. So I'm breathing blood? That copper taste is blood?"

"Kind of. More magic than blood though."

I spit to the side, "Ew! Ew!"

"Buck up," he laughs. "Like I said, it takes getting used to. It's the magical properties you're breathing in that can make you mutate. In fact…" He slides off the mattress.

I lean over the edge and watch Bob lower himself to the stone floor. He lies on his stomach to reach far under the bed. He smiles, his teeth still startling to me, and something scrapes the floor as he pulls out a small wooden chest with a padlock.

He sits up to kneel and plops the chest onto the bed in front of me. The padlock hangs undone and he slides it off to toss it onto the bed. He lifts the lid, and to my surprise, reaches in until his entire arm disappears. Metal and wood and leather rattle as he searches the contents.

He slips his arm free and holds out a gas mask to me.

I grab and examine it, "Does it work?" It's black suede made to mold over the lower half of the face with two filters jutting out at the cheeks.

He closes the chest and kicks it beneath the bed, "It should. It'll help you adjust and maybe even prolong your countdown to mutation."

"Hopefully," I mutter and slip it over my head. Bob hops up onto the bed and helps me adjust the bands and hook in the back. It's not a great fit, but we manage to get a seal around my mouth and nose.

He adjusts the filters and gives me thumbs up, "Comfy? A lot of Earthians wear these. They're also good because they can hide how fresh you are. Plus, they're stylish."

He twists to open his nightstand drawer, which I'm only now noticing, and produces a pair of large tinted goggles. Bob reaches over my head to help me pull those on and adjusts them until my eyes are comfortable and sealed. The room darkens behind the grey lenses and I pull them up onto my forehead.

"So, Earthians?" under the layer of suede my voice muffles. The push and pull of air moves through the filters.

"Yes. You're one of those."

"Not Earthling?"

He quirks his brow, "Earthling? No. Earthling sounds like…something cute. Like a gosling. And Earthians aren't cute."

I narrow my eyes.

"With the mask you can almost pull it off."

"I will destroy you." The mask ruins my scary voice.

"Pardon? Speak up please."

"I WILL DESTROY YOU."

He waves it off, "Like I haven't heard that one before."

I smile, "I believe you." I tick my head to the double doors, "Can I look outside?"

"Pardon?"

"CAN I LOOK OUTSIIIIIDEH?"

"Oh, sure." He takes my hand to lead me to the doors and lets go to turn the handles and throw them open.

"Dramatic," I say.

He smiles and nods to the outside.

I step out and meet a push of hot sticky air on the small balcony big enough to fit a few people. I glance to my right and do a double take to gape. The palace is carved out of the side of an active volcano. In the distance occasional small streams of lava trickle along like veins. At the bottom of the palace a red steam cloud engulfs the base of the structure and grounds around it. Just outside of that cloud a large sturdy wall with guards marching to and fro looms.

"A volcano? This is ridiculous." *Have any James Bond writers been here?*

Bob shrugs, "Nobody lives where the lava is active. And we have magic barriers protecting us from the gas and fumes—among other things."

"Magic huh? Convenient."

He quirks his mouth into a smile, "You have no idea."

I mirror his expression beneath my mask and turn to survey the land out beyond Dr. Doom's palace. We're several stories high. A dark cityscape spans beneath a burnt orange sky. The yellow rays of a setting sun mingle with the red blood of magic hovering in the air. Buildings loom over the huddle of grey little houses and colorful markets made of onyx and black lava glass. Their dull shine in the tinged sky jut out from the city like jagged teeth on the horizon. Houses and buildings are sharp and uneven with hundreds of smoke stacks slithering up in twisting spirals. A dark haze of smoke hovers over the city. Most houses are hard and glossy, others appear to be weaved out of cloth or webbing and numerous are mud huts with thatched rooftops. We're too far up for the noise of hustle and bustle from the sprawling metropolis.

I fan myself. Sweat drips down the back of my shirt, "How can you stand leather in this heat?"

"Well, you get used to it. And it serves a purpose for me personally, but most people here wear a lot less clothing than in your realm. Though some wear leather bracers and such. Lots of things you need protection from. It's like cowboys wearing boots to protect from snakes. Big, mean, nasty, fast, poisonous snakes."

"You're joking right?"

He gestures to the bed, "Think my little Mertyl is an anomaly?"

I shiver, "I think I'll just die from heatstroke then."

"It's not the same as Earthian leather anyway. They breathe. Almost comfortable."

"Almost."

Bob shoos me back inside.

It's cool comparatively. I found the room hot and humid until returning to it from the outside. The red mist creeps in and condensates around the open doors. I walk to the desk and sit in the heavy black chair. Bob shuts the doors and turns the lock.

"Why lock up? We're so high."

He leans against the doors facing me, "You have much to learn about Werdofium. Lots of things and people can fly here."

I wonder how strong the doors are to hold his weight. Bob isn't a small man. *Humanoid. Thing.*

"People?" I ask.

The little air filter pumps away and mist starts to thin out.

"Yeah."

I turn to the desk and flip through a gaming magazine from three years ago. I recognize the cover title.

"What do we do now?" I ask.

"*You* sit and read and do what you like. I have to go report to Thecla."

"Wait, what?" I drag my gaze over to the sleeping centipede, "And what about that?"

"*That* is nocturnal. She won't be up before I'm

back," he runs his hand through his white hair before rubbing the back of his neck. "I have to convince Thecla to let me keep you until this blows over and you can go home."

"Now I'm interested in who this Thecla guy is."

"She's my superior…of sorts. Because you're my property you're technically the empire's property and I'm really not on good terms with the Witch at the moment so…"

"What?" I close the magazine and lean forward.

"It's my fault Rinkai escaped in the first place."

"I'm just getting comfy here and you drop this bomb on me. So you can't keep me? What's going to happen to me? Are they going to—"

"George, relax. Give me a break. I'm doing the best I can while trying to keep both our lives intact. They usually kill fuck-ups."

"Usually, but not you."

"Not me."

He doesn't offer anymore explanation and his hesitance causes my own. I don't prod. There are still many things I don't know about him or his situation. I focus on my own problem of going home.

I slide off my mask, "What will they do with me?"

"Probably nothing. They have bigger concerns than a tagalong, but I need to go through the proper channels. Too many people saw you come through with me in the portal room. I made my claim, but now I have to file the proper paperwork and get approval."

"Well," I snort. "Can't get away from red tape no matter where you go."

He smiles, "I suppose not. Either way, I'll have to mention you in my report about Rinkai to Thecla. She's an Earthian sympathizer. Don't worry about it."

Bob disappears behind the door to the hallway and I sit at the desk to leaf through magazines.

Of course I worry.

I can't concentrate on the words, so I enjoy the pictures. I'm ever weary of Mertyl curled up on the bed, but she never moves.

I can't say how much time passes. There are no clocks. He's been gone for five minutes or five hours. It's hard to say. The consistent red glow coming from the balcony gives away no passage of time. I decide to take another gander.

I pull on my mask and make sure the seals are set before unlocking and opening the double doors. I walk up to the metal railing bordering the small balcony and lean over it for a clear view. Vertigo swims through my brain and I slowly return upright and take a step back.

Nothing changes, but the sun appears larger than it did earlier as it shines through the red mist, closer to the horizon.

My gaze shoots up to movement overhead. High over the palace a set of leathery wings span with an elongated body. It circles as it descends, dodging the columns of steam rising up from the volcano. My mouth hangs open under the mask as I stare.

A dragon? Oh my God, a dragon?

Its scales are black and reflective in the red light. The creature draws closer to the balcony. As I see it clearly "dragon" isn't the correct adjective that comes to mind, but no other can fit it. It lacks the majesty and magic and wisdom dragons exude. Yet it's a reptile with wings. I ponder if the dragons I always read about are possibly hyped up versions of this thing.

It's not impossible to think that people from this place made it to Earth and vice versa. Is this where mythology comes from?

A rider sits atop the creature's back. I shield my eyes as the dragon halts its descent, hovering close. The pulsing wind from the beating of its wings pushes my hair back as I observe the rider.

Under the strategic placement of black armor is gold skin. The helm fans out vertically like a Mohawk and hides the rider's face with a large pair of dark goggles. I can't distinguish the sex. They're astride a plain black saddle that matches the reins of the creature. The rider grips them with one hand and poises a spear over their shoulder with the other.

I approach the railing and grip it. They're watching me as I study them. The spear points at me. I step back towards the door. The rider keeps a moderate distance before spinning downward in a barrel roll into the steam and out of sight.

I can't shake an unease creeping over me. *People don't fly dragons and stare at you randomly. Unless that's a Werdofium thing.*

I go inside and close the doors, sliding the locks back into place. I sit at the desk and put my feet up on its surface, tipping the heavy chair back on its legs.

Bob bursts through the door moments later; I yelp and crash to the hard ground. The back of my head bounces on the floor and pain obliterates my thoughts. The chair cracks under my weight and I roll out of it onto the stone. I moan and flop onto my back.

Bob bends over me, "Sorry George."

I sit up and rub the back of my head. It aches. No blood.

"You need to invest in rugs or carpet. But more importantly, what's going to happen to me?"

Bob helps me to my feet. My head swims and

pulsates against the pain. He tugs the rubber band holding my hair back loose and massages his fingers, careful of his nails, around the back of my head.

"Just a bump."

He gives me the hair tie and I pull my locks back into a lumpy ponytail.

"Bob! Concentrate. What. About. Me?" I sit back down on the floor to cross my legs. It's difficult to keep my balance at the moment, but my head begins to clear. The sharp pain dulls down to a minor throb.

He smiles, "It's fine. Papers were signed and all is well. She has more important things to worry about."

That's...easy.

"Okay, wait," I rub the tips of my fingers together after fixing my ponytail. *My hair's oily. I need a shower.*

Bob turns to the chair to right it. I take the opportunity to smell myself. I wrinkle my nose and wipe off the expression as he turns back to me.

"Yes?" He tests the upright chair and sits in it. It wavers.

"Right, sorry. So what do you do exactly? You said Thebes—"

"Thecla."

"Right, Thecla, is your superior, sort of. Is she a warden? Are you a prison guard?"

He rubs the back of his neck and stands. The chair wobbles, but remains upright.

"Kind of. Imperial prisoners are different from normal prisoners."

"What's the difference?" I study the dark dirt under my nails. *I brought some Lubbock with me.*

"Imperial prisoners are what you call political prisoners." Bob leans over close to me, elbows resting on his thighs.

I hope he can't smell me.

He lowers his voice, "Essentially people the Witch doesn't like." He straightens and offers his hand. I take it and his arm flexes as he pulls me to my feet, "But there are plenty who are a danger to the empire. Not just her personal enemies."

"Like Rinkai?"

"Exactly."

"So you're a security guard?" I ask.

He laughs, "Kind of."

"And Rinkai got away?"

He frowns and shoves the chair in its place beneath the desk. Wood scrapes against stone as he does so.

"Yes. It was foolish."

"What happened?"

Bob kneels and tinkers with the generator by the desk.

"I traded a shift with another…guard, as a favor to him. We didn't change it in the books because Thecla said it wasn't necessary. When Rinkai escaped, it was on the record I was the one who let it happen. Naturally the Witch was angry. Rinkai is a major contributor and leader of the rebellion." He sighs, "The only reason I wasn't killed on the spot is because I'm good at what I do. Really good. I'm impossible to replace and so I was given the chance to get him back."

"What about the jerk who screwed you over?"

He scowls, "He's dead."

My eyes widen.

"When I told the Witch what transpired he denied everything. I have a positive history of serving the empire and he is…was new. It didn't help his mother was already under suspicions of treason. Lilith believes me but, I was still responsible. He was punished. So was

I." He waves off an invisible fly, "In retrospect they might have sent me to get Rinkai anyway."

I nod, "So you just do guard stuff."

"Yes, guard stuff."

"It's more complicated than that. Isn't it?"

"You have no idea," he smiles.

"I probably don't want to know either, huh?"

"Safe to say."

I view him differently. A filter I placed over him as a bumbling idiot lifts and I can see, especially with his disguise gone, how there's more to him than I previously thought. He's complex and capable of things I can't comprehend. I think of political prisoners from my realm and some of the tortures and injustice they endure.

It seems that here Bob may be the person who does those things.

"I'm super stinky," I'm desperate to change the subject. "Can I take a shower or something?"

"Of course. Sorry. I didn't think of it. You must be starving too."

"I didn't even notice, but now that you mention it. Yeah I'm hungry." I'm not surprised. Basic needs like a shower and food aren't at the forefront of my mind. *In fact…*

"Is there a working toilet?" I grin.

He laughs, "Yes. We have plumbing."

"Oh. Thank God." *The thought of dealing with a chamber pot in this sticky heat is unbearable.*

The bath is amazing. I can't recall appreciating one more. In this small, but efficient, bathroom I have running water. Hot water too. Not that I need it here, but it's better than freezing water. The fresh clean feeling revitalizes me until I put my grungy clothes back on. The socks are the worst.

Bob waits for me with two bowls of hot soup. The contents of which he refuses to share with me. *It's likely for the best.*

I sit at his desk on the wobbly chair and blow on my soup to cool it. The steam disappears, then reappears with each breath. I begin to eat and ignore the scalding liquid on my tongue. *I'm so hungry.*

Bob crosses his arms as I pick up the bowl to drink the last of its contents.

I peer over the rim to him, "What?"

"We need to get you some clothes too."

I blush behind the bowl. It captures my voice, "That bad huh?" I set it down and lick my lips.

"We want you to fit in," he nods at my shoes, "Not too many folks wearing tennis shoes. You find the occasional Earthian items here and there, but not an entire ensemble. Unless you're fresh from the realm. We want to avoid those thoughts about you."

I gesture to the desk, "What about all this?"

"I snuck those back myself. And I've bought some from the black market."

"Not a law abiding guard are we?"

"You should be grateful. I'm most certainly breaking laws to keep you to myself," he grins.

I smile, "So it's like that huh?"

"You wish, sweet cheeks."

I kind of do.

"Either way," he continues. "I want to get you a translator. I look silly running around with mine still on. Thecla commented when I forgot to take them off, but at least she speaks English."

I glance at the metal band around his neck and silver cuffs on his ear cartilage.

"What is it with you and saying silly?"

He shrugs, "It's a hip word. And soon enough when you're speaking Werdonic you'll sound funny too."

I giggle at the name of the language. *It still sounds too close to "weirdo".*

"Do you think I'll be here long enough to learn the language?"

I hope not. It's difficult to stay positive. I'm afraid I'll be here as long as he was on earth. On the other side of the fence it's not fun at all. While I enjoyed his company and the safe adventure of having him with me, he was probably miserable. How long do I have to be gone before I make the news? Who will even notice I'm not around? Work? Rachael most likely. But what if no one notices I'm gone?

I close my eyes. Ever since Phillip died I cut myself off from friends and family. They don't understand and they don't deserve my confidence or company. *I drifted away from everyone in my boat of unhappiness long before Bob showed up. I can look at this with disdain all I want, but it's my fault.*

If I get back home, I'll give everyone the love they deserve.

I open my eyes to find tears. Bob stares at me.

"What's wrong?"

I study him before answering. I need to appreciate what he's trying to do for me. *Even though it's his fault I'm here to begin with, but at least he's trying. He can dump me and leave me to be found by slavers.*

"I miss my family."

He smirks, "You've been here two days. I'm sure

they're fine."

I nod, "Yeah."

"And aren't you too old for that?"

"A charmer as always."

"You know me," he reaches into a desk drawer and pulls out a small coin purse. "I have nothing to spend money on anyway. Might as well make it a woman."

"Wow. A dumb stereotype that crosses realms. Impressive. Bravo."

He rubs his smooth jaw, cocks his brow and nods, "Right. I'll be back."

"Where are you going?"

He tucks the small purse into his pants pocket, "To the black market."

I stand up and put myself between him and the door.

"I want to come."

"I don't think it's a good idea. It's dangerous outside."

I scoff, "Tell me about it. Earlier a dragon rider looked like they wanted to spear me."

His brows furrow, "What?"

"I went out on the balcony and this dragon person sat there and just…watched me."

He nods.

"All right. Let's go."

That was easy. Now we little piggies are off to the market.

5. Why aren't they called purple or green markets?

As a child I believed stuffed animals and figurines came to life when I wasn't watching. *The Velveteen Rabbit* was the most cherished of bedtime stories. If I had nightmares, Pinkie, my stuffed elephant, surely protected me from monsters lurking beneath my bed. Pinkie was my knight in shining armor and as an adult I feel vulnerable in my empty house. I can still squeeze Pinkie and cry. When I go to garage sales or second-hand stores I pity stuffed animals and damaged figurines so much I buy them. I imagine when their previous owners weren't looking their tears fell.

I can't get a good view, but recognize an item here or there on the tabletops I'm able to glance. I wear a last minute outfit consisting of both mine and Bob's clothing. I keep my hoodie and t-shirt, but the pants are his and hilariously too long. I have them rolled up and hanging over boots so big they force me to clomp up and down to keep them on. Beneath the hood pulled as far over as it will go, I'm wearing the mask and goggles Bob gave me. I keep my hands inside the jacket pockets. We're trying to convey I'm mutated beneath these hot layers. I try not to think of sprouting tentacles or turning into a puddle or blobby mass as I look around.

I know we're in the market, but staring at the ground the entire way here, it's hard to grasp where we are in reference to the volcano. The dirt at my feet is dark and orange and seems to be the consistency of clay, similar to home. It's still hot and humid. The stench here culminates of foreign spices mixing with sweat, blood, and livestock. I'm happy to wear the mask. The aroma would be worse without it.

It's loud. People yell over each other in shouting matches. I can't understand a word, but no doubt it's about the superiority of their stock and prices. The feet walking close to mine are Bob's unmistakable black boots among hooves, other boots, and the occasional sandal worn by all sorts of different feet. Some have claws, others toes, but most are discolored versions of humanoid.

I wish I could see.

I concentrate on Bob's feet ahead of mine. He said not to touch him or hang onto him. Worse yet, he took his translator off. Even if I want to talk to him I can't. We can't communicate.

Sweat rolls down my back. I can handle heat. I'm from West Texas, but humidity is another creature. Irritation boils within as we proceed.

I'm in another realm on a march and I can't see a damn thing. I want to see!

Bob has his reasons, and they're good ones, but it's like how your parents always told you not to eat the ice cream too fast, but you did anyway and were rewarded with a headache from hell. Except in this case the headache is potential slavery.

All right, so slavery is more extreme than an ice cream headache, but I'm ready for action.

Bob stops and I run into him. I shake my head. *I should have been paying attention.* He turns to the left, making a dramatic sweep with his foot to let me know which way we're going. I follow and find wooden steps. I step up and walk past the threshold through the open doorway. Bob clomps behind me and the door closes.

It's cooler in here, and the hum of a motor alerts me to a filter. Bob takes hold of my shoulders and places me next to the door.

He leans in to whisper, "I be back."

I smile beneath my mask and nod.

The floor creaks beneath his weight as he walks away. His baritone carries over the other sounds of customers shopping and a croaky reply answers. The gruff voice hollers a command and other customers shuffle out. They hold the door open. I stumble when a rough hand takes hold of the shoulder of my hoodie and pulls me out. I stagger down the steps and pause as the others pass me by. My heart thuds in my throat and I'm unsure of what to do. A hand pushes me and guides me to the alley between stores.

I think they're stores.

Then my hoodie yanks in a command to stop. I halt and keep my gaze down. Sweat drips and rolls down my back making it itch. The hand releases me and I stand still. I'm not sure what to do. One scenario after the next bounces around in my head. It's getting late. The orange hue turns dark and shadows cast down the alley as the sun finally sets.

The murmur of the crowd doesn't die with the light

and I remain. My feet ache. The passage of time eludes me and I lean against the wall and slump to the ground. My panic thrives as a thumping in my chest and I try to talk myself down.

Bob won't leave me here. He won't find me too much trouble and just…leave me here. He wouldn't. He won't forget about me. He won't…right?

Insecurities flood my thoughts.

What do I really know about him?

Tears sting my dry eyes. *This world is too much. I don't want to be here anymore. I can't be here anymore.* I'm torn between jumping up and running away or curling up into a ball and hoping for the best. Either way, I don't know where I can run to or to what end being a ball in an alley can come to.

Past the blurry filter of tears, black-booted feet stand in front of me. I bite my lip and am careful to breathe slowly. I can cry like a little girl at his feet in relief, but I don't. He takes hold of my upper arm and pulls me to my feet. I continue to stare down and let him guide me back to the dusty street. The air turns light yellow as torches and lamps are lit to fight the oncoming dark. The thick crowd proves difficult to navigate, but Bob's grip is firm. He turns me into another alley.

A breeze cools my skin and I breathe deeply. Bob jerks me back and makes me face the wall.

I'm going to smother him in his sleep for that.

I turn to the left and face the alley again, but this time several pairs of shiny black shoes greet me. They seem odd against the ground, and a layer of dust covers the toes. The polish shines through. Bob speaks over me to the owners of the shoes. A soft male voice answers him.

Except…*That's not Bob!*

The next few seconds are crucial and I know what's happening.

He did it. The fucker sold me.

Money exchanges in my line of vision. The hands that come from behind me to take it are golden and tan. My chest heaves. In an instant I turn to the street and kick up my heels. The boots are heavy on my feet and the soft flesh of fresh sores are on fire. I don't look back as I dash clumsily down the alley. The opening is only twenty feet away. My hood falls back and commotion stirs behind me.

Just a little more.

Almost.

A black bag slips over my head. I lose consciousness.

Bang! Bang! Bang!

I can't remember the last time I dreamed. As I wake this is no exception.

My ears ring and eyes flutter open. The back of my head throbs and I roll over to relieve it. The cool stone beneath my bare skin comforts in the oppressive hot air.

Bare skin?

I sit up and chains weigh down my neck and wrists. My fingers find a thick band of iron around my neck as I take in my environment. I'm alone in a cell. Iron bars, no windows, and stone walls on three sides surround me. A faint yellow glow lights up the hallway and my eyes adjust to the dark with its aid. My cell is a closet with a pile of hay in the corner. The hum of a generator in the distance allows me to breathe the clean air with ease. The hay is old and moldy. As terrifying as this scenario is the worst of it is…

I'm naked!

I crawl into the corner onto the hay and sit down. Straw pokes as I lean against the wall. I fluff it up around me to attempt modesty and hug my knees when I'm unsuccessful. I rock back and forth. I grit my teeth.

This isn't supposed to happen. This is supposed to be an adventure with dragons and unicorns and handsome knights. I'd take Rinkai over this. But noooooo. Reality has to be a bitch.

I close my eyes. Rattling chains carry in echoes down the halls. Cries follow the crack of a whip. I sob into my arms in silence. I curl up tight and hope they forget me. I'd rather they leave me to starve. I don't want to face what's coming. I know they'll come for me.

Then they'll sell me to the highest bidder.

Freezing water jolts me awake.

With wide fluttering eyes I find two of my captors standing over me, one poising with a newly empty bucket. I follow the drops of water to the stone floor close to me. The other holds a lantern close to me. Fear consumes modesty and I stare like a deer in the headlights. The lantern blinds me against darkness and they're silhouettes, quiet as they converse. The man on the left, with the bucket, squats down next to me while the other holds the lantern closer. It lights up half of his face to reveal black eyes staring from under high thick brows. His long pointy ears stick out from a black mangy mess of hair. Scars cover his pale skin, some fresh, some old, and his white teeth gleam as he smiles at me.

I shift away and draw up my knees.

He reaches out to me with caution. Like I'm a wounded animal.

I suppose I am.

"Parlez-vous Francais?" he asks.

I cock my brow, "French?"

He nods, "Oui, but you speak English I see." His accent leans heavily on the "s".

I answer with a nod.

My mind isn't at full capacity. The overload of constant adrenaline dumps makes me sluggish. He scrutinizes me a silent moment before standing up with a grunt and turning to the man holding the lantern. They speak and turn to the open cell door. The other man is similar to the one I talked to, but no scars. They're twins.

In desperation to find humor I dub them Scarry and Lanty.

Scarry waves to the glow down the hall. A smaller figure runs up with folded cloth, then disappears.

I perk up.

Lanty leans back against the bars while Scarry grabs the clothing and tosses it to me.

I need no instruction. I claw it and hold it up. It's less than I hope for, but at this point I will be thankful for a napkin. There are pieces of soft cotton with attached lacings, but I have no idea how this thing fits. Scarry yanks me to my feet. He shakes his head and smacks my hands away. He straightens out the clothing. He dresses me. The result is a scanty sci-fi outfit. It's a bikini top with a long split skirt providing basic cover. I long for more.

Scarry adjusts the skirt on my hips and nods. I back against the wall as he reaches for my hair. He yanks out the rubber band. It falls loose around my shoulders. He runs his fingers through it.

"We can do this the hard way or the easy way," he begins petting me. "You will follow me. You will eat and go to auction. If you don't do what I say you will be whipped. If you don't answer me when I ask questions you will be whipped. If you misbehave in any other way you will be whipped."

I scowl as I fight back a sob.

"And if you cry you will be whipped."

I swallow back my emotions and nod. I'm defeated. I can only hope to bow my head and endure what I must to get back home.

Oh God. I even miss my job. I miss Bob…no fuck him. He's the reason I'm here. I don't miss him. If I ever see him again I really will beat the holy hell out of him with his own pet centipede's corpse.

I ball my hands into fists as anger replaces sadness. *I'll survive this.*

"Are you a virgin?" Scarry asks.

My resolve fizzles.

"What?"

"You heard me."

"No," my face burns under his gaze.

"That's fine," he smiles. "We'll still get a good price for you."

My stomach churns. I peer up to blink away tears. *Is this really happening?*

Scarry pulls a ring of keys from his belt and turns one in the locks of my manacles.

"Follow me." He turns and steps over the threshold of the cell.

Lanty watches me with a leering smile and lights the way. He nods and steps out of the cell pulling the door shut behind us. I take a deep breath and pad after

Scarry to catch up. I keep my eyes forward, avoiding the miserable, nameless, naked bodies that clink around in the dark cells. The stone floor is smooth and cool beneath my feet.

Dozens of cells like mine line the long and narrow hallway. At the end a glowing torch hangs over an arching doorway. Humanoid guards stand at the exit holding spears at their sides. Their brown leather armor is patched and rough and metal helms shadow their faces in unnatural darkness. Past the frame of the arched door is a spiral staircase. Scarry climbs with dexterity and disappears from view. I approach and peer into the dark, looking both up and down the stairs. Lanty nudges me and I ascend.

A glow cast by the lantern behind me guides as I climb. A sheen of sweat layers my skin as I huff up to the next level. Light from the next room pours into the stairwell when the door opens and I catch the silhouette of Scarry waiting for me. My Jell-O legs wobble beneath me as I stumble up the last few steps. Scarry steadies me. Lanty's hand rests on my back.

I shrug them both off and step into the warm room.

The scent of food runs off with my nose and my stomach growls at the spread. A simple long table with benches on either side is in the middle. On the surface delicious junk food lays out. It's not mystery food like I expect, but spaghetti and pizza and hamburgers among other things. I nearly cry out in excitement and hold myself back. Two sentries guard another doorway across the way.

"Eat," Scarry says.

I'm happy to oblige and sit at the table. It's not the best pizza or spaghetti I've eaten, but I can't care less. It's the best meal of my life. Enthusiastic as I am, I make sure not to eat too much. I have no idea what to expect and being sluggish due to food might be the last thing I need.

I push away my half-eaten plate and glance at the twins.

They wear matching green tunics and brown leather pants with boots. Scarry stands a fraction taller and broader-shouldered than his brother. Lanty's eyes are intense and he holds himself lithe. They're not sore on the eyes except for the fact they're *slavers.*

"Finished?" Scarry asks.

I nod. The wonderful food is strange, but I don't ask and they don't volunteer any information.

I shuffle to the door with guards. A heavy black curtain hangs from the frame. A feminine voice carries from the next room in what I assume is Werdonic. Scarry holds onto my shoulders and looks me in the eye.

"Just stand there. Turn slowly as she tells you. This is an auction and buyers need to see you clearly. If you're crying or weak, no one will want you. And if no one wants you that means you have to stay with us. You don't want that," his smile is sweet as he threatens me. "You don't want to come back through this door. Understand?"

"Yes," my own voice is distant. *I have to be. It's the only way to get through this.* The food's purpose clarifies as I relax into a state of apathy. *To make me close to euphoric for the duration of this hell.*

The twins smile and push me past the velvet curtain.

It's nothing like I expect. Complete darkness blankets the room except for a crystal chandelier casting a yellow circle of light onto the stone floor. The path from the doorway to the spotlight isn't visible and I tread with caution. My nose stings with a sneeze as I walk into the circle. I hold my breath and squeeze my eyes shut.

"Begin turn left," the detached female voice commands.

Her accent is thick. I do as I'm told. I put my arms down to the side and turn slowly. Stepping into the darkness beneath a spotlight is less terrifying than I imagined. I thought I'd be in chains on a stage in front of hundreds of leering buyers.

The woman begins auctioneering in English, but she may as well do so in Werdonic. She's difficult to keep up with and understand. She speaks so fast I only catch a few numbers before a hand reaches from the darkness and pulls me into it.

Silk covers my face as a bag slips over my head. I stumble against whoever the hands belong to and a strong grip on my upper arms keeps me standing. Hands push me forward to guide me.

Is slavery always going to be like this? Stumbling around in the dark? Or is that just life?

The distance is long before doors open and close with the murmur of voices in a small room. We pass through into another and then out into the open. Humidity layers my skin in sweat in an instant, but the air is fresh.

"You will step up into a carriage," the voice comes from my left. It's feminine. *In perfect English too. Probably from the UK.* My heart sinks.

Bought by my own kind.

I reach forward and discover the smooth side of a carriage. Hands keep me steady as I find steps and stagger in. I plop down onto a cushy cloth seat. They release me.

"Stay still and we'll get out of here," says a male voice.

I stiffen. He's across from me and definitely from the States. I swallow and fight back tears as he laughs.

"Jonah, she's scared as it is," the woman says. She's across from me as well, next to him.

The door to the carriage slams shut and we jolt forward. Inertia pushes me back into the seat and the couple laughs at me. I don't find relief they're from my realm. I have an inkling of what to expect, but instead they humiliate me. My fingers reach up to the silk covering my head.

"Don't take it off until we say," the man says.

I drop my hands into my lap and listen to the streets outside the carriage. I just want to know what day it is. I'll settle for what time of day it is. I want to glimpse the outside world for the last time, but they will rob me even of that.

6. I'm Accustomed To Shoes

Betrayal is a festering wound.

Once occurred it can take years to recover. Longer to forget. Bob's betrayal reminds me of when I was in primary school. A friend and I were peas in a pod and went everywhere together. We haunted the swings at recess, ate together at lunch, and had most of our classes together. Her friends were my friends. Every weekend it was my house or hers. We were inseparable. It took a long time to wedge loose the knife she planted in my back.

The couple doesn't converse as we ride on, but I know their eyes are on me. Without conversation or the lull of city noises the drive is dull.

I start awake when the carriage halts and lurches forward. My face burns beneath the black silk from their chuckles. One of them opens the door and the weight of the carriage shifts. Hands find my upper arms to pull me up and out of the vehicle. My foot catches on the steps and hands keep me upright. I'm brought against a lean naked torso. I'm glad the sack is over my head.

The man straightens me out and takes my hand, circling his fingers around it. He pulls me forward. I listen and there's nothing but the sandals of my new masters scraping along the rocky clay at our feet. I grimace as I step over sharp rocks and rough patches of dead vegetation. We walk a few yards before we brush past curtains to enter a cool room with smooth floors. My feet are ready to fall off.

"Okay, enough mystery," the man lets go of my hand and yanks the silk sack off.

Light sears my vision. I squint. I cup my hand over my brow and drag my vision up to the man in front of me. His dark skin contrasts his cream color clothes. His athletic body is sculpted and a sheen of sweat highlights it. White tribal tattoos trace around his muscles and limbs. He's godly, with piercings and a flawless smile. His dreadlocks hang down his back.

My knees shake as I resist my instant attraction to him. My stomach lurches as the thought occurs to me…

I might have to have sex with him whether I want to or not.

I keep my expression stoic instead of mirroring his smile. He crosses his arms and shifts his weight. He's at least a head taller than me, but not as tall as Bob.

Ugh, Bob.

I push thoughts of that traitor from my mind and observe my new surroundings.

We're not in a room, but a large open dome constructed of bright-colored stone. The floors match the smooth stone with mosaic designs and arched openings are evenly spaced around the structure with gauzy curtains blowing in the breeze that cools my skin. I can peek past the curtains to the outside and nothing but burnt orange sky presses down on a barren landscape.

No buildings in sight. The desert is flat, with jagged black mountains in the distance to the west and a smoky haze of the city is to the north in the shadow of the volcano. My heart lurches.

We aren't in the city anymore. Not even close.

A woman circles around into my view to stand next to the man named Jonah. She's hideous, for lack of a better adjective. Patches of aqua hair cover her misshapen body. Remnants of leather and cloth hang loosely from her mangled bone structure. Smooth, light skin covers her disjointed legs. Her knees bend backwards like a cat. Her hands are normal, but her arms extend and she appears to be in the beginning stages of puppet kind.

My eyes widen and she guffaws at me.

"I know," she smiles. "I'm startling."

I furrow my brows and cock my head.

"You must have questions," she says.

I nod.

"Well?"

I glance from Jonah to the woman, "What are you going to do with me?"

They both hoot and holler. I jump at the outburst.

"Hah! I told you she was American!" Jonah laughs.

The woman moans, "But Americans can't ever shut up. She's so quiet."

"Pay up," Jonah jabs the woman with his elbow.

I want to ask, *What the hell?* But I don't want to draw attention to myself. This isn't what I imagined.

Again. That seems to be a theme here.

I expect to be thrown into a room with an old mutated man to have his way with me. Or into a kitchen with manacles slapped on and a tray thrown into my hands to serve, but here I stand. In an open breezy room, hands clasped, watching these two go at it over a bet about where I'm from.

Turning wheels over rough terrain draw my attention behind me and I dare a peek over my shoulder. A dust cloud kicks up behind another carriage. My neck strains as I will my head to do a one-eighty. A pair of large lizards pull the vehicle, running at full speed. I turn to the man and woman in front of me as she forks over a few coins to Jonah.

He gestures to the woman as he counts his money, "This is Katherine. What's your name?" He tightens the strings of his small brown purse and ties it to his belt. My eyes flicker to his abs.

I bite my lip, "George." *An alias doesn't seem like a bad idea.*

"Really?" Jonah cocks his brow.

"Yep. That's me. George. My parents have a cruel sense of humor." *They really do, but not in this instance at least.*

"Like a boy named Sue?"

"Indeed."

Jonah looks past me and I glance over my shoulder again. Several carriages pull up, nearly a dozen. Others guide people like me, scantily clad with black sacks over their heads, out of carriages. Two people accompany all of them. Some of them are mutated and others only partially. There are a few like Jonah who seem normal. They're joking and laughing amongst themselves while the rest of us are stiff. The other slaves pick up their tender feet.

Pairs set up the others in line next to me. All at once they pull the sacks from their heads. We glance at each other with red faces before Katherine clears her throat for our attention.

"Slaves," she begins. "You are very lucky."

People next to her translate what she says into several languages. Languages I recognize. With translating it takes her a moment to speak again.

"You're lucky because you've been bought by the Humane Society for the Advocacy of Earthian Rights. Or HSAER for short," she pronounces the acronym with a silent "h".

Jonah speaks up, "You're not slaves anymore. We've bought your freedom."

I blink. My ears deafen to the translators as my mind processes what they said.

Not slaves? Not slaves?

I cup my hand over my mouth. My vision tunnels. Cries of relief erupt. A small hand cups my shoulder and pulls me down, using me for support. I glance over and it belongs to a slight teenage girl sobbing. Guilt stings me.

And I thought things were terrifying for me.

As an adult I have coping skills. More so than the average person because of my involvement with Phillip.

Phillip…

I put my arm around the girl's shoulder and hold her up next to me. She smiles. I return it and we watch the saviors before us.

Jonah winks at me and I grin like a fool.

"We'll clean you up," Katherine speaks. "Feed you if you need it, and some new clothes. You'll be assigned to bunks and group leaders. English speakers, come with Jonah and me." She nods to the translators who appear to be the respective leaders of their own languages.

The ground shakes our feet and scraping of stone against stone fills the villa. Large slabs of the floor crawl open to reveal descending stairways. The girl next to me breaks off. She doesn't speak English. I'm sad to see her go.

I step up to Jonah and Katherine with a few others. Everyone chatters in excitement.

"God, it feels so good to talk and people know what I'm saying."

"I know, right?"

The others continue their conversations of relief, but I find myself quiet. I wonder what circumstances these other people who find themselves in Werdofium are.

Were they tricked in? Did they want to get in? Or did they get pulled in by a selfish twit who sold them into slavery?

I shake my head and suppress thoughts of Bob. I'm more hurt by his betrayal than I want to believe.

A hand claps down on my shoulder. I peer up to Jonah. In my thinking I'm left behind by the group. He smiles and puts his arm around my shoulders to walk me down.

Underneath the dome is a network of underground tunnels connecting hundreds of rooms. It's a relief from the humidity and heat of the wasteland around us. There's not much at first but the carved out hallways lit by a crude electrical lighting system. We follow our leaders through the maze and I know I can't get out on my own.

Not that I want to.

We pass many people in the halls going about their business. It's crowded down here. In a good way.

"There are currently over two thousand residents," Katherine begins. "They hail from every part of the globe."

We make a few turns.

"Here we craft the translators for Earthian languages to sell on the black market. It's how we fund upkeep as well as buying more members," she continues. "No one knows the location of the facility but a chosen few. Jonah and I are two of those chosen. The Witch, and most other factions of Werdofium, are against us. The last thing we need is to face the fury of any while we build ourselves. Trust no one."

I nod.

Katherine turns and we come into a large open room. The ceiling is still low, but higher than the halls. There are stacks of bunkbeds scattered. At the foot of each is a locker. Lights dangle from the ceiling. It's dim and I don't like it. I place my hand on my chest.

Am I claustrophobic?

"Here is your new home," Katherine turns and offers us a smile. She gestures to the beds, "Any beds that don't have a blanket are unclaimed. You can pick where you stay. Blankets and sheets are in the far corner."

The others dart to beds they fancy. I stand beside Katherine and Jonah as they speak.

"I have to go speak with Sven," she says.

Jonah nods, "I'll make sure they get settled."

"Thanks."

Katherine leaves and Jonah turns to me.

His ready smile disappears, "What's wrong?"

I shrug. I know I should be happy and grateful, but it's dank and dreary in here. The others stake their claim on beds and seem to already be friends. I'm left out.

As always.

"Nothing," I walk further into the room and search for an unclaimed bed.

Jonah frowns and follows me. He steers me

towards the far corner, close to the clean blankets and other supplies.

He points to a bunk, "That's mine." The bed above his is empty. "Why don't you share with me?"

My spirit lifts a little.

"Are you sure? I might snore."

He laughs and nods, "Not as much as me I bet. Sure."

I take a blanket from the pile and place it on the top bunk.

"All right everyone," he raises his hands to grab their attention. "I'll show you where to get your food and other necessities."

The others hop down or stand up and gather round.

"While you're here you're expected to work and make a contribution. So after your tour we'll head down to the assignment station and figure out where you belong."

I'm never excited to figure out where I belong.

Because I never do.

We follow him and Jonah briefly explains English speakers make up the majority of HSAER. Chinese are second followed by Spanish, then French.

"How do we all communicate?" I ask. "Or do we stick to our respective…neighborhoods?"

Jonah shakes his head and we tuck past a group of workers. They smile at us and welcome us home.

"We'll get you translators. We all wear Werdonic translators, so it's like we're all speaking the same language. We want comradery, not division."

I cock my brow, "You're not wearing one."

"I speak Werdonic," he winks at me.

"How long have you been here?"

"Longer than I'd like to be," he says. "Since I was a child."

I pity him. *I'm traumatized by days and he's been here for decades.*

"I'm sorry. No way to get home?"

He shrugs, "The Witch controls all of the portals on this side of the continent. She's not going to grant me one. I can promise you. Although there are rumors of a natural rift that's opened, but it's deep in enemy territory. Impossible for us to get to. For now," he winks. "Until then we're experimenting and doing what we can to make our own."

I nod.

"It's not bad here," he continues. "Instead of American or European or whatever, we're all Earthians." He smiles, "It's nice. We're all on the same side fighting for the rights of the human race. Not just a sect of the human race."

I mirror his smile, "True. I didn't think of it that way."

The others behind us grow quiet as they listen in on our conversation.

"Well, you get the bad egg or two, but nothing we can't handle. And we *do* have a jail," he throws over his shoulder to those following us. "When you get your work assignments we'll give you a packet explaining our laws and punishments."

"Who decides those?" a man in back asks.

"We have a bicameral democracy."

"What?" I ask. *I should have studied political science more.*

"It's like the House and Senate back home."

"Oh."

We come to a cafeteria. There's benches and tables.

On one end of the room the food lays out in a line like you'd expect. People are serving food onto trays. Some of it seems like muck while others are recognizable. I spot hot dogs and macaroni and cheese and mashed potatoes on some trays.

"Food," Jonah points. "This way." He leads us out.

We pass a large open door and I pause. It's a big room, but unlike the others it's bright with fluorescent lighting. Wiring and electronic parts blanket the work-benches. Several people hunch over their work and pay me no mind.

Jonah stops down the way and calls after me.

I catch up to the front of the pack, "What's that?"

"Where they make the translators and other things to improve our lives. Those are our engineers. They have to work overtime. We've had an influx of Earthians in the last few weeks."

We stop at what can best be described as a clothing store.

"Every six months you get a free outfit of your choice. Choose wisely. I suggest waiting until you know your assignment before picking one out."

We all nod and move on.

I wake up in my bunk and roll over.

I catch myself from falling off the side. My heart thuds in my chest as I relax into the cotton sheets. It's not as comfy as Bob's bed, but it does the trick. I slept well.

Bob. Ugh.

I sit up and scratch at the new metal band around my neck. It fits like a choker. The metal cuffs dug into my ears while I tried to sleep, but I can get used to them.

I slide down from the bunk. I slept in my old slave clothes. I share my footlocker with Jonah and open it up. I glance at his empty bed. *I like him.*

My new clothes are folded in the locker. I pull them out. I glance around the room and hide myself behind our bunk. I quite like the privacy of the corner. I change and put my other clothes into the locker. My new uniform is a button-up blue shirt and khaki slacks with a nice pair of black restaurant shoes. I love the support. I tie my hair back into a ponytail with a piece of twine Jonah gave me and head to my first day of work.

My assignment is to run errands for members of our government. *I'm an adult pageboy...lady.* I get lost, but a helpful random woman shows me the way. We pass a wooden box, or the Soap Box Arena, as they call it. It's a place for people to climb up on the box and have their say.

"Ever heard of *Lord of the Flies*?" my guide asks me.

"Yes. I can recall a few things from high school."

She gestures to the box, "Think of it as the conch of HSAER. It gets funny when there's a debate and people try to shove each other off."

I snort, "We should give them padded staves and let them go at it American Gladiator style."

She laughs and shakes her head, then leads me past the Soap Box Arena to a guarded door. Two men, no doubt chosen for their impressive stature, greet us. One has a clipboard.

I thank my guide as she leaves me to the guard checking for my name on the list. I gave them my real last name, but I stuck with George otherwise. He finds it and I sign in on the line. I'm not used to writing George and scribble it. He thanks me and wishes me luck as he unlocks the door to his left. The other guard smiles at me, but keeps his eyes on the Soap Box Arena.

I step through and they lock it behind me. A long hallway with dozens of doors opens up before me with a large one at the end. People are moving to and fro on their own business and I have no idea what to do.

I blink and stand still beside the door, trying to stay out of the way as people rush around. Katherine steps from the eighth door on the left and waves me over. Relief washes over me. I approach.

"Hi. I'm sorry I don't know—"

"No worries," she waves me off. "Step into my office."

I follow her in. It's small and cramped. There's room enough for a small simple desk and a filing cabinet. A single light hangs from the ceiling. It hums as it provides a yellow glow like every other room in the complex.

"You'll be my new assistant," she sits on a stool. "I hope you appreciate it. It's quite difficult to get this position."

My brows furrow, "How—"

"Jonah insisted. He likes you and I like him. So," her smile is empty. "Here we are."

Uh oh.

I glance up to the clock, a copy of every other I've seen in the complex with its eighteen hour slots.

I get to go home in ten hours. Yep, this feels like work.

The day or night, it's hard to tell underground, is spent with Katherine giving me the run around on what she expects of me. She's a member of the democracy and her responsibilities include food storage, prep, supply, distribution, and overseeing the farms.

I glance to the clock, "We have farms?"

"Yes." She's irritated with me and offers no additional information.

Yeah, she doesn't like me. This is going to be so fun.

We work through the hours. I follow her through the complex to the cafeteria, some storage, and then to the mythical farms. They're underground greenhouses. UV lighting keeps it bright and the plants growing. I recognize familiar vegetables alongside the strange and foreign. I follow her with a clipboard, paper, and a crude pencil. I jot down every number they tell her in addition to any notes she has. As we work our way around the complex I can see how I'm lucky to have this job. There are tasks far more laborious than mine.

Though she's catty and impatient with me, it's not bad.

I've worked with worse.

We return to her office and she studies my handiwork.

"Not bad, actually." She offers a real smile, "You seem competent. This won't be as bad as I thought."

I smile and refrain any reply.

"Right. Well, we're done for the day. I have to attend a congressional session. See you tomorrow."

I find Jonah sitting on his bunk when I return to the barracks. He looks up and smiles at me. A fresh bruise mars his bicep.

"What happened there?"

He rubs it, "I'm security and we had an incident."

I suck in my breath and whistle.

"One of the new guys...lost it. For lack of a better word."

I nod. He's the only person in the complex who isn't dubbed by a translator. *I really like him.*

"How was your first day?" he asks.

I reach into the foot locker and dig out my other clothes. I want to keep my work clothes clean and neat. *I think Katherine will like that.* I keep my black shoes on. *So much support.*

"It could have been worse," I disappear behind the pile of blankets for privacy to change.

"But it could have been better."

"I'm in another realm and I still have to deal with politics," I complain.

"What'd you expect? You get sentience, you get politics."

I nod and come out from behind my cover, "Yeah. I know. I appreciate the good word."

He smiles.

I put my work clothes into the locker. I glance at his stuff and catch a picture book about Houston.

"Hey! Houston," I say.

He reaches in and pulls it out. He flips through the glossy pages.

"I'm from Houston."

I sit next to him on his bunk.

"I've been a few times," I say.

"George, how did you end up here?" he asks.

I quirk my lips and consider my answer.

"I was drug here by an imperial guard. He was trying to recapture a rebel named Rinkai. So creepy. He's what's called a puppet kind. Anyway, Rinkai had a hold of me and pulled me through the portal with him," I shrug. "The guard sold me and here I am. Wasn't too bad I suppose, except for the emotional scarring."

I shouldn't complain.

Jonah stares at me, "Rinkai?"

"Yep."

"Who was the guard that sold you?"

"Bob," I answer. "Well, Asrieth I guess."

"Holy shit," he stands.

I watch him pace. He checks the room and bunks around us. We're alone save a few sleeping in silence.

"Asrieth," he whirls around on me and points at me. "What would you say your relationship to Asrieth is?"

I shake my head, eyes wide, "I don't know. I suppose nonexistent now. It wasn't bad though. Why?"

"You're sure he won't come after you?"

I laugh, "He sold me. Why would he come after me?"

"You don't know Asrieth."

No. I don't suppose I do, but I do know Bob.

"And you do?" I stand and cross my arms. "What are you getting at?"

"Asrieth has another name."

How does he know about the Bob identity?

"Jonah!" I snap my fingers, "Focus."

"Come on," he grabs my wrist and jerks me forward to stumble after him.

We leave the dorms and navigate the maze of corridors through the complex. I recognize where we're heading. I just left there.

"Why are you taking me to the democracy? You're being so vague."

Jonah tugs, "Do you have to fight everything? Trust me."

I do trust you. Then again, the last person I trusted sold me into slavery.

"I don't have a choice do I?"

"No. I'll drag you by your hair if I must."

I roll my eyes and smile. I stop resisting and walk next to him down the corridor.

We pass the Soap Box Arena to the guarded door. They don't even check the list and open it for us with a nod from Jonah.

After traversing the long hallway, passing Katherine's office on the way, we reach the large door at the end, which is actually two doors. They're closed with guards. Another nod from Jonah and they open it up to us and I peer down into the coliseum setting of the democratic room. They're in session and representatives pack the pavilion. Jonah pulls me past security down the stairs. We make a commotion and grab the attention of the room as a representative speaks on a bill.

Facing the crowd, and behind their respective podiums, are three judges who regulate the meetings. Two men and one woman all considered to be old and wise. Sven, the oldest and therefore senior judge, confronts us.

"What are you doing? We're in session."

Katherine stands among the rows of representation.

"Jonah. What in the hell are you doing?"

Jonah lets go of my hand and takes me by the shoulders to march me before the judges.

"Hear me out. The man who sold her into slavery was Asrieth."

The crowd gasps. One woman cries out at mention of his name. All eyes are on me and I can only stand like an idiot in my confusion. Jonah puts his forearm across my chest, pulling me to him. People are pointing and cursing at me. I stare as chaos breaks out in seconds. Sven slams his gavel on the podium several times before people sit back down in their chairs and things come to order.

"We'll speak in private," Sven nods to Katherine as she comes down the aisle. "With your representative.

Everyone else clear out. This session is suspended until 8:00 a.m." He bangs the gavel and the crowd files out through the double doors.

A number of them glimpse me over their shoulders. *I feel like a leper.*

Katherine scowls as she descends to stand with us. She glares at me and Jonah pulls me closer to him.

"She's not to blame, Kat. It's not what you think."

"Oh please," she rolls her eyes. "We all know you're protecting your little piece of arse."

My eyes snap to Katherine, "Fuck you. You don't know me or anything about me." I turn to Sven, "I don't know what's going on. Jonah hasn't told me anything."

My safe haven crumbles down around me.

Katherine's lips purse.

Rosemary, the female judge, speaks up in a soft voice, "Let's hear her out, Katherine."

"She has nothing to say. She doesn't know," Jonah begins. "We were only bullshitting."

Katherine shakes her head and crosses her arms.

Jonah glares at her as he continues, "The subject came up of how we ended up here. She mentioned Asrieth. She has no idea who he is or...or what he does. She called him an imperial guard."

The judges exchange a glance. Katherine's eyes widen.

"Or she's lying," she says.

I avoid their gaze, "What do I have to gain from that? I love it here. This is the most I've felt at home or safe since I've gotten to this God-forsaken place. If I was going to lie, wouldn't it be about knowing him in the first place?"

"Look, we never asked her," Jonah continues. "Just like everyone else who's new. We don't ask people. She didn't know. Do you really think Asrieth told her who he was?"

I cast my eyes down, "I asked, but he was vague. I honestly didn't care either. I was so dead set on getting back."

"Like all of us," Jonah adds.

The judges sit in silence.

Everything crashes down on me.

Sure I don't have chapstick, soda, or the internet, but this is a decent place. I don't want to leave. Once again Bob's fucked me over. Unintentionally. That's talent.

"Can someone tell me what's going on? Who is…Asrieth?" His real name is foreign on my lips, "Why are you so afraid of him? He's a bumbling idiot."

The image of being thrown out into the desert sitting backwards on a horse in a giant paper mache helmet shaped like a creepy man's head crosses my mind.

"Asrieth is the Extractor," Sven begins.

I resist the urge to laugh. *It sounds like the title of a Steven Segal movie.*

"He is the Witch's personal tormentor," he continues. "He's not a bumbling idiot, as you call him, but good at what he does. The best. If you possess knowledge of a subject he will make you talk. Asrieth is the very reason we don't tell the populace of our exact location. He can, and will, break you. He is more than an imperial guard, young lady."

"And that's not even half of it," Katherine adds.

My brows furrow as I consider their words.

It can't be. He was vague but…no. It can't be. He's never been that way to me. Ever. He's a bumbling idiot.

I shut my eyes.

I can see it.

If I study him closer, without the filtration of a friend or...romantic interest, I would note how he saunters around the room. His weapons, sharp teeth, and the way he carries himself. I can see a killer in his eyes. The image of Bob fades away as Asrieth consumes my memories of him. From the man who sat on my couch eating popcorn and watching cartoons to a killer. *A tormentor. A person who makes people like me suffer for his livelihood.*

And he's the best at it. Boy I know how to pick 'em.

I try to use reason, "If he's going to come for me, wouldn't he be here by now? If he's following me like you say, he'd be here already. If it's a part of some elaborate plan to out HSAER, wouldn't he strike before you find this out? When he has the element of surprise?"

The judges mutter amongst themselves as Katherine exchanges a glance with Jonah.

"State the obvious, won't ya?" Jonah loosens his grip on me as the room breathes out their held breath. "See? She has a point."

Katherine can't keep her trap shut and says, "Either that or he's biding his time until we get good and relaxed. Then, when we think it's safe, he'll come. It's only been a day."

A shadow of doubt crosses their faces. Including mine.

"That can't be it," I say. I'm turning into one of the sheep as Katherine spits her poisonous words against me. Logical though it is.

"What do we do?" I ask. Behind their eyes cogs turn.

Right now they're trying to decide what to do with me.

I hold my breath a few seconds. I know of my innocence, but people are deceitful. Knowing them only a day hasn't proven any loyalties to them on my part. *I can't blame them for not trusting me.*

Sven clears his throat and speaks, "For now we'll put her in a holding cell."

Jonah begins to protest and the judges silence him.

"Just for now," Sven continues. "You can handle that for us. We'll come for her when we have discussed our options. We'll figure this out." He glares at Katherine's smug expression, "She still has rights."

Katherine frowns, "I suppose I need to find a new assistant."

I'm sure you're heartbroken.

Jonah puts his arm around my shoulders and leads me up the steps. Their eyes bore into my back until we step over the threshold to the corridor. I know where the holding cells are. In the uppermost levels of the complex where there's oppressive heat. If there's an attack the prisoners are most likely to be killed first. In this system of justice there's a strand of blatant cruelty. I know these rules, but didn't care until they applied to me. *Much like politics back home.*

I can't look up as we walk. Jonah keeps his arm around me and stares straight ahead.

"I'm sorry," he says.

I answer him with a shake of my head. I wipe my eyes and condemn myself for stupidity and weakness.

"Honestly, if I knew it would turn out this way I wouldn't have told them."

"What did you think was gonna happen?" I ask.

"I thought I was warning everyone. I thought it was the right thing to do. I'd never doubt you. Katherine's just jealous," he shakes his head.

"I don't understand?"

"We used to be together," he pauses. "She's jealous of you. I like you and she knows it."

I stop and bring myself to peer up at him. In an instant, before I know what either of us is doing, he embraces and kisses me. I close my eyes and lean against him, tilting my head upward. His lips are soft and warm.

We pull apart and I breathe inward.

I haven't kissed anyone since Phillip.

I can't help but wonder what Rachael would think of this. She was so desperate for me to find someone.

We smile at each other.

Then he leads me to my prison cell in silence.

7. Cells Are Boring…Unless They Have Apps

I scratch the 17th mark on my cell wall with a small rock.

I know it's the beginning of a new day because they bring my bread and water. I snarf it in record time. Now I have the other twenty-three hours and fifty-five minutes to sit in the dark and contemplate my life choices.

I think of family.

My little brother was a miracle baby. Years before his conception doctors told my mother she couldn't have any more children due to complications from carrying me. Those were the golden years. My parents loved me then and it's unfair to ever say they didn't, but when my brother was born, I was all but forgotten. *What a surprise.* I was excited at first, of course. It was neat I wouldn't be the only kid in the house. *Finally*, I thought. *Someone to play with!* Until I realized he was more precious than I. More loved. I know it isn't his fault, but I can't help hating him.

I don't have a tragic past to run away from

haunting me during silent times. Only a few regrets. Some of them obvious. *Like helping Bob out. Even if that spell made me do it, I also know it didn't take much convincing.*

I start to think of Phillip...and I can't. I force myself not to.

A scream resonates down the halls.

They're good at keeping us from social interaction. The cell is small with a narrow slot in the metal door. Through that small gap comes my only light source, a single bulb humming with electricity in the hall. In the beginning, a bucket in the corner was my biggest fear of this cell. Now it's that I'll never leave it.

Jonah does what he can for me. I'm left alone and get a half loaf of bread and clean water. As opposed to a slice and questionable liquids. I appreciate his efforts, but his power has limits. He visits me on occasion and a few days ago he informs me the judges made a decision. I'm not important enough to take action, but to keep in lockup.

I finish the scratch on the wall and sit back onto the stone floor. The scream repeats closer. Cries of panic follow. It isn't until smoke creeps into my slot I realize something is wrong. I spring to my feet and peer through the small hole in my door. I tiptoe to look out. The smoke thickens and crawls down the corridor.

Boom!

My ears ring after an explosion shakes the earth. I lose my grip, stumbling back. I recover and jump back up. The guards are running up and down the halls in a frenzy. They begin to open cell doors to free the other prisoners. A guard reaches mine and I stand back for him to free me. Instead he spits through the slot and moves on.

"What?" I'm at the small window again, reaching my arm out. "Let me go! Hey! Let me go!"

The smoke thickens and I cough. I shudder and step back. Cowering down into the corner, I stay under the worst of the smoke. As it thickens I flatten myself to the floor and cover my face. Something hits my side and I dare a peek. It's a gas mask.

I scramble with it over my face and breathe easy once the seals are intact. I find Jonah extending his arm through the slot, holding a small leather satchel out to me. I reach up for it.

He holds onto it, "Don't let anyone have it. Anybody." He lets it go. "They're coming for you now." He retracts his arm and disappears.

"Jonah! Wait!" I jump to my feet and search the cloud of thick smoke. "Take me with you!"

My eyes sting and I back down into the corner of the cell. A thunderous crash alerts me to movement in the hallway. Shadows flicker around in the misty light of the bulb and smoke. The light flickers and my heart stops in the brief darkness.

I reach out through the slot, "Help me! Help me!"

"George," a hand grabs mine.

I know that voice.

My heart aches. Betrayal and hatred attach to him now. I don't want to see him. I quiet and pull my hand free. I sit in the corner of my cell.

A shadow lurks in front of the slot blocking out the dim light of the flickering bulb. The metal door yanks from its hinges. It drops to the side with a clang and the tall figure steps into my small space, filling the cell with his presence. I recognize Bob's white hair sticking out past the black goggles and gas mask. I know it's him.

"Asrieth," I whisper. In his suit of black-studded

armor he looks the part of the monster others paint him to be.

He kneels in front of me and places his gloved hands on my cheeks, over the mask, with a gentle touch. I shake my head.

I don't understand.

I push him away, "No."

He leans down and grips my arms to jerk me to my feet and hoists me over his shoulder like a sack.

"I'm not giving you a choice."

He ducks down through the doorway, careful of me clearing it, and I punch him with all my might. He holds me against him.

"Why?" I ask his back as I relax in his grip. "Why did you do this to me?"

We reach a hallway I don't recognize due to smoke. He sets me down in front of him. I tighten my grip on the satchel.

"To you? How about *for* you?" He crouches to be closer to eye level with me. "I'm here for you, George." He shakes his head and pulls me against him in another tight grip. My eyes widen.

I have myself so convinced he hates and uses me this is not how I thought our reunion would be. *I didn't expect a reunion at all.*

He pulls away and smooths down my hair, "Listen, the place is on fire. Let's get out of here. Don't make me drag you." His warm hand encloses mind and he tugs on me. I grip him and the satchel with my free hand as I stumble behind the man my human friends fear.

We reach the steps leading out to the dome at the entrance of the compound. Bob pulls me in front of him and grips my hips to support me up the stairs. After weeks of no exercise my legs tremble with the sudden movement. He keeps hold of my hand in the frenzy. Smoke billows through the holes in the stone ground and people escape. They're caught by imperial guards in black armor as they crawl out, choking and coughing. I ease my guilt by telling myself this really isn't all for me.

Bob is here by coincidence.

We clear the concentrated groups of humans and soldiers. I glimpse the chaos as he leads me through.

Soldiers step out of his way and avoid him. There are hundreds here, not including those cleaning out the complex below.

A soldier holding reins of an impressive black horse…thing that spits fire and adorned in armor hands them to Bob. I dig my heels into the desert ground upon seeing its mane and tail are flames. Bob glances over his shoulder to me and tugs. The horse stamps his flame hooves and dust kicks up. I read about Nightmares in books and saw them in movies, but this is unreal.

I wonder if mythical creatures from Earth really are from Werdofium. Lost creatures trying to get home, like me.

Bob lets me go only to swing up into the saddle. He sits astride and reaches down for me. I hesitate. Over my shoulder I glance back to the members of HSAER crying in confusion. Some are burnt, most are coughing, but all scream in agony. I watch those few I recognize crawling to what they hope is their salvation to be met by the end of a sharp sword. Katherine stands, a blanket around her misshapen shoulders, staring at me through the haze of smoke. Soot and ash layer her face. The hatred of her eyes burns through the layer of dirt.

I turn my back on her.

Just as she turned hers on me.

I start awake.

We reach the palace gates and my ass is sore.

Bob hasn't said a word since we left and galloped off into the morning sun. I'm sitting on the saddle in front of him as he keeps his arm around me. It's a lucky thing as I dozed off at least once. The horse slows to a walk.

I turn in front of him to catch a glimpse of the city behind us, but meet a wall of vapor instead. *Dammit, I missed it again!*

High, dark, and stone walls surround the volcanic palace. Sentries walk the length above with spears in their hands. A large metal portcullis rises to let us through and we're met with a thick haze of hot vapor. It stinks like the rest of the town, but once again my mask filtrates the worst of it. We dismount Bob's horse, a helpful guard keeping me on my feet until Bob can take over, and we disappear into the mist.

Bob seems to know exactly where he's going and I follow him as always. Were I alone in this mess, I couldn't get anywhere. The dark palace door looms ahead of us out of the vape and opens. We enter into a great receiving hall that has seen better days. Ragged and threadbare black carpet covers slate floors. There are no decorations. No paintings. No tapestries. Not even candlesticks. Torches are hung creatively along the walls in a staggering pattern. Their smoke rises to the high ceiling covering the paintings of long ago in a haze.

As we pass through, most of the palace is this way. Once grand, now dirty and neglected. We pass several guards and others who have business on the grounds. I discover who some of the hooves and claw feet belong to. Satyrs and imps and many manner of creatures I thought to be the vivid hallucinations of ancient peoples.

We pass a minotaur close to Bob's room and I can't take my eyes off of him. He towers over even Asrieth and his blue fur is brilliant in the glum atmosphere. His clothes are well-tailored and black silk. Bob smiles and opens a door before pushing me into the room.

I look around.

Ah, familiarity.

He shuts the door and locks it, "It's rude to stare."

"Sorry," I shrug.

I shuffle over to the bed and flop onto it. I'm not sleepy. I had enough sleep in that lovely cell of mine. This fatigue is something different.

I feel loss.

I can't be sure who I am or who I can trust. Nothing is what it seems in this place.

Bob's weight sinks the mattress beside me and he takes off my mask. He takes off his own with the goggles and drops them all to the floor next to the bed. He brushes stray hair from my eyes. I glance up at him.

"Are you okay?" he asks.

I nod.

He glances to the closed balcony doors and hovers his hand over my forehead, "Did they hurt you?"

I want to ask him why he cares. *Maybe I should.*

"No. They didn't hurt me."

"Didn't think I'd come, did you?"

"I don't understand why you did."

From his boot he pulls out a large knife that would make Paul Hogan proud and uses it to clean under his sharp nails.

"I don't understand why I wouldn't."

"Did you sell me to find them?" I sit up to lean back on my elbows.

He keeps his eyes on his nails, "I didn't sell you."

A floodgate opens and I launch myself onto him. It's all I need. My arms circle his neck and the knife clanks to the stone floor. He's frozen.

"Why?" I shouldn't ask.

I think I know, but I want to hear him say it. I need someone else to say it. It should be him.

He turns and encircles me in his arms. I feel safe.

"Because I care about you, silly."

"Nobody says silly anymore."

"I don't know why you think I sold you. I would never do that." He loosens his grip and pushes me to lie back down.

"What happened?" I sit up on my elbows. He presses me down again.

"I went into the store to get you a translator. I've used that man before to get other Earthian things. I didn't even think of it because I'm usually alone, but he always closes the store for me when we do business for privacy. He kicked you out with all of the other customers. I thought he left you alone but," he glances to the satchel lying on the bed next to me, "I was in the back room and didn't see what happened. As soon as I realized you were outside I went to look for you. You were gone."

I nod. *It makes sense.* Guilt passes over me as I recollect the hate and doubt I cast over him.

"I did revel in finding HSAER's base, but it was only a perk. It was easy to get the Witch to loan me some soldiers for that. It's important people don't know about you George. I have many enemies who would love to get their hands on you. They may be who took you from me."

Saying they took me from him is a flattering way to put it. *It means I'm important enough to him to be taken away in the first place. If he really is what they say he is.* Then I cross my arms.

"Took me from you? Like I'm a glorified wallet."

He laughs, "You know what I mean."

"How did you find out where I was?" I ask.

"I have my ways." He smiles, careful to keep his teeth hidden.

I have difficulty pushing back images of people from the market tortured at his behest.

"What do you remember?" he asks.

"What?"

"The person who kidnapped you. What do you remember?"

"Can't we just forget it?"

He nods, "If you feel it's not important."

"Well, it is, but I don't see what good will come of it," I sit up and lean against the carved headboard. I prop a pillow behind me and settle down. "Are *you* okay? You seem different. More, manly maybe. Or at least more coordinated."

Bob smirks, "I missed you more than I thought."

"Gee, thanks."

"You know what I mean."

I smile with a nod. My eyes wander around as he stands and the mattress bounces up without his weight. The room is almost new to me. I spent only a couple of days in it before the kidnapping. It's messier than I recall. Paperwork is scattered in clumsy piles on the desk that used to be covered in trinkets and magazines. A pile of weapons leans against the corner opposite the desk. I can't discern what's in the mess of wood and steel. I swallow when I note a sword poking out, imagining it covered in blood to the hilt. It reminds me of Asrieth, not Bob. And what he represents to my fellow Earthians. Mertyl curls up on the corner of the bed, immobile, as always.

"Can I ask you something?" I venture.

He kneels in front of the generator humming along beneath the desk and turns the knob to stop the motor, "Of course."

"Promise you won't get mad?"

His black eyes glance at me before he pulls the motor out from under the desk. He yanks out a blood-red square of cloth from the machine.

"Well, I can't promise, but I'll try."

"Maybe I shouldn't ask."

With the flick of his hand the sheet is white and a small liquid sphere of red floats in the air next to him. I haven't seen magic in the time I've been here. HAESR didn't have a grasp on it, but they were trying. The theory is magic is available to all of us in this realm. Most Earthians don't take the time to learn from someone who knows or cares to teach us.

Bob reinserts the square and pushes the filter under the desk. The knob clicks when he turns it back on and the motor hums to life.

"George, unless you're going to insult my mother—and even then I don't care—I don't think I'll get mad," he smiles.

He opens the top drawer of the desk and withdraws an empty glass vial. The bloody liquid squeezes down through the opening and he stoppers it.

"If you're sure…"

He sets the vial down on the desk.

"Oh c'mon. What are you afraid of? What did those

Earthians do to you?"

It's the emphasis on "those Earthians" that causes me to frown and cross my arms, "Go fuck yourself."

"That's more like it," he chuckles. "What did you want to ask?"

"About Asrieth."

His smile dies, "You know I'm Asrieth."

"Yes. I know, but I think...I think if we're going to be this—" I motion between the two of us, "Then I need to know more about you. Isn't it fair? You know me better than I know you. You lived with me for weeks and when you asked, I told you about me. I'm tired of the mystery. The vague answers. I know you're doing it on purpose. I heard terrible, horrible things about you. I need to know if they're true."

Bob stands and pulls the broken chair out from the desk. He straddles it, leaning on the back with his arms, and keeps his balance on the wobbly legs. The wood creaks under his weight.

"And what terrible things did you hear?" his voice is soft and stare intense.

I shift under his scrutiny, "Well...that you are, you know."

"Maybe I don't know. What am I exactly?"

I glimpse the darkness within him. His face is stoic, and though they're black, his eyes gleam in the dull red light. I can't help a glance to the sword and wonder.

"Do you doubt me even now?" he asks, breaking my spell of fear.

I can't answer him truthfully.

He frowns and stands, the chair creaking. His boots echo off of the stone walls as he approaches me with caution. Slow and careful.

"George, I turned this city upside down searching

for you. I know it seems unbelievable. That I can care for a puny little Earthian so, but it's true."

"Why?"

"Because what they said is true." He holds his breath and stops short of the bed, looming over me as he confesses, "Because I am what they say. Whatever it is they said. If it is horrible and terrible then it is true. I have done what they think and beyond their imagination. I am an awful man. Everyone is afraid of me. They should be."

I shrink from him and grip the satchel, hugging it to my chest.

"Everyone, but you. Don't do that. Don't be afraid of me too. You didn't used to be. I'm the same as I was two days ago, I promise." He runs his claws through his unkempt hair and sits on the edge of the bed close to me.

I choose not to run in fear.

"Please, I'm like everyone else..." He reaches out to my white knuckles.

I don't flinch. *This is Bob. He laughs. He's goofy. He's fun. And I declared him a bumbling idiot more times than I can count.*

"I need someone in my life that doesn't run from me, or use me." He smiles, "I can't remember the last time someone smiled at me genuinely. The last time I was...hugged for fuck's sake. Before you, there's nothing."

I let go of the satchel and sit up. I take his hand in both of mine. I look down at them together, my tan in contrast to his pale skin, and squeeze. My lids flutter as I try not to cry. I don't only have pity. It makes me feel good to be so important to another person. I can't imagine what his life is like.

Worse than mine.

I don't seem to care, or mind at least, the reason for his pain is his own evil wicked bad man actions.

I suppose I don't give a shit.

"I'd like to say I understand, but I'd be lying." I'm disappointed to find tears rolling down my cheeks despite my best efforts.

"Aw, jeez. Don't cry you big baby."

I look up when his thumb brushes my left cheek.

"Yeah, well, maybe if you weren't so pathetic I wouldn't have to feel so sorry for you."

He smirks, "Keep it to yourself. I have a reputation to uphold."

"Absolutely."

"George, no matter what people tell you about me, I would never do those things to you."

I nod, forcing a smile. *What will he do if the Witch asks him to? Hopefully I'll never find out.*

I release his hand and reach down for the satchel. A dark layer of soot covers the light tan leather and I brush it with my fingertips.

Bob wipes at his comforter, "Can you please not get that stuff all over my bed?"

I glance at him and work the straps loose. The bag is far too big for the item inside and rolled up and tied tight to make up for the excess fabric. I cross my ankles and stretch my legs out to allow room for the satchel on the bed in front of me. Curiosity eats at me as I unroll the satchel I forgot moments ago.

Bob nods to it, "What's that?"

"Heck if I know," I shrug and loosen the straps to untie the string, "Jonah gave it to me right before you found me."

"Jonah?"

"A friend."

"Is that all?"

"Yes."

"You sure?"

I peer up at him. He's studying my face. I don't know why I lied. My thoughts linger on our kiss.

"I'm sure," I stick my hand into the satchel and search for the item inside. "He was the jackass who put in me in jail in the first place."

Satisfied, Bob nods. His brows furrow while he watches me feel around the bag.

"Then why did he give it to you?"

I shrug.

"Did he say anything when he gave it to you?"

"Yeah, not to let anyone have it." Any lingering feelings for HSAER faded with my sanity in the cell.

Especially Katherine and her bitchy bitch bitcherness.

My fingers find something cold to the touch, and smooth. Like ice. It's unnatural in this humid and hot environment. I retract my hand, sucking in my breath. I reach in again and my fingers circle the long thin item, finding sharp points scattering up and down its length.

I withdraw my hand and stare at the punctures covering my palm and fingers. Bob snatches the satchel and opens it to peer inside. He pulls out an unnaturally large rose. Red petals and greens leaves are vivid and stark against each other. Never has a redder rose existed. The size of my fist, the petals on the head of the flower are large and blooming and the stem stretches to a yard in length. A layer of shine coats it as though someone dipped it in a light layer of glitter. A thin steam rises from its cool surface as it hits the hot air. Its thorns are over an inch long and I glance at my pricked hand. Bob holds it up between us, his grip tight over the stem, and we stare at it.

"Is it…frozen?" I ask.

He shakes his head, "I don't know. What the hell is it?"

"A flower?"

"No. It's more than that. Did your little friend tell you anything about it?"

"Will you put it down at least? Are you bleeding?"

He sets down the rose on the bed and studies his hand, "My hands are callused from work. So not much."

I stare at the rose and try not to think of his work.

"What should we do?"

He shrugs, "I don't know. I've never seen it. Nor heard of it." His fingers brush against the stiff petals. "It must be important though. I wonder how important."

As his fingers slide around the folds of the petals, the red color brightens. He stops and hovers his hand over the flower. The petals grow bright until it glows a pale red, light bouncing off of the hard surfaces of the room. It's different from the bloody copper that normally blankets us. The air around us shifts. My hair lifts in weightlessness. My brain runs laps around my head and I reach up, feeling I can fly. Bob's white skin washes in rose color and he seems akin to the Devil. His black eyes widen and look up to me, his own hair lifting and framing his face.

"Can you feel that?" his whispers.

I nod. My voice is distant, "Yeah."

"That's magic."

I smile and enjoy it.

Bob touches the glowing petals. The runic and tribal tattoos that adorn his skin glow the same red color. I can't comprehend the significance of what's happening around me. I giggle and enjoy my new high. The color brightens to a blinding white and force knocks

Bob back to crash into the wall behind him. He makes a dent in the stone and a few pieces clatter to the ground around him. I lean forward, hovering over the rose as my body lifts from the bed.

"Whoa."

"Don't touch it," he picks himself up. The glow of his tattoos dies and the pale red light bathes him again. The petals dim without his touch.

Bob nods to me, "Take the pillowcase off of that pillow."

I laugh at him. *Why would I do that? Pretty...*

He comes round to me and yanks the pillow beneath me. I float and laugh harder at him and roll around in circles, spinning in the air. He grips the soft pillow and peels back the case. He flicks his hand and the rose levitates in front of me. I stop laughing and stare. I reach out to the pretty flower.

"I said don't touch it!" he snaps.

I blink and swallow, still spinning, but keeping my hand out.

Bob holds open the mouth of the pillowcase and the flower levitates inward, the brilliant red glow shining through the cloth. Bob grips the opening of the pillow-case and closes it. The weight of the rose drops into it. The glow fades and it's once again a lump in cloth.

I drop onto the bed with a bounce.

The shiny spell of the rose ebbs from me in seconds. Gravity is too much. I lay face down and breathe against the soft comforter. My head explodes in staggering pain and I curl up, gripping the sides of my temples. Screams ring in my ears.

They're mine.

8. Doooom Flowah

I probably dreamed, but I can't recall.

I come to with lingering thoughts on college. I hate writing prompts that are deep philosophical questions. Questions that are impossible to answer and more so for a teacher to decipher unless they understand the inner workings of your psyche. Since classes are large and we're only numbers to them, I doubt that's possible. One such question I loathe is "If you could go back in time and do anything, what would it be?" followed by a dictated word count far too low to answer this properly.

How can I explain the biggest regrets of my life in five hundred words or less?

I stretch on the bed and snuggle deeper into the soft sheets as I recall where I am. *Not in HSAER.* I don't need warmth, but I like cocooning in a sheet burrito. It protects me from monsters lurking beneath the bed.

Does the sheet burrito defense hold up in Werdofium? Probably not.

I open my eyes.

Sweat adheres the sheets to my skin and I sit up to

peel them from the contours of my body. A spiking throb remains from the migraine that shoots through the mush between my ears. I snatch a breath of air and push my palms against my temples. My recollection of how I passed out inches its way back into reality the longer I remain conscious. I close my eyes.

"Magic headaches are the worst."

I creak open an unwilling eye and find Bob sitting on the wobbly chair at the desk. He hunches over a large book with several others piled around him.

"I never took you for the scholarly type," I regret speaking. Pain shoots between my ears like an icepick. I double in on myself and grit my teeth.

"Don't talk. It only makes it worse. Even if it's to joke about me."

My face twists as I resist crying out. I do my best drugged cat impression and wish for the headache to go away. My stomach rumbles. I will myself not to vomit from bullets of pain whizzing around in my head.

"There's nothing you can do but sleep it off," he pushes himself from the desk, the scrape of wood on stone rings like an explosion in my ears.

I cry out.

"I can't give you anything for the pain, but I can make you sleep. Would you like that?"

I can only moan.

"George, last time I used magic on you, it made you angry. I won't do it again unless you explicitly say."

I clamor and suck in my breath, preparing for the price I must pay, and say, "Asshole."

"I'll take that as a yes."

Sweet, beautiful, painless, blissful darkness.

I wake up in better spirits.

The headache contains to a minor ache in the back of my head as I stir. My eyelids are heavy while they flutter open. Distant and groggy, I kick off the sheets. I roll to my side, facing the balcony doors, and sling my arm over the edge of the bed.

Bob sits at the desk again, reclining in the wooden chair with a book in his lap, facing the bed. It disappoints me he doesn't have spectacles on.

"Bob?"

His dark eyes glance at me and peer over the edge of the book, which is large and leather and typical of a tome found in a thirteenth-century library back on Earth.

"How's your head?"

I clutch my tangled hair, "It's fine, but I still feel weird. What happened?"

He places the open book on his desk and turns back to me.

"You were over-exposed to magic."

I nod, "Would you care to explain that professor?"

He smiles, "I guess. If you've not had exposure to magic, too much at once can do damage. It must be taken in doses like most other things. That rose…well, that's just the thing."

"What is?"

"It's a source of magic."

"And that's significant?" I ask.

He points to the open book, "Very. In this realm magic is a naturally occurring element. Like water and air. You don't find an object that produces water out of nowhere. It has to come from somewhere. Same with magic. It doesn't come out of nowhere. It takes time to build back up, just like any other natural resource. Those who are gifted in magic don't possess more of it; they're able to channel larger amounts of it through their bodies without causing themselves harm. And they're not always successful. There's only so much magic to go around. Like water."

I'm too groggy to get this. Or care. "Bob…"

"This means that whoever possesses this rose, or whatever you want to call it, has access to unlimited magic." He grows excitable as he talks, "If someone can learn to control how much magic that thing outputs, they can become godlike. I just want to know where in the hell it came from."

He stands up and paces.

"Where did HSAER get it? Gods, if only there's a way to find out."

I prop up the pillow without a case behind me and lean against it.

I think my body is going to mold its form into this mattress.

"I don't know about magic, but that sounds…bad."

Bob stops pacing and looks at me.

"You're right. It can be. In the wrong hands."

"And what are the right hands?" *I have a feeling I know already.*

"The Witch."

Bad feeling confirmed! "Are you serious?" I ask.

"She's not as bad as she's painted to be."

"Yeah, and for the Nazis Hitler hung the moon. It's all about perspective."

"Exactly. Listen to yourself. Everything you've heard about her is from someone else. You can say the same of me," he says.

"Okay, fine. That's fair, but she is the one who gets you to torture people."

"You're in denial if you think your leaders are more innocent."

I bite my tongue. *I am ignorant as far as politics are concerned. I can't say what goes on behind closed classified doors. In my realm, my country, there are "information extractors" just like him. Men and women who go to work in dark basements and come home at the end of the day to their families.*

At least Asrieth doesn't pretend to be what he isn't. As far as I know, as always.

"So what's your deal with her then?"

He shrugs, "I don't know what you mean."

"Oh please. You always jump up to defend her." I fake a gasp, "Are you in love with her?"

He snorts, "No. She's more like a mother figure. She and my mother are good friends. I knew her as a child and I knew her son. She's not what people make her out to be. She only has unorthodox ways of getting things done."

I smile, picturing an old woman bending over a cauldron with a giant wart on her giant nose.

Of course he isn't in love with her.

"So, you really think we should take it to her? That's our best course of action?" I push Jonah's warning to the back of my mind. I don't fault him for what happened, but he's not here. My self-preservation is.

"Yes. And it's the only one. She's the only person we can trust with it."

"Who else is there?"

"Her generals. Advisors."

"Oh. Are they evil and conniving? They always

are," I perk up.

Bob frowns, "This isn't a fairytale and shouldn't be treated as such."

I nod. *He's right. I need to stop making comparisons between this reality and stories I fancied as a kid. Stories I still fancy as an adult.*

"But, you still don't trust them? Her people?"

"In my line of work you can't trust anyone. Except for hapless women you drag into your dimension against their will," he winks at me.

I laugh.

Because Bob does, in fact, know the Witch personally we find no resistance getting an audience.

Oh! An audience! We're going to court. We're going to court!

It's strange to make an appointment with a witch. I remind myself on occasion as we walk down the palace corridors that she is in fact a world leader and not some old lady stooping over a cauldron poisoning apples all day.

I'm happy to walk out in the open. Since my kidnapping, Bob isn't leaving me alone again. *Or so he says.* I protest I at least need to be alone during bathroom time. Bathroom time is off limits.

I wear the gas mask, but no more hoodies or boots that are too big. I get a look now and again, but one glance from Asrieth sends them in another direction. Everyone really does seem to know him and what he does. He looms beside me as a man who fears nothing.

But I know better. He has fears.

The palace remains a series of mazes inside the

volcanic mountain and I don't know why I expect it to be different this time. The decorator went out for a few centuries by the looks of dust. I think perhaps as we grow closer to the Witch things spruce up, but no.

Has this carpet ever been vacuumed? Even magically? I know magic cleans because Disney says so.

We go upstairs again and again.

It's because of these stairs we're running late for our appointment. They're dark and steep inside the stairwell, lit by dim candles on sconces. I huff and puff, hanging onto Bob's belt. He drags me upward as the rose in the satchel bangs against my hip every step.

Bob glances over his shoulder, coming to a halt, and whispers, "We're here."

I straighten up. He grips his pants and pulls them up. I make an effort to breathe in and out of my nose to avoid panting like a dog.

From the stairs we enter a cavernous room carved out of glassy lava rock. It's smooth and black with white veins. Massive columns are placed with strategy around the room to keep the mountain above from crashing down. My eyes wander and find nothing. There are no guards, no carpet, not even a secretary. Next to the entrance float large white balls of light a yard wide chained to the wall with dainty silver links. Beyond the columns lays darkness. I look down and find our reflections in the shining surface of the floor. I frown when I see up my skirt and step my feet together.

"Where are the guards?" my question echoes down the walls of the massive room.

Bob keeps his reply soft, "She doesn't need any."

I swallow and nod.

"I should let you do the talking."

"Yes. Unless she asks you something directly."

I nod again and inch closer to him.

He glances at me, "If she asks your name tell her it's George."

"That's the plan." I make a mental note to ask him the significance of that advice later. I tug down my gas mask to hang around my neck since there isn't any red mist in here.

"Where is she?"

In answer a low grumbling akin to rocks grinding against each other drifts to us from the darkness. I stiffen and my hand shoots up to curl around Bob's bicep.

"What was that?" my whisper hisses into the room.

"Her pet," he answers. Bob relaxes next to me and glances down smiling. My other hand curls around his forearm and I sidle closer, keeping myself partially behind him.

"Don't worry," he says. "She never shows it to anyone who isn't going to get eaten."

"Stop bullshitting."

"No really. She feeds her enemies to it."

"You love this."

"Absolutely."

The grinding stops and I squint into the darkness until a humanoid saunters out of it.

She has every right to saunter.

My eyes widen and take in the form of the Witch.

She'd make a perfect spokesman for an MMO.

Jewels and precious metals adorn brilliant pink hair pulled taught from her dark face into an intricate braid. Against her black skin the shade of her hair is neon and bright in the dark room. Strips of pink silk held together by thin silver chains and small brooches, pinning fabric together over strategic places, compliment her curves. A length of flexible metal runs from her wrist to her upper arms like metallic sleeves. Dozens of silver rings on her ankles run along the length of her foot with chains attached to toe rings.

As she grows close I catch a gasp in my throat.

She has no pupils and only the whites of her eyes look upon us. Large leathery wings sprout from her back and blend into the darkness behind her.

The Witch's pouty lips stretch into a white pearly smile of sharp teeth as she approaches. She holds out her hands, which glint with rings, metal, and precious stones so numerous she appears gloved.

"Asrieth, my little love," her voice is smooth and dripping with honey.

Bob steps forward and takes her delicate hands in his and leans down to kiss her cheeks.

It disappoints me she isn't an old crone.

I don't like her.

Bob lets her go and she faces me, the only true indication she's looking at me, smiling.

"And this must be?"

"George," he answers.

"How nice to meet you. I'm Lilith. You may also call me Lady." She beckons me with her glittering fingers.

I glance to Bob before stepping toward her with caution.

"Come now. Don't be shy," she closes the distance between us to take my hands.

The palms and underside of her dark fingers are free of jewels and metal. The touch of her skin is cool. It's smooth and stiff, reminding me of a snake. She pulls me forward and gives a light hug, patting my back. With a stiff motion I tap her shoulder blades above the arching cartilage of her wings. She pulls away and keeps my hands in hers as she talks.

"What brings you here? Ulai said it is important."

Bob clears his throat and nods to me, "We have something I think you need to see."

I take the cue and slip my hands from her light grip. I reach around into my satchel and pull out the rose, still wrapped in Bob's pillowcase, with care. Lilith arches her brow and clasps her hands. I hand the rose to Bob who offers it to her.

Taking it she unwraps it and with the flick of her fingers levitates it into the air. The pillowcase falls to her feet.

"This rose—" Bob begins.

"I know what it is."

He shifts his weight and crosses his arms, "You do?"

"Oh yes," she smiles. "It was stolen from me."

Bob tenses and the temperature of friendliness drops in her voice, "Where did you get it?"

I hold my breath. Bob's brows furrow as he considers his answer.

"George was kidnapped into slavery. She was bought by HSAER and brought this back with her. I'm sure you remember giving the go ahead to clean them out? I found her and the rose was in a satchel she carried."

I want to curse at him for not lying about my involvement, but at the same time I suppose it's wise of him to tell the truth. She seems skeptical at best.

She turns her white eyes to me, "And where did you get it?"

I lick my lips and think, "I liked where I was, no offense," she nods with a cold smile. "But they found out about my association with...him," I tick my head to

Bob because in my panic I can't remember his real name. "So they locked me up and told me nothing. Then out of nowhere there's screaming and smoke and…things happening. A friend, someone who felt sorry for me you could say, slipped this satchel through the slot in my cell and disappeared. He didn't say anything about it."

She purses her lips before puckering them to relax her mouth.

"He said nothing? There's nothing you can think of?" she crosses her arms as irritation supersedes friendliness. The air cools around us.

I'm lost in her white eyes, "Well, he did say something."

"Go on," she nods.

"That I shouldn't let anybody have it. Anybody," I shrug. "That's it."

"And yet here you are."

"Obviously."

The Witch grins and glances at Bob, "I like her."

He smiles and shakes his head.

"She's candid and I don't get much of that."

"That's because she doesn't know any better," he says.

Lilith laughs and her cool demeanor dissipates. She closes her fingers into a fist and the levitating rose disappears.

"I believe you," she says. "And I suppose you have no reason to lie to me."

I shake my head, "No. They locked me up without hearing my side of things for a long time. I have no loyalties to them."

"But they're your fellows."

"Tell *them* that. No friend of mine would lock me up."

Bob nods in agreement, "My Lady, while we're here, I wonder about opening up a portal to get George home."

I'm surprised. The thought of going home slipped my mind.

Just when I accept my new lot in life. I was hoping for a cool mutation like wings or laser hands.

Lilith shakes her head, "I'm afraid I don't have the resources to…spend. And," she hesitates, "We have a situation in the portal room. All activity suspends until further notice."

Just as well. I'm getting attached to the idea of laser hands anyway. Maybe I can start my own school for mutated humans. I shall dub us…E-Men. Women. People. E-People. And I shall be Professor G! Not gonna shave my head though…

Bob's brows furrow, "I didn't hear anything of this."

"You wouldn't," she shrugs. "There are…inconsistencies with some of my staff and I've kept a few things under wraps. The room is off limits to everyone except…"

I see where this is going.

"Except?" Bob takes the bait.

"Except subjects I know I can trust."

I pipe in, like an idiot, "Like people who just brought you something stolen from you?"

Her sharp teeth gleam in a smile, "Exactly, George."

"My Lady, you know whatever you ask will be obeyed," Bob offers.

"Every once in a while it's refreshing not to force someone. Isn't it, Asrieth?"

Bob frowns. I can't read the hidden meaning to her

words.

"I wouldn't know," he says. "But I'll gear up and go see about the problem."

She dismisses the gesture, "Nothing to gear up for really." She glances from me to him and back again. "Oh, I know! Why don't you both go and have a look around. I'm sure it's not dangerous."

Bob forces a smile, "Of course, my Lady."

She smiles and lays her hand on my shoulder, "It should be fun for you too, George. How many times have you been through a portal?" She walks us to the entrance.

I peer down into the dark recess of the stairwell.

"Oh, just the one time," I answer.

"Well, thank you for returning the rose," she says.

I smile, "You're welcome." I rest my hand on the frame of the doorway and take a step down.

"You know," I begin.

Bob towers behind Lilith and shakes his head.

"Bob had nothing but nice things to say about you. And he's right," I finish.

The ends of Lilith's pouty mouth curve up into another smile, "Oh he is? Well, I know sometimes people can misread the direction I take the country in. How refreshing and honest you are."

I nod with a goofy smile and make my way down the dim stairwell with caution. Bob stays behind a moment, as I expect. His heavy steps follow me after a few minutes. I sit on a step leaning against the warm stone wall.

My thoughts race in the dark and drift to home.

What is my family thinking right now? Am I fired yet? Is there a missing persons report?

I smirk at the thought of terrible Christmas pictures

of me plastered all over the local news stations. My smirk disappears when I think of Mrs. Morgan.

What did she tell the police? Would they think she's crazy? Why wouldn't they?

Guilt sits on my shoulder and whispers into my ear when Bob stops at the step above me.

"Well, that could have gone better," he sighs and sits next to me.

I catch a whiff of leather and spice.

"What do you mean? I thought it went great," I try not to sound too cheerful.

He glances at me with his black eyes and scoffs, "You would."

"What does that mean?"

"You don't know her like I do," he says.

"What? You were the one saying nothing but good things—"

"She assumes we had something to do with the rose disappearing in the first place. I'm not sure what she's thinking, but knowing her she thinks we stole it and returned it so I can gain favor to get you home. Or it's something else entirely. I don't know," he sighs.

I clamp my mouth shut.

"Yes," he continues, "She's sending us to deal with it as a test. It's dangerous. Very dangerous."

"She told you all this?"

"She doesn't have to."

I drop my face into my hands and take a deep breath, "What are we gonna do?" My palms grow sticky from my breath.

"Do what she wants us to. We don't have much of a choice," he says.

I sit up straight and wipe my hands on my lap, "So, what now?"

Bob snakes his arm across my shoulders and pulls me against him.

"It'll be okay. I won't let anything bad happen to you," he promises.

Heat in my cheeks spreads to my neck, "I know."

He gives me a squeeze and stands up, letting me go. Bob offers his hand and I take it.

"So, if she didn't tell you all that, then what were you actually talking about when I left?"

We start our long walk down. I keep my hand along the wall for balance.

"The situation. In the palace we have a room specifically for portal use. There are natural portals that occur, but 99% of them are made by us or other political entities."

I make a mental note to ask about other political entities later.

"Last night a portal came from nowhere in the portal room. It wasn't summoned, nor did it use any of our materials. It pushed another open portal out of existence. We know it's not natural because those are jagged. Misshapen. This one is pristine. Perfect. Lilith can sense magical properties flowing from it. Our summoners already tried to send in a probe—"

"Wait, like NASA?"

"Yes. We do have technology you know."

I recall the generator in his room, "Oh yeah, but that advanced?" I slip on my gas mask remembering the reason for the filtration.

"George, can I continue?"

I wave my hand.

"Thank you. Now, as I was saying, nothing metal can get through this new portal."

"And that's…unusual?" I ask.

"Yes. Yes it is."

We stop for a Georgeneedstobreatheatsomepoint break. I huff and sit down on a step.

At least coming down I have gravity on my side.

Bob sits next to me and rests his forearms on his knees, "Lilith did seem...skittish."

"Yeah?" I continue to puff.

"I know this doesn't mean anything to you, but Lilith is afraid. She's thousands of years old. Gods only know how much power she truly possesses. She fears what might be behind the portal."

I show my teeth beneath my mask, "Bring it."

9. Ooga Booga!

We make a quick stop at Bob's room for supplies.

I have to give up my gas mask since it has metal, but Bob found a leather replacement. It doesn't work as well as the rubber and metal mask, but it's better than nothing. I put it on and feel like a ninja. I stand in the bathroom, checking out my new ninja moves in the mirror while Bob gathers things. He pokes his head in.

"You have to take off your translators," he nods to me in the reflection.

I touch the metal band around my neck. I study the cuff attached to my ear.

"How are we going to talk?"

He shrugs, "With the English you taught me?"

"So, fifty words. Awesome," I sigh. "Why are these made of metal anyway?" I lean forward over the black stone sink and examine the band. It's plain and clasps in the back to fit like a choker. There's nothing special about it as far as looks are concerned.

"On the inside runes are carved into the metal," he says. "We can make them out of other materials, like leather, but the runes wear off quicker. The runes can also be more precise on metal."

"So it's magic with a scientific application?"

He leans against the doorframe and crosses his arms, "Yes. If runes aren't precise they don't work as well. If we had more time I could commission a leather one for this trip, but we don't. So take them off. Let's go."

"Wait," I hold up my hands and turn.

His arms are bare and tattoos run up the length from his fingertips. A whip hangs at his hip and I force myself to push thoughts of archeology from my mind.

"This is ridiculous. We can't possibly go into a dangerous situation without being able to talk."

"Sure we can," he walks to the bedroom door and I follow him out into the hall.

"No! No we can't. What if you say 'run' and I think you mean 'don't move'?" I ask.

He shrugs and pulls the door to his room closed.

We begin the long journey downstairs.

"You can keep your translators on until the last minute. You'll get them back the second we return," he says.

"*If* we return. Assuming I don't die a horrible agonizing death because I thought you were talking about chocolate bunnies instead of zombie bananas."

"Were you dropped as a child?" he laughs.

"Zombie. Bananas," I insist. "Who eat my face!"

"That would be a shame. I happen to like your face."

His compliment and sharp smile disarm me into awkward silence for a moment.

That's probably what he wants.

"Don't you have work? And stuff?" I change the

subject. "Responsibilities?"

He laughs, "I get time off like everyone else. I did wipe out HSAER. And what do you call this? I don't go through strange portals as a hobby. This is a part of my responsibilities."

"So you get time off? With pay?"

"With pay."

"Ooooh!" I laugh.

It's funny how some things carry over between realms. I'm about to go on a whirlwind adventure and I'm talking to him about paid time off.

We continue to traverse the levels of the palace. Bob keeps my mind off of our task by talking about his acquisition of Mertyl. He's so effective before I know it we're descending down rough worn stairs and stepping into a cavern located who knows how far underground.

The jagged features of a room carved out over time from water jut from the ceilings and floor. A stadium can fit inside of this space. The floor slants, sloping down towards the middle like a shallow bowl to a black lake. Warm yellow globes hold onto the walls with chains and cast the occasional shadow. My eyes widen.

Silver portals, not unlike the one that drug me here, hover around the room. Some are close to the ground. Others are horizontal over the lake.

There are a few dozen people, or things, or people-like…people scurrying around doing their business. My gaze wanders to a crowd surrounding a portal. Lilith is among them.

I swallow an urge to turn right around and go back upstairs.

We approach, Bob sauntering as I struggle not to fall on the loose gravel sliding around under my feet. I'm so busy staring at my shoes when we reach the crowd I look up to all eyes on me.

I glance from face to face, "What?"

"My Lady, you can't be serious," a man speaks up. He's tall with a golden tan and small curving horns protrude from a mess of black-tamed hair. Black lines his golden eyes and dark tattoos slither up the sides of his torso. A falcon perches atop his shoulder over a leather guard. Other than the horns, he can be the painting of an Egyptian tomb come to life with his white linen wraparound adorned with blue and gold details.

"She's just a child," he points to me.

I huff, "Child? Excuse me? Who are you talking to, junior? I'm an adult and can take care of myself. Thank you very much." I repress the urge to tell him to get off my lawn.

Bob snickers.

"I see," the man laughs. "Never mind. She's perfect."

My stomach lurches and I resist hugging myself, "We're not going in alone, are we?"

Bob glances to Lilith, "Are we?"

"Of course not," she smiles.

A heavy hand rests on my shoulder and I turn to an Amazonian woman grinning down at me. She's not as tall as Bob, but fills out with muscular definition. Her vibrant, blood-colored hair is wild and kinky, tamed down against her head with twine. Her eyes are the orange of a burning fire and a glow comes from behind her irises, standing out in the dimly lit cavern. I search for any mutations, but find none.

Unless you include the fire eyes and super warrior princess look.

"Thecla," Bob mumbles to me.

I nod, recognizing his boss's name. I give her a

quick once over. *She can totally run a prison.* Scars cover her dark golden skin and she seems all too happy to accompany us on our task.

"Hey, you must be George," she drops her hand to shake mine.

I nod as she releases me.

"Pleasantries aside," Lilith's silky lilt gets us back to the task at hand. "I wish this to be done within the hour."

She flicks her gilded hand towards the portal.

The gathered group splits itself to allow a clear path. I look up into the reflective surface of the portal and glance myself standing between the two imposing figures of Bob and Thecla.

I study myself. I'm still wearing the clothes, in all their funky glory, I was in when Jonah jailed me. The split skirt and scanty top with the supportive black shoes given to me by HSAER when I arrived. The mask covers my smile and my braid hangs down my back. Bob rests his hand on my shoulder. I nod with newfound adventure resolution and approach the portal.

"Let's do it."

The Egyptian painting steps up, "Ah, ah, ah." He holds out his hand, palm up. "Your translators please."

I halt mid-step.

"Unless you want your head removed the moment you step through," he smiles.

"I'll get them," Bob offers. His fingers slip the collar and cuff off with dexterity. He hands them over to the man and mutters something in Werdonic.

The man replies, closing his fingers around the items, not taking his gaze from me. I frown under his stare and he smiles. I glance back to the portal.

I lean in towards Thecla, "I was told you speak English?"

"Yes! I do," she smiles. "I am happy to practice it on a native." Her accent is heavy on the "h", "Do you have any Werdonic learned yet?"

I shake my head.

Thecla frowns and throws a phrase to Bob over my head.

Bob rubs his hand on the back of his neck and shrugs a reply.

I know they're talking about me. Dammit, what are they saying?

Lilith crosses her arms and watches them bicker for a moment before raising her hand to silence them. The Witch glances over her shoulder to the crowd and asks a question. Everyone searches through their pockets and robes in a hurry to please their ruler. The Egyptian painting leans towards the Witch, producing a blue permanent marker. I cock my brow and glance at Thecla.

"Hold still," she says.

The Egyptian painting approaches me and tips my chin up towards his face. I stare into his eyes. I blush and throw a glance to Bob, who keeps his face stoic. Bob mutters something and the man glances between me and him. Egyptian painting's eyes drop to my neck and he slides his finger from my chin to pop the cap off of the marker. He bends his knees to get closer to my height and places the soft wet tip of the marker on my neck a couple of inches below my jaw.

"Hold your breath," Thecla says.

My chest sticks out as I suck in my breath and hold it. I repress a giggle as the velvet tip of the marker runs along my sensitive skin. It cools as the fresh ink dries. The Egyptian painting bows my head down and forward as far as he can. The soft tip of the marker glides over the back of my ears. He purses his lips to blow on the last of the wet ink. His hand rests on the base of my neck.

I glance to Bob for help.

"Okay, that's enough," he steps in and pulls me away from Egyptian painting.

"Asrieth," the man replaces the cap of the marker, "You're overprotective. I'm not going to hurt your pet." The marker levitates out of his hand and disappears.

"We don't have time for this," Lilith snaps. "We've spent enough time on this girl. We have more important things to worry about than your eternal pissing contest." Her blank eyes narrow and she points her gilded hand to the portal. "In. Now."

My heart thuds in my chest and Bob's hand slides from my shoulder to the small of my back. He nudges me forward and I study the horrified expression of my mirrored self as we approach each other.

Thecla speaks, "Okay, Asrieth is going first. Then you, then me. Okay?"

Bob nods and disappears into the glassy surface without hesitation. I look up to Thecla and she smiles, but it strains.

If she's scared, why am I not panicking?

I do.

I dig my heels into the loose gravel and shake my head.

"No." In the corner of my eye, Lilith's hand flickers before an unseen force jettisons me into the portal. I scream and clutch the satchel Jonah gave me, now filled with food stuffs, water, and a trauma kit.

The first time I shot through a portal it was beautiful and vivid with purple hues and distant stars.

This time it's nothing but darkness. When the world opens up below me in a bright yellow atmosphere, I shut my eyes against the pain of contrast.

Another problem is the world opens up *way* below me. The air whips my hair and clothing around as I fall thousands of feet above the ground. I take in a breath of air and scream.

This is a perfectly appropriate time to holler. Anyone tells me otherwise, they haven't been a mile above the ground with no oversized airmattress below them.

I faint.

I come to in Bob's arms. It's sweet until he smacks me on the cheek.

"Wake up."

"Am I dead?" My eyes flutter.

He frowns and looks up past me, "I see the runes are working."

"Yeah," Thecla answers from behind me.

With Bob's hand supporting my back I sit up. The blinding yellow color around us is sand, but seems a light taupe from here. Sand dunes surround us in a valley. We're on a dark paved surface. The horizon is bright and blue with no source of light. No sun and no clouds dot the blue sky. The pavement beneath is cool to the touch. I glance down wondering why my skin isn't simmering like an egg on drugs. A warm breeze is the only source of heat and it blows Bob's hair around as he checks my eyes.

"I'm fine," I mutter.

He drops his hands. His white hair and skin are stark in this light, and Thecla darkens.

"Last time you went through you had blindness, remember?" he asks.

I blink. *That was a lifetime ago, wasn't it?* "Yeah. I

guess so."

"She's been in Werdofium for weeks," Thecla pipes in, "She's had enough magic exposure by now. It shouldn't shock her anymore."

I shiver. *If I have more I'll start to mutate too.*

Bob stands and wipes sand from his leather pants, "True." He looks around.

I brush myself down.

The pavement stretches down the valley for over a mile. Behind us it ends. I glance down and notice the pavement isn't dark, but stained. I survey the surrounding area and notice the edges of the darkness meet the normal gray tone of pavement. I jump up on the realization it's stained with blood.

"What the fuck?" I dash to clean pavement and brush along where my body made contact with the tainted ground.

"Strange," Thecla observes. "These are blood stains. Some of them fresh, but no bones. No bodies."

Bob nods.

I crouch and cover my face with my hands, "Why am I here?"

"Because Lilith requests it," Bob answers.

I peek at him through my fingers. He watches me.

I stand and turn to the valley. Jagged dark, tall objects sprout from the ground like withered fingers.

I point, "Tally ho then…I guess."

Thecla pats me on the back with an expression far too cheerful for the occasion.

"Tally ho!" she says. She hooks her arm with mine and we march forward.

Whether I like it or not.

I glance back over my shoulder to Bob and catch him smiling at us.

At least I'm not the only one trying to make light of this.

We march, then skip, and then break down to a walk before we get within a hundred yards of the dark objects. We grow close. Bob makes a quick step in front to shield us and he stops, cupping his hand over his eyes. I step up next to him and mimic his pose.

"Dead trees," he says.

I nod, but can't see a damn thing against the bright light and heat waves over the pavement.

Thecla comes up behind me, "Let's approach with caution."

Bob and I both nod.

"And let's be quiet," he adds, making a point to glance at me.

I narrow my eyes at him, going unnoticed as he unhooks the nasty whip hanging on his hip. He unfurls it.

"As least we know magic works here," Thecla says.

"How do we know?" I ask.

"How do you think we kept you from splattering all over the ground?" Bob replies.

I shrug, "Point made."

Bob jerks his head towards the trees, "Let's get this over with." He runs his deft fingers up the length of his whip to roll it in his hand.

We move forward, one awkward step at a time. I'm not sure if they're experiencing what I am, but my legs vary between heavy as lead and light as a feather. Of their own accord my limbs switch from wanting to stop in their tracks to running away like a repeat of my great run in Lubbock. My heart thuds in my chest as we near the sparse grove of trees. We approach and I count seven spaced along the width of the pavement. They aren't large, maybe a few yards tall. They jut up from the pavement like charred hands. Something swings from their branches. I squint. Old antique toys whose paint is chipped and tin rusted over with time. They swing on white yarn in the breeze.

Our pace slows as we walk past the trees, their only movement the swinging toys.

I catch a glimpse of a few up close and gasp. *I recognize some of these.* They're the kind of toys my grandparents had. Little metal cars and fire trucks. Small tricycles and dolls with tattered dresses. Metal tops and jack-in-the-boxes sway from the dark limbs. Once vibrant paint is faint and the lines of happy little drivers' smiling faces are only a trace on the old metal. I swallow and drag my eyes forward. From the line of trees a stone block sits fifty yards ahead of us.

I lick my chapped lips and stop mid-stride when, a few yards away, I recognize a sarcophagus before us. It takes a minute to distinguish what it is because it's a large square block of plain gray stone a yard and a half high.

Bob and Thecla stop, turning to each other.

"Do you feel it?" Bob whispers.

I shake my head, but listen. I will myself to possess the sixth sense they seem to share. I sense nothing but my beating heart. I shift my weight and look down to the ground crossing my arms, grumpy I'm not one of the cool kids.

"Maybe I should wait here," I say.

Bob and Thecla exchange a glance before Bob holds out his hand to me.

"C'mon George. We do this together."

I take a shuddering sigh and peer past him to the sarcophagus. The outline of the lid clarifies at close proximity and carved into the sides of the block are worn pictographs. I close my arms tighter around my torso and bite my lip. Hopelessness and loss wash over me. Tears well up in my eyes and I cry.

I have no idea why.

I crouch to the ground and hug myself as I wail into the quiet desert afternoon. *Or it seems like an afternoon…and a desert. I can't be sure. Of anything. Ever.*

A pulse blips from the ground, beating against my feet in a faint rhythm. An unexpected outburst of tears floods my vision and I flutter my eyelids. The pebbles at my feet bounce in the beat and overwhelming sadness fades with each strike. Euphoria replaces hopelessness the sarcophagus sends out waves. I jump to my feet as I rise. I want to let it out. Let out the wonderful thing unlawfully caged away inside of that stone box. Prison.

I lurch forward with the momentum of ecstasy. The leather belt holding up my slinky split skirt jerks back and I fall back against Bob. His arm circles around my waist. He holds me tight against him. The pulse grows in volume and vibrancy. The base of pounding tickles my feet. I reach out for the sarcophagus, my fingers willing themselves to stretch out far.

The living, breathing rhythm of the prison beats its way up my feet through my legs and torso to plug into my puddling brain. A loud moan escapes from deep within me. Bob tenses up and rests his lips on the crown of my head. He swears in a whisper above me. He lets me go as his own desire hardens behind me. I don't give it a second thought as I stumble forward to the sarcophagus.

I draw near and whispers of promises bypass my ears to my manipulated mind. Endless nights of pleasure, physical and mental, vivid imagery of myself drowning in money, being worshipped, having lusty sex with any man or woman I ever think possible floods my vision. The promises fade when my hands drop to the smooth warm surface of the stone. I stare at a small symbol burned into the lid. A backwards "c" with seven small circles surrounding its backside. My fingers follow the charred grooves of the symbol.

A hand covers mine and my eyes trail upward to Bob on my right. His jaw clenches and expression remains stoic. The muscles in his arms tense and relax in the same rhythmic beat at our feet.

"We must be strong, George," his tone is a soft whisper above the music filling my mind and clouding my judgement.

He's weakening. Good. Very good. Help me open the sarcophagus, the box, the prison. I need your strength.

I reach up to tug my mask down around my neck. I lick my lips and gaze up at him through my eyelashes.

"I need you," I whisper.

His black eyes shoot to me and his hand clamps around mine in a fist.

"I need you to help me," I try again.

I turn to him and he faces me in automatic compliance. I raise my free hand to the back of his neck, tiptoeing, and pull him down to me.

Yes. This is how we get him to do what we want.

His lips brush against mine as I whisper to him, "I need you, Asrieth."

His arms circle me in a tight grip and pull my body against his. He leans in to kiss me, and with cruelty I turn my face to the stone prison. His lips plant on my jaw and he growls into my ear. Asrieth kisses my jaw again and loosens his arms. He drags his eyes to the massive stone prison and blinks rapidly. An inner struggle wages behind his dark gaze.

You need…I need one last push. Convince him.

I sidle against him and lower my hand to his crotch, pressing against it.

"Please, Asrieth."

With brute force Asrieth shoves the lid of the sarcophagus free. It doesn't go crashing to the ground as expected, but flies away in the breeze like a plastic bag. We peer in to find an endless pit of darkness with a sea of twinkling stars. Asrieth lifts me up in his arms and backs away, holding me against his chest. He stops and grips me as the wind howls and darkness furls out of the tomb like dye spilling into water. At a brief glance, Thecla crouches, her hands and arms around her head. I can't decipher the words over gusts of wind as she mutters over and over again.

I drag my unblinking gaze back to the sarcophagus and the darkness seeping out of it. Asrieth doesn't flinch as it finds and envelopes us both in its warm embrace.

I'm nothing.

And then I am again.

My body jerks as it floats in milky darkness. The air thickens until I'm swimming in it, aware of it gliding against my skin. My limbs flail to find a sense of gravity. I still at the sound of his voice.

The voice.

"Thank you," it purrs and crawls around on the surface of my skin. "I knew he was the one, but you. You are his key."

I gasp. Unseen hands grab my wrist and pull me against a hard male body. Blood rushes to my face as I recognize naked skin beneath my fingertips. Without any consent from me, my hands roam around the contours of his muscular form. Lips latch onto my neck and large hands lower to the curve of my backside. My body entangles with his in reaction to the pleasure he sears into me. I flush and cry out at his touch.

"Oh my darling," he says before I disappear into the nothing.

10. Polite Awakening

I know this is a dream.

And so I cry.

Everything blurs around the edges of my vision as I walk down the street in Lubbock. When I had my try at college I lived in a neighborhood close to the university, paying way too much to rent a room in an overcrowded house. There was a corner store close by. I walked there every afternoon after class to get a coke.

This is when I meet Phillip.

I brace myself for one of the happiest moments of my life. I walk through the sliding doors and he looks up with a smile. *He's new. Just started.* I smile at him with a nod and walk to the back of the store to peruse the soda selection. I pick out my bottle, not thinking of soda at all, but of the man behind the counter watching me.

His smile is contagious as I approach and he makes casual conversation. I'm a hard person to talk to, and in turn I don't talk to people often. He makes it so easy.

The dream swerves from reality when he asks me on a date.

But this doesn't happen for weeks…

I start to cry.

"But you're dead," I say.

He smiles, "What are you talking about?"

It's so good to hear his voice…

"You're dead," I repeat. My heart breaks as I say it over and over, "You're dead. You're dead."

He doesn't understand.

Stabbing cold water breaks me from the trance of my dream. My head dips under the surface and I swallow water before understanding I shouldn't try to breathe. A faint warm glow hovers above and a hand plunges in searching for me. I reach up and it grabs hold of my forearm to yank me up. I break the surface of the water and gulp in air. The hand drags me up to the rocky shore of the portal cavern and I collapse. I get up on my elbows before I turn over to retch up the excessive water I swallowed.

A hand soothes my back and shoulders, coaxing me as I dry heave. They guide me further up the shore to smoother ground where I curl up on my side and shake. The rock beneath is warm and I press my cold cheek against it closing my eyes. The hands guiding me pull a soft wool blanket over my body and whisper words of comfort. In Werdonic. They might not be words of comfort, but their tone is nice. I crack open an eye, recognizing a man that isn't Bob.

Egyptian painting smiles down at me.

I stare at him. The scene in the desert seeps back into my memory. The beating pulse at my feet. The desire and happiness ripping through my inner most self. My actions. I search for Bob.

"Wait…" Imagery of what I did grows vivid. I'm horrified with myself. "No no no no no. I didn't…" I search the cavern.

Bob's sopping wet form bends over Thecla, who's laying out on a rock like I am. Her eyes are closed and she lies still on her back, her chest moving up and down in the soft rhythm of unconsciousness.

I sit up and shiver. The dark caress of the coffin man, the thing, lingers. I want to crawl out of my skin and slide back into clean water. I pull the wool blanket tighter around myself. A cold metallic band slips around my neck and fastens. I glance over my shoulder to the Egyptian painting. He dangles my ear cuff translators in front of me. I nod and turn my ears to him. The metal cuffs slip over the cartilage and he pinches the ends together to secure their hold.

"Better," he says. "Your runes were gone when you came through."

"Thanks," I hug myself. I watch Bob sit back and close his eyes.

Won't you come see if I'm okay?

"I'm Seneh," the painting offers.

I turn up to him, "I'm George."

"Yes, I know."

"Well, okay then."

He smiles, "But that's not your real name."

"Maybe," I pull the blanket up to wrap it around my shoulders. "Can you tell me what happened?"

He frowns, "I'm not sure. We were hoping you could tell us."

I ring out my hair, trying to focus on the portal above the lake. It hovers over the black glassy surface horizontally.

"Why do we always land in water?" I ask.

"Ah," Seneh leans over and offers me a red fluffy towel. From where he got this towel I don't know.

"When we exit portals we are usually jettisoned by the inertia of the pull. If we don't land in water or somewhere soft, we can land on our heads and potentially die. Or break something at best."

I nod. I watch the portal, wrapping the towel around the bottom of my braid to soak up excess water. The reflective surface shimmers and I blink to be sure. It wavers again and this time it grabs the attention of others.

Bob jumps to his feet and the room fills with silence.

"Do you feel that?" he asks.

I shake my head and try to erase the conjured image of the same question in the desert before I gave in to temptation, consumed by ecstasy of the beat.

Others watch as the portal distorts above the water. Seneh tenses next to me, but I can't take my eyes off of it. The silver surface grows dark and fades into a pitch black hole over the lake.

Pop! Pop! Pop!

I cover my ears as a thunderous boom rings through the air and reverberates off of the cavern walls. Bob crouches at my side in an instant, pressing me down to the warm rock. I lay flat and cover my head. Wind howls and whips up around the cavern. Despite our weight, it pushes us back. Water splashes downward and further up the shore as the portal presses against it with an unseen force, creating an oval around it. Pebbles fly away from the lake, stinging the skin as they whip past. Bob lays low and presses his hand on my back to anchor me.

Pop!

The portal vanishes and the wind slows to a breeze.

Pop! Another portal, gone. Pop! Pop! Pop!

Sonic booms precede each portal disappearing. Every one vanishes. The wind ceases and the cavern calms. I shake with involuntary panic. I reel from the desert and this new excitement. Bob's hand leaves my back and panic rises without his touch. The rocks shift as he stands.

I snap my hand up to grab his leather pants. I tug.

He peers down at me with wide eyes, "George?"

"Don't go," I whisper.

His mouth opens and closes. Seneh's eyes are on us, but he remains quiet. His smirk speaks volumes of amusement. Bob shoots a glare to him and reaches down to hoist me to my feet. I cling to him.

"I'm sorry," I stammer. "I'm embarrassing you, but please don't go. I can't take this. I can't take anymore of this."

He smiles small and pets my hair, "It's fine. Stop being so whiney."

I laugh and nod, tears welling in my eyes, "Right. Sorry." I let him go and tighten the blanket around me.

"I'll let it go. Just this once," he winks.

Lilith's command rips through the air, "Get out."

The cavern's innocent occupants scramble to squeeze through the narrow stairwell. Stragglers slow with nonchalance to buy time, hoping to eavesdrop on Lilith's business. Our business.

Bob and I start for the door with Seneh as Lilith walks up, pointing to the three of us.

"Not you. You, stay here." She points to Thecla's still form, "Get her to the infirmary. Let me know when she wakes." Two subjects nod and rush to fulfill her order.

She turns back to us and crosses her arms, "What did you do?" Her gilded hands gesture around the empty room. "Every portal is gone. Have you any idea the millions of coin those resources cost?" Her blank eyes narrow and she re-crosses her arms, "Explain."

"It's more serious than money lost, my Lady," Bob says.

She smiles.

I don't like it.

"Asrieth, dear. You know I love you like a son," her smile fades. "But don't think for a moment I won't gut you and put your insides back together with a hot poker for giving me a smart tongue."

He nods, "I know, my Lady. I don't forget it for a moment."

"I appreciate elaboration."

He glances at me before he begins, "There's an old god inside that realm. I think it's a prison. Or was."

Lilith's chest rises and falls with a sigh, "And you released them."

"Potentially."

"Darling, I need a straight answer."

Bob shifts and crosses his arms. He keeps his black eyes on hers, "It knew our deepest desires and took advantage of them to get what it wanted."

Blood rushes to my cheeks and I wrap the blanket tighter around myself, willing it to hide me. Seneh keeps his gaze on Bob steady with an occasional glance to me.

"And that was?" Lilith asks.

"To set it free," Asrieth answers.

"You absolutely couldn't resist these little desires of yours?" she pushes.

"Apparently not," he mumbles.

"So what did you do?"

"We…lifted the lid off of a sarcophagus," he continues. "And then everything went black. A barrier broke. I can say with confidence we passed through several magic blockades on the way to this sarcophagus, but they were weak and ancient."

I cock my brow. *I didn't feel a thing. Then again I am me.*

"Very weak and very old," Bob continues. "It took no effort to pass through them. This god has been locked away for a long time."

"Hmm," Lilith uncrosses her arms and saunters to the water's edge of the black lake. She stares down at her reflection. "I suppose this isn't our problem for the moment. We have more pressing matters. Seneh," she glances over her shoulder. "Begin rebuilding the portals at once."

He nods, "Yes, my Lady."

"If we need more materials you can send Asrieth and dear little George to fetch them from the count."

"Yes, my Lady."

"We need to concentrate on our own plans right now. Asrieth, George, you two will be responsible for this 'god' should they be of any more cause for concern. Do you understand?"

"Yes, my Lady," we both answer.

Our walk back to Bob's room is awkward and silent. Dread fills me since I know the inevitable talk about the events in the desert fast approaches.

Our deepest desires? Does that mean I'm his?

I try not to think about it. Fear grips me. Perhaps this little incident in the desert ruins our budding relationship. I steal glances at him as we walk.

He's handsome. A little pale. He's been nothing but nice

to me. He's done his best since I've been here to keep me safe. Is it so terrible to be more than friends? Of course not…but what if he rejects me? Maybe it's not a question of me wanting him, but him wanting me.

Old insecurities I thought left behind in Lubbock creep back up my legs and into my heart. I sigh before running into the door post of the entryway to the stairwell. We pass another floor before Bob's quarters. He chuckles from behind me as I rub the throbbing ache on my nose and forehead.

"Shut it," I say.

"I don't know what you're talking about."

I glance at him over my shoulder. His smile is contagious and I mirror it.

Why am I so mopey? I shake my head and inse-curities loose. *I have no reason to feel awkward. We were both out of control. He misread what happened.*

"Out of la la land yet?" he asks as we climb stone steps.

"Yeah."

"I know what you must be thinking," he begins.

I continue to climb, "Oh yeah?"

"But your ass really does look amazing at this angle. You shouldn't be so hard on yourself."

"Hah!" I can't stifle a chuckle, "You know what? You're absolutely right. Thanks. I'll try to remember that."

"Anytime."

"So," I brush my hand along the dark wall for balance. "Are we gonna talk about it?"

"I'll wager not anytime soon."

"I'm okay with that."

"Good."

We shuffle into Bob's familiar room and he flips on

157

the filtration. I tug free the leather mask hanging around my neck. I forgot to put it back on when we came out of the portal. I stare at it, wondering if it even does any good.

"How long have I been here?" I ask. "I can't keep track."

"Round about a month I'd say. On your calendar."

"My calendar?"

"A month isn't thirty days here."

"Ah. Well, it feels like much longer," I toss the mask onto the bed.

"It might have been less. Still in a rush to get home? With all this excitement around?"

I sit on the edge of the bed and pull off my adventure satchel, setting it on the floor.

"How long does mutation take?"

Bob sits in his wobbly desk chair and leans back, his black eyes cast up to the ceiling. "It varies, but I would say the longest for it to take is a year."

"Wow, how vague."

"I don't know what you want from me. This isn't exactly my area of expertise."

I try not to think of his messy area of expertise. My gaze wanders to movement in the corner. A large centipede slinks from the desk towards the bathroom.

Mertyl in action!

I curl my legs up onto the bed, "Holy shit! It's moving!"

Bob chuckles and leans further back, defying gravity on the tips of the chair legs.

"She's gotta eat too you know." He leans forward, the wooden legs of the chair smacking the hard ground, "You can't leave yet."

"Why not?" I ask. "I mean, other than the obvious

reason."

"You've spent more time with those humans than me since you've been here. That's hardly fair."

"Those humans? Can you sound more derogatory?"

"I'm half if it's any consolation," he shrugs.

"I hardly need to be consoled for being human. It's interesting you're half. How did that happen?"

"My mother is a midnight lady and my human father was her slave. It happens."

I blush. *Answers any question of our anatomy fitting together.* I shake my head and put my hands over my burning cheeks.

The door bursts open before Bob can mock my reaction or I can ask what a midnight lady is. I jump to my feet and Mertyl hisses from the bathroom doorway. Bob remains in the chair, but his hand rests on the whip hanging from his belt.

Thecla's chest heaves and her eyes are wide. She leans against the closed door.

"What is it? What happened?" he stands up scooching the chair back. "Why aren't you in the infirmary?"

Thecla shakes her head, "Rinkai's escaped."

"Impossible," Bob's brows furrow. "He's in D block. I secured him myself."

"He found a way," she takes a moment to catch her breath. "And worse, no evidence he was ever there. We are in deep shit," she slides down the door and cups her face in her hands. "I have to do something before Lilith finds out."

How is this our problem? We have enough to worry about.

"She'll think it's glamour or one of our own helped

him," she continues.

"Shit," Bob strides to his pile of weaponry and shuffles through it. Metal clanks and wood bonks against the hard surface of his floor as the pile shifts around.

I give in, "Sorry, but what does this have to do with us?"

"Asrieth brought him in. If they think Rinkai was a glamour all along guess who's in trouble?" Thecla stands and leans against the door. "And if it's found he's not a glamour. Asrieth has to go to work. Real work. On our own people."

I frown, "Okay."

Thecla's body lurches forward into a stumble as the door bursts open a second time. She catches herself and whirls around to cut Seneh, our new intruder, a nasty glare. His eyes search the room and land on me, but I'm positive he's talking to them.

"New portal opened up on its own," his hand lingers on the door handle.

"Fucking eh," Bob swears. "What's next? A visit from my mother?"

"Actually…" Seneh begins.

"Fuck you," Bob snarls.

Seneh chuckles, "My Lady wants you down there. Now. Oh, and bring George of course." He disappears into the hall and leaves the door ajar.

"Bring me? Why do you always have to bring me? I think we all know how useless I am."

Thecla shuts the door and smiles at me, "You don't give yourself enough credit. Sure you're useful."

"As bait, maybe," I cross my arms.

"Can't go fishing without the worm," she offers. She sits on the bed.

I roll my eyes.

"What do we do?" Bob turns back to his pile of weapons, searching.

"I don't know," she answers.

I pipe in, "Maybe Rinkai made the new portal to escape? Does he know how?"

"He does. See George? You are useful," Thecla's face lights up.

Bob smirks and shakes his head. He pulls out a long thin strand of gold ribbon in a tangled mess.

"Are we really going after him?" I shiver with the memory of long bony fingers grasping my ankle.

Bob begins to untangle the ribbon, "No. Thecla is going after him."

"What?" She stands up and points at Bob, "I'm your superior. You don't tell me what to do."

"My superior who let him get away. Twice. You're also the one who tested him and signed off on him not being a glamour."

"Don't you dare stick this on me," Thecla crosses her muscular arms. "This is bullshit."

Bob hoists himself off of the floor and offers her the ribbon, still tangled.

"Here you go."

Thecla's face hardens into a scowl. She glowers past the ribbon to Bob. They're close in height and I find my eyes bounce between them. Without breaking the staring contest, Bob smiles and grips Thecla's wrist. He twists her palm upward and places the ribbon in her grasp. Her fingers close around it, scrunching the gold strand.

"Fine," she sighs.

"Come with us to the portal room," he says. "George could be right." Bob crosses the room and kneels next to the bed, leaning over and sticking his arm underneath.

I scoff, "Don't make it sound like such an anomaly." My stomach growls and they both glance at me. *I can't remember the last time I slept or ate.*

"I'm hungry too," Bob makes a face and pulls out the small trunk. He opens it and buries his arm digging around. Yanking out a leather piece, he holds it up, "Here we go." He twirls it around to his back and shrugs on a dark brown leather tunic. White bone buttons run up the right side of his torso and his fingers are nimble fastening them.

"Wow, a shirt. You're moving up in the world."

He smiles at me, "I need to be able to remove it fast and these buttons allow that."

"And why do you need that?" I wriggle my eyebrows.

"Not for that," he laughs. "Well, not usually. I need to access the magic runes on my chest in case we come across trouble."

Thecla snorts at us.

"Ever hear of Velcro?" I ask.

Bob shoots a glance at me and grabs a small purse of coins from his desk, "We'll get some fast food on our way to the portal room."

Bob's idea of fast food and mine are worlds apart. Images of hamburgers and French fries in portions way too large for me with a nice carbonated beverage dominate my thoughts while we walk in the halls. Thecla all but mopes behind us while she continues to unravel the ribbon. We go downstairs and veer off down into a long hallway.

The smell of…*something* wafts to my nostrils and I take a deep breath in before gagging.

"What is that?" I cough and wave the stench away. I pull the leather mask from my bag and settle it over my face. "That smells like road kill warmed up by a hair dryer."

"It's not bad," Bob says.

"I can say I'm a much better host than you. How can you forget the marvelous fatty delights I fed you back home?"

"Sorry George, we don't have those things here. I'll get a nice fat one for you, okay?"

My stomach lurches, "A nice fat what?"

"Spider," Thecla makes noise behind us. She chuckles, "They're not too bad if you salt them first. Spider gristle is always a treat for Asrieth."

I stop mid-step, "Oh my God! You're not expecting me to eat that?"

Bob stops and glances back over his shoulder, "You didn't complain about the soup."

"The soup? You mean when I first got here? That was spider?"

"Well, some of it."

"Traitor!"

"It's full of protein and nutrients. You were in shock, you needed them."

Thecla begins to wrap ribbon around her forearm, "What do you think you ate in that little human paradise?"

"I saw the vegetables, but I never thought to ask…about…the meat…" I swallow.

We reach a small door at the end of the hall. Several patrons of questionable ancestry push past it and the door swings on hinges. They reek of alcohol and who knows what else as they stumble past us. Bob reaches for my wrist and yanks me back out of the way to let the crowd pass. Thecla remains in the middle of the hall, messing with her ribbon, as they avoid her.

I stare after them and notice a few human-like features, "Mutated?"

"No," Bob answers. "Eventually you'll be able to tell the difference."

"Honestly, I wasn't planning on being here that long."

We approach the door and Bob pushes it in to let me pass before him. A wave of steam billows past me into the hall as I step through. While I expected a dining hall, nothing as massive as what lays before me. It's as big as the portal room, maybe bigger. Tables and disgusting manners in full swing line the hall. A few humans are serving their masters and my heart skips a beat.

I hover next to Bob, who comes in behind me. He lets the door go and it smacks into Thecla, who continues to try organizing the ribbon. She protests and pushes her way past the swinging door.

"Asrieth, I know she's all you see, but give me a break."

We both ignore her. Bob rests his hand in the small of my back and urges me forward. I hesitate and dig in my heels. I keep my gaze on the manacled humans.

"Slaves?" I point.

Bob glances down to me and follows the line of my hand, "Ah. Yes. Most likely."

I nod and tick my chin to the end of the room, where the food lays, "After you."

"They can't get you."

"If it happened once, it can happen again. What if

I'm not lucky?" Panic grows at the thought of being a mutant's sex slave, "What if I'm lost and you never find me and I rot in a prison of finery?"

Asrieth takes hold of my shoulders and turns me to face him. He bends, lowering his face closer to mine.

He smiles, his sharp teeth pearly, "They won't because I will kill them. If that's not enough, I will kill them and any who were involved."

"And most likely stop their family line," Thecla mutters.

I glance at her and Asrieth tucks his finger under my chin to turn me back to him, "Don't worry about it."

Thecla ties off the end of her ribbon and tucks it under, "That felt like a mile of ribbon."

I bite my lip and nod. *This is supposed to be comforting, but it makes him scary instead. Thank God he's on my side…but what if there's a time when he isn't?*

I wonder about the families affected by his actions. Any lives that might be torn apart to prove the point you didn't mess with him and his own.

I feel like a glorified taco getting fought over at dinner. Now I have the imagery of Bob standing triumphant on a table holding me up with a whoop and holler for his prize.

"We going to eat or what?" Thecla asks.

"Why are you still here? Don't you have business finding a political prisoner?" Bob snaps.

"I'm coming to the portal room with you."

"Yes. To the portal room. Not to the dining hall."

She sighs, "See you later then. Good luck, George."

"Thanks," I smile. "Do I need it?"

"Always," she turns round and slips past the swinging door. A few patrons enter and walk to the long line.

"That door is so tiny considering the traffic," I say.

Bob shrugs, "It's actually because this room was originally a death pit. See, the equipment they use to cook and butcher the spiders was used on prisoners in the old days. So, one door is ideal to bottleneck the masses should things get out of hand. The door didn't always swing. That's new."

I can only stare at him, "Death pit?"

"Don't worry. It's been a few decades since then."

"Decades? Time doesn't make things less horrifying."

"Well," he rubs the back of his neck. "The equipment is sterilized?"

"That's not what I'm saying."

"Oh."

I question Bob's moral judgement and decide it's best to not think about it. *People back home ignore things all the time for money and other gains, why can't I?*

11. Don't Adventure On A Full Stomach

True hunger isn't picky and I eat my spider meat with salt.

I watch the others catch glances at Bob and I as we eat. Bob sits silent, eating some kind of meatloaf with bread.

I remember once I woke up to the sound of glass breaking. Never a fun experience for anyone living alone, especially in a new place. It was a few days after I rented the house from Mrs. Morgan. I wasn't ready to deal with a break-in, so I cowered down into my blankets and feigned sleep. I couldn't bring myself to walk to my cell phone on the desk to call 911. It was the most intimidating ten-foot distance of my life so far.

The intruders never came into my bedroom and I lay still until the morning sun crept into the window. It glowed purple through the comforter I pulled over my head and I grew brave. I got out of bed. I didn't hear anything for hours, but I was careful. Surprise overtook fear when I entered the living room. The TV and DVD player, gaming systems, and packed boxes all remained untouched. I wondered if it was my imagination.

I turned the corner to the kitchen. I stopped in shock, a foot hovering over the tile. The window was in fact broken, but the glass was swept into a pile in the corner. The thieves thought to tape a plastic bag over the hole in the window. They taped a note to my pantry door.

It read: Sorry, but we're really hungry.

"It's okay," I said to the note.

I sprinkle salt on my soup and slurp. They aren't spiders in the traditional sense. *Or at least in the "Earth" sense.* Insects don't have actual meat on their nonexistent bones to my knowledge. *But spider is definitely the best way to describe the creatures being cooked and served.*

I feel guilty eating while high-pitch squeals ring in the room as a fresh batch cooks alive. *Maybe they're more like lobsters.*

I overeat and walk to the portal room in misery. Armored guards block the entrance to the last stairwell. They uncross their pikes in unison and let us pass. Bile rises on the way down. *I should have digested before going through so much activity.* Bob chatters about his first "spider" kill. In detail. It doesn't help with my nausea and I don't catch the whole story.

Seneh greets us upon stepping into the cavernous room. Other than guards lining up in a circle around the portal situated away from the lake and level with the ground, he is the only one here.

"It's my Lady's wish for you two to go in and investigate. She says she senses the old god within and wants you to be the guinea pigs."

Bob frowns, "Of course."

"Why?" I ask. "Why does she keep sending us in alone? If it's super dangerous."

"She's still punishing Asrieth for his mistake. Be grateful it isn't worse," Seneh answers.

He seems too happy about it.

"She knows I had nothing to do with it. Not to add I'm the one who corrected the problem," Bob says.

"Yes, there is that. But alas, you never rise up to your full potential and now she has leverage to make you do so," Seneh smiles down at me.

It doesn't answer my question, but I know there's too much history between them to explain in the next five minutes.

"I've been thinking about you, George, and remembered to get you this," Seneh reaches into a small leather pouch hanging off of his hip.

My eyes linger on the contours of his sculpted lower stomach, but snap to his hands. Bob tenses next to me and his hand rests on his whip. Seneh pulls out a leather collar and bone ear cuffs and offers them to me.

"Oh! For my translation. Thanks, this will really help," I nod at him.

Seneh's smile is smug and Bob remains hostile. The falcon on Seneh's shoulder spreads his wings and readjusts his claws over the shoulder guard. The angrier Bob appears, the happier Seneh is.

I pretend I don't notice and take off my metal translator and cuff to replace them. I lay them in Seneh's waiting hands and he gestures to the portal.

Bob grumbles about a "kiss ass" under his breath and puts his hand on my back to nudge me forward. I step on the loose rocks towards the circle of guards. The portal appears to be like every other, but as we approach a whisper hisses. I stop and Bob bumps into me. He's been staring down Seneh.

"What is it?" Bob asks.

"Do you hear that?" I ask. *I have regrets wanting to hear what he did earlier.*

He cocks his ear towards the portal. He shakes his head, "No. I hear nothing."

I nod and bite my lip.

"What is it?" he asks, watching my face.

I shake my head, "Nothing." *Maybe it is. Right. I hope. Please Jeebus.*

As we approach the whispering grows fervent and insistent. It's incomprehensible.

I finger the choker around my neck and look up to Bob.

"Testing. Testing," he says with a smile.

"One. Two. Three," I reply.

"Perfect," Seneh grins. "More permanent than a magic marker I'd say."

I nod and turn to the portal.

There aren't as many strange faces staring back at me. Lilith is missing. Thecla is missing. The guards are standing back. I see only Bob, myself, and Seneh.

"Why does she keep doing this?" my reflection lip syncs.

"Who? Doing what?" Bob asks.

"It doesn't make sense. This isn't your job. And I have no skills."

"But Asrieth does," Seneh adds. "You really don't know what's going on?"

"Seneh, I will tell her when the time is right."

I cross my arms, "I don't know. Now might be a good time."

"Isn't it though?" Seneh agrees.

"This is none of your business," Bob snaps at him.

The casual atmosphere dissipates. Seneh's falcon flaps his wings and lowers his head towards Bob.

"I change my mind. Let's talk about this when we get back. Lilith wants us to hurry so…" I step to the portal. "Let's get to it before we get in trouble."

Seneh smiles. He bows and gestures to the portal again, not taking his eyes from Asrieth's.

I grab Bob's hand and pull him forward with me. The portal's mirrored surface ripples us into deformed reflections while we approach. I hold my breath and walk through after Bob.

Once my body passes through, the hand holding onto Bob's empties. Just like the last portal, there's only darkness. No vibrant colors. It pulls me in several directions at once.

Well, this is new.

Pain sears my joints while unseen hands yank and tug, push and press my limbs.

As I open my mouth to scream, buzzing rings in my ears and hundreds of tiny insect feet crawl around in my mouth and over my tongue. Bugs flutter around inside of my head and crawl down my throat before I'm shot out of the portal's purgatory.

Bob breaks my fall and we land in cold mud. It's dark and I'm not sure if I'm blind again. I reach out and see the faint shadow of my hand.

"It's okay. I'm right here," the wet environment soaks up his quiet voice.

I spit out muck and recall the bugs. I sit up and check my limbs and joints. Everything is accounted for. Not a bug to be found. My sight adjusts to the faint light source covering the sky in a haze of sick green. A swamp surrounds us with trees in a little clearing we landed in. Cold and dark mud covers my body. It's a couple of feet deep. Bob grips my upper arms to hoist me to my feet. The suction of the wet earth beneath tries to anchor us in place.

We both watch as the portal lowers down close to the ground.

I point at it.

"Is that normal?" I whisper.

Bob wipes muck from his arms, "It is if someone controls it."

The occasional splat of muck drips from tree branches. Bob holds onto my shoulders and studies our surroundings. It's difficult to see anything beyond the thick line of trees.

My eyes wander up to the green sky in search of a sun or moon. No celestial bodies to be found. A movement shivers in front of me below the horizon and my gaze snaps to one of the trees. My heart thuds in my chest and goosebumps layer my body.

"I just saw something move," I whisper.

Bob slides his hands to the top of my shoulders and glances back over his to the horizon of trees black against the green sky.

"Not surprising."

The tree my eyes settle on twitches.

"What the fuck," I struggle to back away.

He holds me in place, "Shh. Shh. Listen, George, I need you to be quiet and calm."

I shake my head.

"Yes. Now. Do me a favor and take a few deep breaths. Okay?" he smiles.

So fake.

I try my best and nod. I can't tear my eyes away. My eyelashes flutter. With so little light I have trouble with vision. Everywhere I look are shadows. Bob takes hold of my chin. The mud from his hands smears on my face.

"Look at me."

I drag my gaze from the creepy shadows to him. He seems at home in these surroundings. He's black and white in this dark place that lacks color save the eerie sky.

"You're going to be okay," he nods, moving my chin up and down so I join him. "Okay? You understand this, yes? Because I need you to be calm."

I nod. "Yes," I tell him as well as myself. *He can handle anything this place throws at him.* "Yes. I'm fine. And I'm calm." I clench my hands into fists and force my lungs to breathe in deep.

"Good," he drops his hand back to my shoulder. "Stay as far from the trees as you can."

"I think that's going to be difficult considering we're in a swampy forest of death."

"I'm being serious."

"I know," I frown. "So am I. What's wrong with the trees?"

"They're alive."

"Of course they are."

"I mean, *alive*."

I suck in my breath, "Oooooh." I clear my throat and lean forward to whisper, "How am I not supposed to panic?" My heart crawls into my throat, closing it as I try to speak words that don't come. My hands wander up to his belt and grip it.

"If we keep quiet and mind ourselves they may leave us alone." He slides his hand down the length of my arm and grips mine, "I need you to walk with me."

My deep breaths turn shallow, "Okay. Okay." I nod and count each breath in and out in an attempt to control them.

Another tree twitches. Then another.

I whine and shake my head, "I can't do this."

Bob pulls me against him, leather and mud separating our warmth.

He rests his chin on the crown of my head, "I know. It's scary. But they can feel your fear. I don't know if they're malignant or not."

I jerk, but he holds me to him.

"How can I not panic?" *I don't want to be here anymore. I want to go home. Real home. On my couch eating fast food and watching terrible cable TV. I want to go to work tomorrow morning and deal with selfish customers and treat myself to ice cream afterward.*

I want some fucking chapstick.

Mud smears between us as I struggle against him.

He holds me against him, his lips in my hair, "Shh. Shhh. Please."

My energy zaps and I shudder against him.

"I'm sorry," I whisper, sputtering as I try not to cry. "I'm so tired. I'm so scared."

"I think you're taking this pretty well," his voice rumbles against my ear.

I hiccup and try to recuperate my breathing. *The last thing he needs is for me to pass out. Again.* I pull myself together and grit my teeth.

"Okay. I'm okay," I hiccup again. It irritates me. I'm happy irritation replaces fear. I hold my breath and free myself from his grip to put my arms above my head. He glances down at me with a smirk and I glare. Things are returning to normalcy.

Other than the scary ass trees surrounding us.

With my hiccups under control, Bob takes my hand and starts to cut a trail in the thick mud. The little clearing is larger than I thought, but it's hard to judge distance in the dim light. The sky never alters with its steady green glow as we wind our way through the trees. We get a few feet from them, but now I know they're living. They twitch and a deep sigh or cough escapes them. When I look skyward the silhouette of branches aren't jagged and varied like trees I'm familiar with. They're all smooth and thick like tubes jutting out against the sky. I lose track of direction and follow Bob through the thicket.

"Where are we going?"

We pause. He points upward in front of us. Past the thicket of branches, looming over the tree line, a tower stands black against the green sky.

"Oh." *I'm an idiot.*

We don't stop, not even to catch our breath, until a wide path leading to the tower opens up before us. It's distinguishable by the spacing between the crooked rows of trees. The muck remains deep and up to my thighs. We hover near the mouth of the path before proceeding.

I huff and puff. My body starves for oxygen.

"What is this place?" I gasp.

Bob remains unaffected by exercise. His brow furrows, "I have no idea, but I figure this is where we need to be."

"How do you know?"

"Do you see anywhere else we should go?"

I sigh, "No." *Not that I think we should be here either.*

The looming tower stands over thirty stories tall. It's plain and cylindrical with smooth sides. Its width is a few city blocks. The material is too dark to distinguish what it's built out of. *Assuming I would know anyway if I could see it.* At the base red light spills from a large open doorway. Steps lead up to it from the mud. Vibrant light mutes the hazy green atmosphere above us and turns mud at the bottom of the steps to a glowing pink.

I swallow, "We're going in there, aren't we?"

"Yes," he looks down to give me a smile. "Thought we'd stop by. Try to sell them cookies. Inquire about some old god type and be on our way."

I can't muster a laugh for him, but a smile creeps up.

He squeezes my hand and we slosh forward. Our eyes dart around in the darkness to shadows beyond the scarlet light. Trees sigh and sway beside us, whispering and betraying our presence as we pass. We near the steps and Asrieth releases my hand to place his own on the whip hanging at his hip.

That's not a good sign.

I crane my neck to peer at the top of the tower. A faint red glow coming from a single window captures my attention. Bob rises out of the muck onto the steps and turns to help me. My thighs burn as the mud's suction resists walking.

More like a mockery of walking. I'm pretty sure I waddled.

He lets go of my hand and turns back to the open doorway. I bend over to wipe a layer of sludge from my legs.

"I'm so tired," I whisper.

He does too, "I know. A little further and then you can rest."

I nod. *I need to do physical training at some point.*

Asrieth's pale skin turns pink as we approach the doorway with caution. Massive doors are swung open. I peer past them to a cavernous room with black marble floors and tapestries on white walls lined with lit sconces. In the middle an altar sits atop a single step dais.

Whoosh!

Bob knocks us to the ground. A flying sword dives from inside the building. I cover my head and curl up into a ball. I watch Asrieth get to his feet, whip in hand. The sword twirls through the air and swings back around towards us. Bob widens his stance and cracks his whip, his wrist circling with expertise. The sword slices down. Asrieth pulls back the whip and cracks it above him, the leather tip circling around the black leather hilt.

My jaw drops.

Muscles in his arm flex as he yanks on the enchanted weapon, causing it to crash to the ground at the top of the steps. The fall forces the sword to bounce around the hard surface with a clang. Bob's eyes remain on the sword, his hand running along the length of his whip to roll it up as he approaches. He slinks up the steps and the sword lies still. Asrieth kneels in front of it to loosen the length of braided leather from the hilt.

I lay frozen. Sharp corners of the steps dig into my body. I can't take my eyes off of him as he reaches his hand out to the sword. I hold my breath as his fingers circle the black leather hilt. He lifts it and we both release our held breath as it hangs limp and lifeless in his grip. He straightens out and turns his gaze to the large room beyond the doors, keeping his back to me.

I hoist myself up from the steps and my joints creak. One foot at a time I bring myself to the landing and stand next to him. He glances at me. Whip coiled in one hand and gripping the sword in the other, Bob starts towards the open door. I follow him with caution, still eyeing the sword in his right hand. The curved blade is four feet in length. Silver twine wraps around a long hilt. I purse my lips remembering that kind of sword is called a scimitar in the books I've read.

Together we pass through the doorway towering above us. The room opens up before us, but I don't have time to focus on the details before a black mist catches our attention near the altar.

"Get behind me," Asrieth commands.

I obey and peer out past him.

The mist solidifies into a humanoid form. Details sharpen as remainders of haze swirls around a man with four arms. Other than the extra set of limbs, his second most striking feature is his scarlet skin. Giant horns protrude from his slick black hair. I cock a brow when a red tail with a point on the end flicks behind him, bringing my gaze down to his hooves. His yellow eyes fixate on Bob and his sharp teeth are discolored and too big for his mouth.

He tries to speak nevertheless, "And what is it you seek here?" his gruff question reverberates back to us several times.

"Convenient. You speak Werdonic?"

The man shrugs, "I speak many languages. What do you seek?"

"We're searching for the god we released," Asrieth answers.

A wicked grin spreads across the man's face, "Am I the god you seek?"

"No," I blurt. I slap my hand over my mouth. *I didn't mean to say that.*

"No," Bob repeats. "No, you're not it."

The man's smile disappears, "But I am a god. A god of war." He gestures to the walls around him, but we don't dare take our eyes off of him.

"If you are, then why this weak spell?" Asrieth holds up the sword. "Simple boundary magic."

The man clasps the bottom two hands behind his

back while the others face their palms upward.

"I do not usually have guests. Only wild animals and trees. Maybe something like her," he gestures to me. Bob steps in front of me, "I need nothing more complicated than that. But you," he points to Asrieth. "You're different."

Bob lowers the scimitar, "Then what we seek isn't here."

The man frowns.

"How did you open the portal?" Bob asks.

"I opened no portal."

An invisible finger traces up my spine beneath my clothes, covering my skin in goose bumps. Bob shudders at the same time. My fingers hook around his belt. I tug.

"Let's go," I whisper.

He glances over his shoulder to me and nods. As he turns back the man towers over us, inches away.

I yelp and jump back. Asrieth stands his ground with a white knuckle grip on the whip and sword.

"We have no business with you," he says.

"I am a god," the red man's hate-filled mouth spews spit. "You leave when I say you leave. If I say we have business, we have business."

"You are disillusioned. Perhaps you were once worshipped by primitive peoples who long since left this place, but you are no god."

I shake my head, eyes wide, "No Bob. Please. Let's go."

The yellow eyes settle on me, "After I destroy you the little creature can be my pet." His red lips pucker.

My gut wrenches. *Fuck him up, Bob.*

Asrieth unfurls the whip, "Fine. If it's a fight you want—"

The red man raises his other arms, each bearing a

scimitar, and slices upward towards Asrieth. He doesn't waste time lunging forward in attack. Asrieth tucks and rolls away without a scratch. Time slows as I watch the man slicing through the air, Bob dodging.

Rustling behind me grabs my attention and I turn around.

Trees fill the doorway. They're different shades of human flesh patched together with crude needlework. Branches are limbs of humanoid creatures. Trunks shift with movement underneath the patchwork skin. The roots are arms and legs flexing and twisting in impossible ways to crawl along the ground. They remain behind the threshold, but reach out for me.

My stomach tries to claw upward into my throat and I hyperventilate. I back away and turn to metal clashing. Asrieth lost his whip and it lies next to the altar. A careful glance back to the door and trees press against the invisible boundary. I turn back to the fight.

Across the room the red man presses his twin swords against the blade Asrieth holds up to block. I dive for the whip and notice puddles of red congealing residue puddled along the floor. I zigzag around them. Asrieth flings the red man away and slides out from beneath his massive form. He seems fatigued.

I have to help him. I refuse to be a damn damsel.

I close my eyes and pray, "Please don't let me fuck up." I grip the handle of the whip and stand up, the altar coming up to my chest. I draw my hand back and flick it forward; a crack follows and echoes around the room. Relief washes over me as I realize I didn't cut myself open in the process.

The red man turns his attention to me and gives Asrieth time to back away. Bob reaches to the bottom of his tunic and rips it away, the bone buttons popping.

The red man turns back to watch him run his pale fingers across one of his many tattoos. As he does this, his lips move. Runes glow red beneath his hand before disappearing into his skin.

His black pupils grow and fill in the whites of his eyes. Black claws on the edge of his fingers extend and black feather wings burst from his back, tearing through his pale skin. He fists his hands and howls for a moment before flexing the massive wings and opening his mouth to let loose an inhuman growl.

My eyes widen. I can't decipher if I'm afraid of or attracted to him. I duck behind the altar, the whip hanging loose in my hand, peeking over the edge.

The red man dives forward as his feet hover over the ground. Asrieth meets him with speed and his wings whip back and forth, allowing him to jump towards and away from his attacker without being touched. The red man grunts and redoubles his efforts. Asrieth bares his sharp teeth and draws back before snapping forward, his blade slicing through the red man's upper left arm.

I cover my ears as his piercing scream echoes between the walls of the tower. The red man backs away, dark blood gushing from his amputated bicep. Gritting his teeth the man waves his hand over the wound, cauterizing it. Burnt flesh sizzles and an angry scar remains where his arm once was. I move my hand to my nose.

Just in case.

"Formidable," the red man says as he jettisons over to the altar.

To me.

He draws his hand back and I duck down behind the altar covering my head. A squelch echoes around the room before warm blood and innards spew all over me and the altar. I close my eyes and mouth tight and freeze. Heavy footsteps walk around and I wipe my eyes to open them. Asrieth stands in front of me, panting, holding the red man's severed head by the hair. Blood covers him head to toe; bits of red man guts slide down his body to the floor.

"Are you all right?" he asks.

I gape.

"I wasn't sure you could...by yourself...I..." I sputter.

"Have a little faith will you?" he asks. He smiles and spits.

I nod. *I do now.* I cough and slide up the altar, dropping the whip to the dirty floor. Copper scent of blood overpowers my senses and I press my lips together, fighting the bile rising up.

Asrieth whips his sword and blood slides off the blade and through the air, landing on me with perfect accuracy.

"Thanks," I mutter.

"Anytime."

I search the room speckled in pools of congealing blood and tapestries of human skin depicting battle scenes. I squeeze my eyes shut and open them to focus on the doorway. The trees remain, but still. Asrieth follows my gaze and cocks a black brow.

The bulbous trunks and infected wounds on the trees are too much.

I bend over, my hand gripping the edge of the altar, to vomit. Asrieth gets close to me and takes hold of my hair with his clawed hands. The sword clangs when he drops it to smooth his palm over my back.

"I'm sorry. I should have warned you," he strokes my shoulders.

I can't say anything as I continue to fight for air between takes.

"I, however, am very pleased," purrs a masculine voice.

I drop to my knees and continue to gag and cough, my stomach empty. I spit and peer up to the source. He's handsome and in a pristine black tux complete with a red bowtie and matching cummerbund. His ebony hair is wavy and slicked back, every strand in its place. His black shoes shine in the dull, red room.

His eyes are icy blue and tongue smooth as he speaks, "Hello again, my dear."

Every muscle in my body tenses and my insides scream.

I know that voice.

12. A mother's intuition for…violence?

"It's her," Asrieth whispers.

I scoff at him, "Her?" I point, "That's a he."

The man chuckles and it reverberates off the walls, "I'm both. I am as you think I should be."

We exchange a glance and look back to him. *Or her. Whatever.*

"Both?" I ask.

He smiles. It's disarming.

This guy is rocking at least a 20+ charisma. Minimum +5 modifier.

"I appear however your mind perceives me."

I nod, not understanding.

Asrieth's wings flick next to me, a puff of air helps along the blood drying to my skin.

"Who are you?" he asks.

"I have thousands of names. You can't comprehend who I am, but only who you've heard of."

I shake my head, "You're not making any sense."

"I am Darkness," he says. He puts his hands in the pockets of his trousers and smiles, "I am the Devil. The

Night. Angra Mainyu. Mara. Iblis. Biki. Aoden. Craig Blaize. I can go on if you like."

I swallow. An image of a fallen angel dominates my mind.

"Lucifer?" my voice is small and quiet.

He nods, "Now you're getting it. Or at least the concept."

"What do you want with us?" Asrieth asks.

"Why, you set me free. I thought we can be friends."

"I'm not going to be pals with the Devil," I cross my arms.

His smile fades, "I understand. You can't fully comprehend who I am. You never will. You're simply not…evolved enough. You humans have tried for centuries to analyze us and our motives."

Us.

Logic hits me over the head, as it so rarely does. *If he's Evil, then his opposite must also exist.*

"Observant," he smirks.

I clutch my blood-covered hair, "Out of my head."

"I can't help it. You think so loudly." He turns his gaze to Asrieth, "But you, you're a smart boy. You know how to keep them quiet."

"I can't stop you if it's what you want," Bob replies.

"You're right, but I don't want that. I want excitement. Chaos. A little death maybe, but definitely chaos. I think you two can help me."

I hold my ground, "I don't think so. You're fucking Satan."

"Are we having a theological discussion here?" he purrs. "I'm not Satan. I'm not any one thing. This is only a physical manifestation of what I can be. I may inspire what you perceive as Satan, the Devil, Lucifer, but I'm not that simple. I'm the only being in the universe who is simply, Evil."

A vision of a new exciting television show on Fox, "Just Call Me Evil!" flies through my brain.

"Okay, I get it. I'm a dumb human. Thank you very much."

To my surprise he laughs, "You don't envision me as scary. Some people find me so terrible they faint or simply die of fright."

"Why don't you show your true form then?" I ask.

"I don't have a true form. I don't really have a body. I manifest what you see me as."

What is Bob seeing?

"A woman who looks like his mother," Lucifer answers.

I cock a brow and glance at him.

Asrieth shrugs. "You're not angry with us then?" he asks.

"Of course not," Darkness answers. "They trapped me in that ghastly prison for ages. I'm quite happy with you."

Speaking of prisons. "So you're the one who made this portal. Did you help Rinkai escape too?" I ask.

He smiles, "Yes. I did."

"Why?" I ask.

"Do you know what your comrades are planning?"

I shake my head. Bob remains silent.

"Your Lilith is going to use the Earthian realm as a ferry."

My heart leaps, "What? What for? Why? What do you mean?"

"She's going to open up a portal from her palace as another opens up in Celeste. She will then march her vast army through your realm and pop out on the other side. Conveniently attacking the unsuspecting citizens of Sumirah."

I don't know these places, but hold my tongue. I glance at Bob.

"This is her plan. Nothing's changed. It's impossible to get through their barriers to open up a portal on the other side."

"Oh, things have changed," Satan smiles.

"So you're going to war?" I ask my companion.

"A slaughter is more like," Lucifer chimes in.

"I'd think you don't have a problem with this," I mutter. "No offense."

"None taken," Darkness straightens his suit cuff. "And you're right, I don't. But I do so love chaos. If Lilith has her way she'll be in and out of your realm in a matter of hours. Rinkai, wanting to take her place, plans on closing the portals and trapping her and all of her soldiers there," he smiles. "Wouldn't that be so much fun?"

"The rose," Asrieth answers himself. "The rose is what's changed."

"Yes. It will magnify the portal's strength. An army can pass through it with ease. And with distractions on the other side, it's possible for the portal to break their magical barriers."

"So she can't do this without the rose?" I ask.

My gut wrenches. *I just handed it over. Like it was nothing. Jonah told me not to…Then again, if he had only said so…*

He shakes his head, "No. She can't without it, but to ease your guilt I promise she was looking into other ways after its disappearance."

My mind reels from the Q&A, but here is a man, woman, being who has all the answers. He's willing to

187

give them.

"Don't you know since you've told us we're going to try to stop it? Or at least I will," I say.

"Of course I do," he smiles.

"Then why tell us?"

"It's the least I owe you for my freedom," he rubs his fingers on his temples. "But we're done. I suspect you have enough to go on?"

"I don't think Satan does something because he feels obligated."

"You're right. I do have ulterior motives, but if you must give me a label I like Lucifer over Satan. It rolls off the tongue a little better I think."

"Okay."

It's a strange conversation. He seems so ordinary. *Sure good looking, but not extraordinary. I'm more intimidated by Asrieth than this guy.* I narrow my eyes. *But then, that's the point, isn't it? That's how he works. He gets more out of you this way than if you faint or run away screaming.*

"Right again," he says before fading away like smoke on a breeze.

"Out of my head!" my command echoes along the walls of the tower.

"Lilith can be bad, but I would never say she's evil. She does have her reasons for wanting war," Bob ditches the sword and retrieves his whip before he walks me to the open doorway of the tower. He picks up the remains of his tunic and slings it over his arm.

"Always have to have your shirt off," I smile. "And now you speak! You were awfully quiet back there."

He shrugs, "I feel the less someone like that focuses on me, the better."

The trees disappear and are back in line as we cross

the threshold.

"So what can possibly be worth all this? Worth what he's talking about?"

"Her son."

"Oh great. A sob story," I sigh. We reach the bottom of the stairs and I glance down to the mud. I dread the cold. "Let's hear it."

Asrieth ignores the question and bends over behind me. He hooks his arms under my knees and arms to lift me up.

"I have my wings out. Might as well use them."

"About that," I begin. "Is this a disguise or what?"

He crouches and the massive wings flap up and down, air stirring around us. The trees moan as he launches off of the landing and we lift above the tree line. There's a chill to the wind whipping around us. I cling to him, searching for the portal. Asrieth spots it first and lands with a nice glop into the mud. It splatters the back of my legs.

"Woo! That's cold," I slide down and peer up at him. "So, is this…you?"

He sighs and nods, "Yes. This scary son of a bitch is me. The real me. How I truly look."

I bite my lip, "Why didn't you tell me?"

"I know it scares you."

I shake my head. "Not really," I lie.

He cocks a brow.

"Okay, so it does a little, but I know who's under there. That's what matters," I pat his bicep. "I know you'd never hurt me."

He smiles. It isn't as charming as he hopes.

I return it anyway, "So why the disguise all the time? It wasn't just for me was it?"

"Oh, no. I usually keep it on. It represses my

natural magic channeling, which can get out of control. The less magic I have the more humanoid I become. And most doorways aren't made to fit wings. I get tired of walking sideways all the time."

I laugh.

He pouts, "It's true."

"I know, I know," I take a breath. "That's what makes it so funny. I can picture it."

He holds up his hands. Caked blood covers black claws, "Look at these. I can't hold utensils worth a damn."

I guffaw and he smiles.

"You promise you're not afraid of me?"

"I promise."

We slip through the mirror surface.

I've gone through enough portals to hate them by now. Every time I dive headfirst into something or other. *At least it's always water on this end.* Once again I'm drug out of the lake, but this time it's Bob. Seneh kneels next to us, offering mystery fluffy red towels. Asrieth refuses, but I grab one and try to wipe mud and blood off.

I'm disgusting.

"Seems like something happened," Seneh says. His falcon agrees by shrieking.

I wonder if you can track Seneh by a trail of bird poop.

"Where is my Lady?" Asrieth asks.

"In her chambers," he answers. "But she can't talk to you until tomorrow."

"Why?"

"I don't think it's any of your business."

Asrieth smirks, "You don't know."

Seneh dismisses us with a wave and turns to the portal hovering above the lake. He flinches when it pops and disappears.

Asrieth helps me dry off and I shrug the towel around my shoulders. We approach the door and he tucks his wings in to his body, but he still walks sideways to pass through. He has to up the stairs too.

I feel bad for him.

As a fantasy lover, I always wonder what it's like to have wings like his. I never think of the inconveniences. Like going through doors.

Is it hard to sit, sleep, shower?

We ascend the stairwell with Bob walking sideways and come out into a familiar hall. We shuffle into his quarters and he kicks the door shut behind us. Mertyl is curled up on the corner of the bed and I eye the bathroom wherein lies the precious bathtub.

"Can I?" I tick my head to the open door.

"Sure."

"I don't suppose we can eat again…"

He smiles, "I bet your stomach's empty. We should talk about a few things anyway. Why not over dinner?"

I head to the door and pause, resting my hand on the frame.

I glance over my shoulder, "Do you need to clean up too?"

"I can use magic."

"Really?"

"Yes. How do you think I keep the leather so clean? In fact, toss me your clothes when you're done."

"Why have the bathtub?"

"I didn't build the palace. It came with the room."

I smile and slip into the bathroom, closing the door behind me. Beyond the door he shuffles around the room as I remove my clothes. I peer in the mirror. I don't look like myself. I've lost considerable weight and my hair is long and unkempt. Pale lines define where my clothes lay on my skin in contrast to the blood and muck layering me. I stick out my tongue to my reflection and start the water.

It's the best bath of my life so far.

When I finish I wrap up in a towel and open the door. Steam billows past me into Bob's room. From beneath the desk drifts the hum of the motor. Bob sits on the foot of his bed, peering down at runes on his chest. He's back to the version of him I'm most familiar with.

"I'm finishing up," he glances at me and looks back down.

I hold my dirty clothes and wait. Near the head of the bed sits a large tray with two hot bowls of soup.

"Yay! Food."

He chafes his hands and stands up, "I'm starving."

"You're starving?"

"Epic battles burn a lot of calories."

"I bet," I duck into the bathroom to grab an extra towel. I sit on the bed and drape it over my lap for modesty. I set a pillow in front of me and the tray on top of it. I inhale the steam.

I never knew spider bits could smell so good!

"So," I take hold of the spoon and dip it, "What is it we need to talk about?"

He stands next to the bed and his dark eyes drop down to me, "I'd rather you didn't have hot soup near you when I say this."

I still my hand, "Say what?"

"It may upset you."

"Oh great," I lay the spoon down, resting the handle on the edge of the bowl. "Now what?"

"That's not helping."

"Out with it!"

He crosses his arms, "Lilith sends you with me on these missions as a hostage."

"Say what?"

"When you first got here, the only way I could keep you is if I laid some kind of claim to you or bought you as a slave."

The color drains from my face, "And?"

"I knew you wouldn't like being my slave—"

"Damn skippy."

"—so I said…"

My heart thuds against my chest and ears in wild rhythm, "You said what?"

"We fell in love in Lubbock and I'm going to marry you. You're my fiancé."

"*What?*"

"I'm responsible for you. I thought it the best way," he keeps his distance.

"But you don't mean it, right? I will get to go home, right?"

"Of course. I don't see any reason to believe otherwise."

I peer down into the bowl of soup. I'm blushing. *Why am I blushing?* My eyes widen. *I'm not repulsed by this. In fact I quite like the idea…does he feel the same?* I can't bring myself to look up at him.

"And how," I swallow, "How is she using me to make you do things?"

"Lilith is the one who arranged your kidnapping. She tested my resolve to get you. She doesn't think I know, but I found out…from people. When she saw what I did to get you back she realized…"

"Realized what?" I part my lips. I'm not getting enough air.

"She can use you to manipulate me into doing what

she wants."

I shut my eyes. *Relief or disappointment? I don't know.*

He gazes at me, but I keep staring down into my bowl of soup, "Why can't she make you anyway? Isn't she your ruler?"

"She is my ruler, but my mother is her biggest ally and supporter. As am I. She's never been able to force me to do what I don't want to. She doesn't want to rock the boat. Or didn't."

"Isn't she rocking the boat already then?"

"Yes and no. My mother doesn't know about you and I hope she never will. Lilith knows that."

My eyes snap to him, "Why not?" *Feelings, crushed.*

"Because she will use you against me too."

I nod, "Oh."

"My mother isn't a good person, George."

I sigh. I want him to say my real name. *Even though he doesn't know it. Nor does he seem to want to.*

"Why does Lilith have to force you anyway?"

"I know her plans. They're not for the good of your realm. I have attachments. I refused."

Pain ignites in my chest and stomach. *Guilt.* "I'm even more attached, believe me. Now I'm single-handedly responsible for its ultimate demise," I cup my hands over my face. "Speaking of which, what other plans does she have?"

"I know nothing other than the ferry. Only there's more."

I huff, letting the guilt of all he's enduring on my behalf wash over me. *I'm so pathetic.*

"I'm sorry," he offers. "I have to take you with me because Lilith said if I leave you behind and don't do as she asks, she'll kill you."

Tears sting my eyes. *I had no idea. I've been*

complaining and being difficult. I've given him hell this whole time about how things aren't going my way.

"Of course I'll do as she asks," he continues. "But I'm afraid she'll sell you again. Or worse, one of my other enemies will find out about you. Lilith would be merciful. They wouldn't. I know it's risky, but I need to take you with me."

"I'm sorry," I whisper.

"Don't be," his fingers circle my wrists and pull my hands from my face.

My eyes are puffy and ready to burst.

"Please don't be sorry. I got myself into this and I'm only trying to keep you from getting caught in the cross-fire."

I nod and bite my lip. I glance up to the ceiling to clear my eyes and thoughts.

"Why do you feel so responsible for me? I thought…"

"You thought what?"

"I don't know. I don't expect you to go through all of this for me. It's so much trouble," I glance down to my cooling soup.

He lets me go. The pillow and tray levitate off the bed and over onto the surface of the desk. Asrieth sits in front of me and offers his pale hands, palms up. I drag my eyes to him.

"Do you really want to know?" His face remains stoic, serious, guarded.

I lay my hands in his, palms down, and his fingers curl around them.

I know where this is going. I've walked this road before, but the man I took the journey with is dead. Asrieth is unusual, but he's a real person. Not a fantasy. He's alive and looking me in the eye. Afraid, but with resolve.

I inhale and push the air past my lips slowly. His expressionless face readies for my reply. I know he's expecting a negative reaction. It's eternity before I muster an answer. To be ready for our relationship to take a turn for better or worse.

There's no turning back.

"Yes," my lips tremble. He grips my hands.

"Because," he draws in a breath and pauses. "I love you."

I close my eyes and tears fall down my cheeks. I shudder with a sob. I'm so happy I can't respond.

It's been so long.

Hot tears drip onto our hands and his grip loosens. Past my blurry vision his resolve falls and his expression wears down to disappointment.

I shake my head, "No. No." It's all I can say. I blink and cry.

"I'm sorry," he whispers.

He releases my hands. I can't speak for lack of air. The vast emptiness of words to describe how I feel fills the room with silence. I lunge forward onto his lap and wrap my arms around his neck before he can stand. I lean in and cry against him.

"This is a good thing?" he asks.

I smile and pull away. My fingers card into his thick wild hair.

He smiles and his hands snake across my back to grip me. He leans down and brings his face close. I close my eyes and his lips hover over mine before he kisses me. It's soft and sweet. His strong grip crushes me against him, but his lips are gentle.

He pulls away to tuck his thumb beneath my bottom lip. He presses it down to open my lips and he leans in to deepen the kiss. I yield, arching my back, and pulling him to me.

Goodbye, Phillip.

.

13. Well Laid…Lied…Set Down Plans

The last night I saw Phillip alive was the night I told him I loved him.

It's a memory that pains me. We ate dinner before our show and over pancakes at the Denny's on 50th and Slide, I blurted it out. I didn't know where it came from. We were talking about people's obsession with their cars, but I said it and stared at him in horror with my fork in mid-air.

He smiled and said, "I know."

Then he changed the subject. I took a moment to recover and chatter on about mundane matters. We sat through the movie in the usual way, holding hands, leaning towards each other. It was an action/comedy and easy to get my mind off of it for an hour and thirty-seven minutes. The credits rolled and when we were alone in the car, silence screamed at me.

I was mad at him for his noncommittal reply. Even "I don't feel the same way" would have been something of an answer. He didn't go one way or another. I was in emotional purgatory. As a result of my anger I didn't invite him in that night. He died because of my petty selfishness. It's my fault.

His parents broke the news when they found his body, face down in a ditch, off a highway in Colorado. We kept in touch after his disappearance. We were the only people in the world who cared for him. The three of us. During those times I felt closer to them than my own family. They didn't tell me about his death over the phone, but asked to meet up saying they had news. I knew. They came to my house and I refused to sit.

They held hands as they told me. His mother shed fresh tears and his father held himself together. I stared at the scratches on my coffee table. One of them, I can't recall who, set down a small red velvet box in front of me. Their words are a jumble to me now, but Phillip was going to ask me to marry him. He loved me dearly. They felt awful for telling me. They felt awful it was how I found out and it came from their lips instead of his, but they thought I needed to know. They hoped he would tell me himself one day.

They left me, and the ring, to sit in silence and thought. I couldn't bring myself to cry. Crying acknowledges he's really gone. It validates that he will never say my name again.

I draw away from Asrieth when he nicks me with his razor sharp teeth. He releases me and I roll my tongue around my teeth tasting copper.

"Sorry. Sorry, I got a little enthusiastic," he leans in and pecks me on the lips. "Who can blame me?"

"Actually, I think I can," I begin. He interrupts me with another kiss, "Why me?"

"Oh come on. Don't ruin the moment," he says.

"Humor me."

"Why not you?"

I slouch in his grasp, "Do you really want me to list the reasons?"

"No. I don't want your excuses for not accepting my…," he pauses. "My love for you."

I cock my head to the side, "Still hesitant? It's not too late for a takeback," I lie.

"No, it's not that. I've never said it before."

"I know. Or if you did you're sly and I didn't notice."

"I mean ever," he grins. "It feels nice. I can see why people do it now."

"Do what?"

"Say I love you," he kisses me again. "You don't have to reciprocate. I'm happy you're not running away in terror."

I smile, "That's just silly. Why would I do that?"

"Nobody says silly anymore," he frowns. "I still don't think you quite understand who I am."

"I do," I can't stop staring at his lips. "And that's how I know…" *It's my turn. Can I? Do I really love him? Are these just fuzzy feelings riding on the moment?* I think of Phillip. *No matter how mad at him I was he knew I loved him before he died. Maybe it was a comfort. I can't deny Asrieth this.*

"I love you," I say.

He kisses me in reply. My lips find sharp teeth, but I don't care. He pulls away for air. I savagely jerk him back to me.

We don't have sex.

We lay down to make out enthusiastically before falling asleep holding onto each other. We're exhausted from both physical and emotional fatigue. It's a great way to end the day. No regrets.

I'm not sure either of us is ready for it anyway.

I wake up hours later alone.

The towel I fell asleep in falls off and I twist in the sheets. They're soft and warm. I smile to myself. I still and listen for signs of movement in the room before opening my eyes.

He's gone, but my clothes are clean and folded on the corner of the bed. I sit up and frown at the indenture of sheet wrinkles in my skin. I lean against the head-board and yawn.

Do I feel as passionate now as I did last night?

It's terrible to second guess my feelings, but I won't do either of us justice if I dive in headfirst without thought. I give it careful consideration.

We're from different worlds. Literally. Is it realistic to hope we'll end up together?

I get up and dress in peace.

I sit on the bed to pull on my shoes. My eyes shoot to movement on the edge of the bed as Mertyl climbs her way onto the soft comforter. She walks in circles like a cat before settling down. I proceed yanking on my footwear, having trouble getting them over my heel. I lay flat out on the bed with my feet in the air trying to use gravity. Somehow.

Do insects get more intelligent as they get bigger?

Asrieth opens the door, holding a bowl of soup, and kicks it shut. He's wearing his usual pants and boots with a studded leather tunic like last night. He laughs at my exertion.

I glare and sit up, "Don't make me destroy you."

"Ah yes. I forget about your cataclysmic abilities."

"You would do well not to," I give him my best

maniacal laughter.

He smiles and sets the bowl down on his desk.

"Just one?" I ask sliding from the bed. I plop into the wobbly desk chair and freeze. It creaks beneath my weight, but remains steadfast. I rip the spoon he offers from his grip. I'm starving. "So where did you go?" I proceed to inhale my meal.

"I had to report to Lilith."

I nod and swallow my mouthful of soup, "So what now?"

"Nothing. She wants us to sit and wait."

"So she can carry out her evile plans?"

"Evile?"

"Yes. A little more umph to it than evil."

"I see. And what makes her e-vile as opposed to only evil?"

I frown, "I know you're not from my realm, but I'm still partial to it. I don't want to make it through all of this bullshit to go back to ruins with no internet."

I set my empty bowl on the floor next to the desk. I saunter to the bed and tug a pillow out from under the mess of covers and plop onto the mattress.

"I see you have your priorities straight then," Asrieth frowns at me.

I squeeze the pillow.

"You still want to go back?" he asks.

I swallow, "Of course I do."

"I see," he nods and keeps his expression neutral.

"It's not like that. Give me the benefit of the doubt here," I laugh. "I don't want to grow an extra set of limbs or something."

"I don't blame you," he smiles.

"Let's not forget there's still the doom of mutation hanging over me."

"I'd still feel the same about you if you had those extra limbs."

Heat flushes my cheeks and I glare. *I hate it when he makes me blush.*

He grins, happy to continue, "Or a couple of noses. Even better, a tail."

"Kinky."

"Don't knock it until you try it."

I smile, "But seriously. We have to do something."

"I know you feel compelled, but there's nothing we can do." He doesn't seem a bit sorry.

"Can't you morph into Super Asrieth and create havoc? Get me a ride home?"

He flinches, "Why are you calling me that?"

"Super?"

"Asrieth."

I pause, "It's your name."

"I suppose it is," he nods.

"You mean to tell me you like Bob better?"

He shrugs, "My name is said with such…" he considers his word choice. "Disgust. Fear. Contempt."

I know he's earned that reputation, but just look at him. That's not who he really is.

I smile.

"Asrieth," I singsong.

He cocks his brow.

"Asrieth," I continue. "Asrieth." I toss aside the pillow and keep my eyes on his as I stand. He crosses his arms and leans back against the door, watching me. I can't remember the last time I tried something like this without being awkward. It's natural to want him to feel better and second nature makes my hips swing as I repeat his name.

"Asrieth," I draw near to him and run my fingers

203

up his stomach over the leather of his tunic. He drops his hand to catch my wrist. I peer up at him through my eyelashes.

"I love you, Asrieth," I whisper.

He smiles and leans down to brush his lips to mine. I tiptoe and push him against the door, wrapping my arms around his neck. His hands slide up and down my back as we continue to deepen the kiss.

He's breathless against my lips, "Well, if you put it that way. I guess my real name isn't so bad."

I wriggle my eyebrows and he laughs, "Want to know mine?"

"I do," he straightens up and looks down at me with a sigh.

"Don't sound so enthusiastic," I roll my eyes and turn away, but he keeps hold of me.

"I really do, but you have to understand. I can't."

"You can't? It's easy. It's—"

"No," he stays my lips with his finger. "I mean it. Never tell anyone here your name. It's important."

I pull down his hand, "Please, be more cryptic."

He frowns, as do I.

"If someone knows your real name, and they know magic, they have power over you."

I blink. *I've heard that before.* I read it in old school stories about magic and wizardry.

"That's true?"

He nods.

"Well, what about you? People know your name."

"It's different."

"Oh yeah? How's that?" I ask.

"I can defend myself from such magic."

A dark thought strikes me, "So these spells. They have to do with some kind of...?"

"Mind control is most common."

"But you can still do those without the name."

"Yes, but the name makes it more powerful and easier. You can find the person at any time or place. The distance of power is also greater."

"And these spells," I swallow. *I don't want to say it. I don't want to ruin things, but I feel compelled.* "Can be like the charm spell you used on me?"

He drops his hands, "Yes. What are you getting at?"

My heart thuds in my chest. *I don't want to do it, but I have to ask.*

"And since we're here, in your realm, you can charm me more effectively. Right?"

"I don't like what you're implying."

I take a step back, "Are you charming me?"

He slumps against the door and wipes his face with his hands, "No. I'm not."

"What I feel is genuine?" *I'm such an asshole.*

His expression dissolves into pain. I built him up moments ago to tear him back down.

You're as tough as they come, but I've hit your weak spot. Like a bitch.

"Yes," he answers. "What you feel is genuine."

I cross my arms, "Well I'm sorry but—"

"I understand. If it's any comfort, charms don't work that way anyway."

"They don't?"

He shakes his head crossing his arms, "I can make you do actions. Such as say yes. For example, saying yes to let me live with you, but I can't make you have feelings for me. I can make you lust for me, but not love me. What you feel is real."

I blush. In my cell in HSAER, I thought about

205

Lubbock and chalked up all of the things I felt about him to a charm spell. *But this joy of knowing he loves me and fear of losing him is real. This is real. Real. No more excuses. I shouldn't have said anything. Too late.*

"I never should have charmed you," he says.

I peer up at him, "I wouldn't have helped you if you didn't. It's just as well."

"No," he shakes his head. "If you didn't help me you wouldn't even be here."

"It doesn't change anything. I'm glad you forced me to help you," I smile. "I would rather be here right now, than never know you."

He's skeptical, "Really? After everything that's happened?"

I nod, "Yeah. I think the good outweighs the bad. Don't you?"

Someone beats on the door he's leaning against and we both start. He steps back and opens it to Thecla, whose fist hovers in the air.

"Oh, hi," she smiles.

"Howdy," I pipe in. She waves to me.

"Bad news and good news," she begins. "We haven't found Rinkai, but Lilith can't care less right now. So, we're off the hook."

"You mean *you're* off the hook," Asrieth nods. "That's all?"

"What? Oh, no. Lilith says it's time."

"Time?"

"Yes, time."

"Oh, as in *the* time."

I cock my brow, "For her big plans?"

"Yes," Thecla glances at me and glares at Asrieth, "What have you told her? What does she know?"

"Nothing, believe it or not," he answers.

I raise my hands, "Only what the guy in the other dimension said."

"And what did he say?"

Asrieth answers, "Lilith is going to use George's realm as a highway for her army. Soon."

Thecla nods.

"What about Rinkai?" I ask. "Isn't he a political big shot?"

"George," Thecla begins, "There are a lot of political big shots who want to see Lilith fall."

"Wait, so what's it time for again?" I ask.

"The briefing," she answers.

Asrieth glances at me, "Give us a minute then."

Thecla gives us a once-over before nodding and slipping out. She closes the door and Asrieth turns to me, crossing his arms.

I peer up to him, "You're going to really do this?"

"Do what?"

"Terrorize my home."

He cocks his black brow, "I'm sure it's not going to be like that."

"So what's it going to be like, exactly?" I cross my arms.

"Not raping and pillaging if that's what you're thinking. I have my reasons, but I don't understand how you can still be attached to that place."

"That place?"

"Yes."

"Because that place is my home."

"What do you care? When I stayed with you no one came round after your accident to see how you were. Not. One. Person."

"Rachael called—" I stammer.

"Who is left for you? Who do you care about more

than me? My gods, George, what if I really was…" he clamps his mouth shut and turns to the closed balcony doors.

"What? Really was what?" I press.

"I was going to say psychotic killer, but…" he laughs bitterly. "But that's exactly what I am. I am a psychotic killer. I'm ruthless."

"Don't say that," I point at him.

"It's true."

"It's not true!"

"You don't know anything about me except what I've let you see."

Tears sting my eyes and he's blurry in my vision.

I shrug, "So what? So the fuck what?" I wipe my eyes. "I don't know what you want from me. Do you want me to love you or fear you? I don't care who you are or what you are. If you're a killer, you're a psychotic killer who loves me. And that's hard to do. Don't do this to me. Please don't make excuses to get rid of me," I cry into my hands.

He grips my wrists and pulls them away from my face. I keep my eyes shut and turn down. He tucks his fingers under my chin and tilts my face up.

"Look at me," his voice is soft.

I shake my head, but flutter my eyes open. I drag my gaze up to his and he smooths his hand over my hair, pushing it back.

"I will never get rid of you."

My face twists and I shake my head.

"Never," he continues. "I will do anything to keep you all to myself." He rubs his thumb over my wet cheek.

I nod. *I don't want to believe him.* I search for any excuse for this not to work. *We're both afraid it seems.* He pulls me into a tight hug, resting his cheek on the crown of my head. I wrap my arms around his middle.

After a moment he pulls away and we straighten ourselves out. I wipe my face.

"Can I come with you?"

"To the briefing?"

"Yeah. Do you think Lilith will mind?"

"No," he takes hold of my hand. "She expects you there anyway."

Dozens of people crowd Lilith's residence, surrounding a long table with a large map suspended in the air at the end of it. There aren't any seats. We all stand, Asrieth and I near the door. Thecla leaves our side to stand by the table. Everyone settles. Lilith makes a dramatic entrance from the darkness behind the map to stand next to it. I squint at the large painted canvas hovering near the Witch. I refrain from crying out in delight.

Earth.

I know those continents to the pride of my third grade geography teacher.

A man, tall, thick with muscle and overweight beneath his black armor, hoists himself up from a single chair at the head of the table to stand next to Lilith. He's older, his skin rough and grey like an elephant, and a thin black braid runs down his back from the base of his balding head.

He seems important. And like a total badass.

As if reading my mind, Asrieth leans down to whisper, "General Ulai."

I nod and watch Lilith wait for the crowd to silence

before speaking.

"Everything is in place," with the flick of her hand another map hovers from behind Earth's to float next to it. She clasps her hands behind her back.

I narrow my eyes.

I've seen this before.

It's the continent of Werdofium, which resembles a misshapen upside-down horseshoe. I glimpsed it once during my HSAER stay hanging next to the map of Earth in the democracy's pavilion. At the time I found myself too busy fantasizing a triumphant return home to study the map of where I resided. *Like an idiot.* I imagined how devastated everyone at work and my family are since I went missing. Then, after a minute of staring at Texas, I realized they might not care.

What if people don't flock to me or miss me when I get back? What a letdown. I'm fired for sure.

I blink, bringing myself back to the present.

Lilith points to the map of Werdofium on the right side of the horseshoe. A range of mountains dominates that side of the continent.

"Sarai is currently on the Rapillan border to quell a distraction our intelligence department created," she nods in recognition to a woman standing at the head of the table. The woman is breathtaking. White hair, white skin, and ruby red lips. Her eyes are black and clothes are clever like Lilith's with their strategic placement.

She belongs on the cover of a fantasy novel.

The woman returns Lilith's acknowledgement.

"General, if you please," Lilith steps back from the map.

Ulai nods and takes her place. He points to a large dot close to the southern tip of the right side of the horseshoe.

"Sarai tried to slip unnoticed from his hold. A powerless double sits in his stead. We amassed over a hundred thousand troops for this mission. Lilith will lead the frontal assault with twenty-five thousand elite cavalry."

Do some of the people here count as the mounts or the riders?

"Our spies inside Celeste will use chaos to distract their sorcerers and get the barriers down."

Asrieth and I exchange a glance. *No mention of super rose I see.*

"Once done we'll port the remaining troops directly into Sarai's hold."

That's a buttload of people.

Ulai walks over to the map of Earth. My stomach turns.

"Here," he points to the western tip of the Sahara. "Is where we'll have the troops ferry and wait."

I form a mental list of questions to ask after the meeting.

Lilith steps forward, "Thank you, Ulai. Everyone knows their tasks to see to." She dismisses the small crowd with a wave.

Asrieth shuffles us into the stairwell with the others. Thecla hovers close. Lilith calls to him from behind the sea of "people" filing out of the room.

"Asrieth, come see us."

He cringes and his eyes snap to several targets, "Can you?"

"I'll take her," Thecla nods.

He slips through the crowd. Thecla puts her hand on my shoulder and smiles down at me, "Let's go."

14. All Georges come with free shipping!

On the way back I bombard Thecla with questions about geography.

"And who's Sarai?"

"The sorcerer of Lumirah," she answers.

Right, because I totally know what Lumirah is.

I quirk my lips.

She smiles, "Lumirah is the country we're invading. Celeste the city. They're the bad guys."

"Check."

"And Sarai is their version of Lilith."

Okay, now that makes sense. I'd want someone powerful like Lilith out of the country if I was going to take over.

"Wait, won't someone try to take over here with our own sovereign gone?"

Thecla laughs, "Aw, George. You're starting to think of yourself as one of us eh?"

"Oh well, I mean, not really. You know what I mean," I stammer. "Answer the question."

"It's a possibility, but trusted people will be left behind to ensure something doesn't go wrong while she's gone."

We get back to the room and Thecla digs through Asrieth's bottomless chest to pull out a folded map. The map isn't paper and I don't care to think of what it's made of. She unfolds it and lays out the large map on the bed. Mertyl hisses as Thecla swats her out of the way and slinks into the bathroom.

Mertyl reminds me of a cat.

The horseshoe is clear and Thecla pulls spectacles from her pocket.

"Werdonic to English. They'll help you read. I've been meaning to lend them to you."

I thank her and slip them on. Reading the labels, I notice a group of tiny countries covering the upper curve of the horseshoe. Its title reads "Rapillan Province" in fancy inked lettering, but this title is crossed out. "Cluster Fuck" is written over it. I quirk a brow and glance to Thecla.

"Ah. These little provinces are broken up because of an ongoing civil war. The lord who ruled over them died and his twelve children have been fighting over it ever since. Each one thinks they'll unite the land once and for all, but always fail miserably. The map lines are always changing. It's dangerous and we avoid it when possible. That's the name it earned over the years," she explains.

I nod and look closer. The map shows only the continent in detail, but I catch bits of other lands on the edges.

I point to the left part of the horseshoe, "So we're here. In Mythreale right?"

"Right."

"What's going to happen to Earth?"

She pauses and straightens up, "Well, the idea is to

move all of the troops over from here first. Then Lilith will head through to the gates of Celeste, the capital of Lumirah, and do her thing. The other troops will wait for the barrier to go down and then they'll port into the city."

"And why don't they port straight in to begin with?"

"The barrier we keep referring to prevents ports from happening in the city and surrounding area. Not only us, but other countries interested in their coffers."

So Thecla doesn't know about the rose either.

"Oh. So what about Earth?" I ask.

"I'm sure you noticed we'll be in an unpopulated area. Lilith has no real interest in Earth at the moment. No need to raise alarm."

"No one will get hurt?"

"I didn't say that. There is a town nearby they will no doubt ransack. You can keep seventy-five thousand soldiers occupied for so long. It depends on how long it takes those on the inside in Lumirah to work."

I frown, "That's no excuse."

"We're at war, George. There are casualties."

"Usually casualties of war are expected between the two peoples warring."

"Oh please. That doesn't always happen and you know it," she puts her hands on her hips. "Don't worry about it. You'll be staying here anyway."

"What about all of the innocent people in Celeste? It's a capital. It must have a big population. What about all the kids?"

"Casualties of war."

My heart starts pounding in my ears, "How can you be so casual about it?"

"I don't have a choice. I'm not in the cuddles and

fluff business here. And there's no guarantee all of them will be killed. Some will escape, be taken into custody, that sort of thing."

"Oh well, that's *so* comforting," I mumble.

I want to give her hell, but I don't know this world. *Or what these Lumirah people are even like. I'm just glad I won't have to be there, directly involved. Although, is it really different back home? I remember watching the news and thinking how awful people are to their fellow man, turn off the TV, and not give it another thought. Sure, I condemn and curse the people who cause so much pain to others and don't do a damn thing about it afterward.*

She frowns, "Don't judge me."

"I'm not," I lie.

Thecla folds up the map and sticks it back into the chest. She drops it to the floor and kicks it beneath the bed as Asrieth comes in. He's scowling and kicks the door shut.

"They want me to go," he announces.

"Of course they do. What did you expect?" Thecla asks.

"I expected it, but I hope to weasel my way out."

"Like always," she says.

"Yes. Like always."

"I don't know why it bothers you," she glances at me.

My glare betrays my emotions.

"Oh."

"Thecla, I'll see you tonight," he opens the door.

Taking the hint, she gives us a quick farewell and slips out.

I cross my arms, "You're not really going are you?"

"Excuse me?"

"You heard me."

He cocks his brow.

I brace myself.

"And why won't I be going? Earth won't be harmed."

"It isn't just about that."

Confusion crosses his face.

I roll my eyes, "What if you get hurt?"

He gapes.

"What? What's that look?" I ask.

He shakes his head, "I've...It's a new thing for me. Concern. For my safety."

"And," I begin, "I don't know if I can..." *If I can prevent the deaths of some innocents, aren't I bound to? If I can save his life...*

"You can what?"

"Will you hurt anyone? I mean, kill people?"

He sighs, "That's what you do in war. You don't throw daisies at each other."

"But I mean innocent people. Can you really barge into their homes and slaughter them like sheep?"

His brows furrow as he frowns, "I will if I have to."

"Have to? What possible circumstances can make you think you have to?"

"Have you ever been in battle, George?"

Words catch in my mouth. *It's a fair question. I'm being judgmental of everyone having never been through it myself.*

I hold my ground, "I don't want you to go."

"I don't have much of a choice. Lilith wants me to and I can't tell her no."

"Why the hell not?"

He crosses his arms, "You know why."

"Well," a lump catches in my throat, "Don't martyr yourself on my account."

"That's hardly what I'm doing."

"It's different if they're attacking us. Why is this happening in the first place? Why go to war?"

"I can tell you and the war will be over by the time I finish. The only thing you need to know is they're the bad guys."

"That's what Thecla said."

"Because it's true," he walks over to the pile of weaponry in the corner. He digs around.

"Then why were you hoping not to go?" I ask.

"Because war is a nasty business. I don't like it. Lilith knows that."

"So you've done this before?"

"Why are you doing this?" he asks.

"What?"

"Interrogating me. I understand. You don't want me to go, but I have to. I might do things I'll regret. What soldier hasn't? But I'll do them…for the one I love. At least this time I have real motivation."

I uncross my arms and clasp my hands, "Please, Asrieth. Don't go."

He withdraws a sword with small hooks cut into the blade down its length. *I'm positive if you stab someone with it, it will yank their innards out.*

"I have to," he replies.

I imagine families having afternoon tea or another harmless activity in a living room when the sudden alarm sets off seconds before soldiers tear into their home. Demanding blood and glory.

Like the Kool-Aid Man from hell.

My stomach lurches, "It seems so unprovoked."

"They have something we want. Because they are our enemies we take it. People on Earth do the same thing. Your own country."

"What if it happened here?"

He glances up, "What do you mean?"

"Well...how would you feel if while you're off to this stupid thing I'm slaughtered just because I'm here? Say I'm reading and because I'm in this palace, in this country, no other reason, I'm cut in half."

His eyes narrow, "You're not being very fair."

"It's the same damn thing isn't it? What if they retaliate while you're gone?"

"No one said we're going to commit genocide. We have a specific goal in mind and once it's accomplished we'll leave."

No genocide is better but..."You're not a soldier either. You're something else. You work in the prison. That's different."

"True."

"Asrieth, you don't have to go."

"Please."

"I won't look at you the same," I blurt. *I shouldn't have said that. I shouldn't use that. I'm an asshole.*

He freezes and stares at me.

That's what he needs. If that's what it takes to keep him here, so be it. It's the right, if not most horrible, thing I can say to convince him to stay.

I close my eyes.

I'm an awful person.

I open them and he remains still. Cogs turn behind his eyes as he wars within himself.

"All right," he concedes.

"All right?"

"If it's important to you, I'll stay."

I close the distance between us and hug him.

Thank God.

He drops the sword and it clangs to the stone floor.

He wraps his arms around me.

I'm happy and guilty. *Not just because of what I said to make him stay, but the other thousands of families who don't have this option. But I don't care. I can't lose him. This can't happen to me twice.*

I peer up at him, "Will you get in trouble?"

"Not any more than usual," he grumbles. "I'll get stuck with bad jobs for a while, but I don't think even Lilith has the guts to kill me."

I gasp, "Oh shit. I didn't even think of that."

"You so rarely do."

"What?"

"Think things through. Or think."

I punch him in the gut and he smiles down at me without a flinch.

"You can at least pretend to feel pain."

"I do. I'm hurting. On the inside."

He rests his hands on my shoulders, "I'll make it as though I want to stay behind to see about quelling any ambitious rebels that may come along. Rinkai is still loose after all."

I nod, "Sounds good. What time is this going down?"

"Everything is ready. There's another meeting tonight. Tomorrow morning the portal is going to open and everyone will head out."

"All right then. Go forth and tell Lilith you're not going forth. Should I go forth with you?"

"Go forth?" he laughs.

He insists I stay in his room. Lilith doesn't need to know I forced him to stay behind.

I sit on the bed in his absence, leafing through one of his books. I push the glasses up the bridge of my nose.

I hate glasses. I had Lasix for a reason dammit.

The book I'm reading is about the proper art of sword sharpening.

How they jam packed all of this action into 997 pages is beyond me.

My mind wanders. I lay the heavy leather bound tome on my stomach and relax back against the head-board.

I should have asked if I can hitch a ride back home with the soldiers. But then I'd be stuck in the middle of the Sahara without any Matthew McConaughey eye candy to keep me alive. There aren't exactly any payphones lying around. Not that I have any change. Or anyone uses payphones anymore. When was the last time I saw one?

A hesitant knock at the door rouses me from my thoughts. I close the book and plop it next to me on the bed. I approach the door to the hall and knocking continues, but from the balcony doors.

"Um…" I search for Mertyl, who's nowhere in sight. *Awesome. Right when I need her.*

The eternal red sky outlines a dark silhouette beyond the frosted glass of the balcony door. I close the short distance to it. As I draw close the figure becomes clear. It's a man, a head taller than me with wild bloody-red hair and black feathers sporadically sticking out of a tangled mess. I can't tell if they're a natural part of his anatomy or decoration. He wears leather common in Mythreale. Nothing stands out about his pants or black boots, but he's wearing a long-sleeved hooded tunic with fingerless gloves.

"Who is it?" I ask through the glass.

He pulls the dark tinted goggles up to his forehead, "George?"

I nod.

"You gonna let me in?" the glass muffles his voice.

I shake my head.

"Really?"

"Tell me who you are first," I put my hands on my hips.

"You're smarter than I thought."

He leers at me and licks his lips. My eyes widen and I step back as his fist shoots through the glass. He curls his hand to unlock the door. I screech and dash for the door to the hall. The back of my neck stings and burns. I rub my hand to find something crawling around biting me. I grab it. A large spider with a thin long stinger jutting out of its oversized abdomen crawls around in my palm. I chuck it against the wall and as I reach for the handle of the door my legs fall out from under me. I collapse. The burning sensation of the sting shifts around my insides. Every vein in my body betrays me as it carries venom.

I can't move. I can't blink. I stare up at the ceiling while the stranger approaches. He squats and searches my bag.

"No weapons. Hmm," he clicks his tongue and shakes his head. He removes my glasses and tosses them. "You're a bit of a celebrity you know."

Even if I can respond, I'm reeling from shock.

I can go from reading about the fundamentals of sword sharpening to a lying puddle of George. Asrieth left a while ago and I hope he walks through the door, but the man takes his time assessing me with his emerald eyes. Under other circumstances I might find him attractive.

Who am I kidding? I think he is anyway.

"This is a little too easy, but a job's a job," he reaches down under my arms to hoist me up.

He jilts my body to find a good grip before he stands, slinging me over his shoulder. The burning sensation passes. I can't move, but I can feel. He kicks the balcony door further open and dumps me over the side of the railing casually. I fall. I would scream if I could.

I'll even settle for fainting.

Instead I hurl through the air for a terrifying five seconds before I find myself in the clutches of a flying lizard. I stare at the sky and the horizon is upside down.

My gaze fixes on two suns lighting up the burnt orange hue over the cityscape. A purple moon looms translucently on the horizon.

Two suns? What? Two! Two suns! I'd give anything for a camera!...Or for the ability to move. I'd settle for that.

I'm more flexible than I give myself credit for. I bend back until my head and legs dip far down while the creature grips my torso.

I'm a semi-circle! This is totally what I wanted to do with my afternoon.

The man leans over far in the saddle strapped to the belly of the wannabe dragon.

"How ya doin?" he asks over the wind rushing past my ears.

He grins, his sharp teeth gleam protruding from black gums. His goggles are settled back over his eyes.

My own water because I can't blink while the air rushes by during our flight. We fly away from the volcanic palace and over the city in minutes. I had no sense of how large and sprawling the city is until now. The wings of the lizard flap and a headache beats against my brain in the same rhythm. Now lightheadedness as blood rushes to my head. The man leans over to peer at me again.

"Uh oh! Thar she goes!" he laughs seconds before I pass out.

Jostling stirs me from unconsciousness.

I'm in a fucking box.

My body tingles in the most painful way. Feeling returns to my numb limbs. I beat my hands against the sides of the wooden crate. It's a cramping yard cubed.

"Asshole!"

I've never felt more akin to shipped goods. Oh my God, I am shipped goods.

"Shhh," a he hisses. He's right next to me outside the box. "Dammit. I knew I didn't get the venom dose right. She's already awake."

"You sorry son of a bitch!" my heart leaps into my throat. I vibrate in my prison with panic. I try to tip it over, but a force outside of my confinement prevents it.

"Tell her to shut the fuck up," a gruff voice carries from further away.

"Let me out!" I try tipping the box again.

The box creaks at the top as he puts weight on it, pinning it to the floor of whatever we're riding in.

"Listen, George," my kidnapper hisses, "We need to be quiet now."

"Fuck you," I spit.

"Gods, she is spunky," he chuckles.

The other man grunts.

"As I was saying, you need to be quiet," his tone lowers. "Because if you're not, I'm not sure I can get you to our destination alive. I distinctly remember a deep discount on my pay if you're not breathing when we get there."

This gets my attention.

"Are you threatening me?" I don't mean to sound

so mousy.

"No, no. Not at all. I don't make threats, but this is a dangerous area," he snickers. "I know you can't see where we are, but trust me."

"I'm sorry, but why should I trust you?" I smack the side of the box.

A howl shrieks in the distance. It rumbles the walls of my box. I clamp my mouth shut and hug my knees in the darkness.

"See?" he says.

We travel for hours. I need to use the bathroom so bad each bump in the road is torture.

The clopping of a horse's hooves ring on a hard surface.

We're in the back of a wagon or something.

Additional clopping joins ours as traffic increases. The murmurs of other travelers float by. In the time since I've sat in this darkness trying not to get depressed, I comfort myself with the knowledge Asrieth will come for me.

He has to. Right? Oh no…I'm not the hero of this story. I'm the freaking damsel. Noooooo! I'm the bait. The motivation for the main character. Now I have more empathy for Princess Toadstool. Or is it Peach now?

I want to ask the man questions, but I'm afraid of the answers.

Assuming he'll even answer them.

He keeps to himself with an occasional comment to the driver or me about mundane things. I perk up when the telltale sounds of a city draw close. I'm ready to get out of this box.

I start banging against the sides again, "Let me out!"

"Shhh," my kidnapper hisses. "Be quiet."

I curse and rock the box. The weight holding it down is gone and it tips over. The hard surface meets my face. I moan, but keep slapping my hand to create as much noise as possible.

"Help me!"

"Halt," a man orders. "What's all this?"

The red haired man answers, "Nothing. Just…banging out a rhythm." He beats on the box like a drum.

"No!" I say. "Let me out!"

The wagon shifts as my kidnapper jumps out, "Good luck."

"What?" I ask the darkness.

They call after him. People run past the wagon. The driver curses and swears he has no idea what's going on. The wagon dips under new weight. The box cracks and splinters as the tip of a crowbar pries the top off. I shield my eyes from the light. I keep them closed like a bat with a spotlight on it.

"What's this?" a man standing over me asks. He grabs my upper arm and hoists me to my wobbly feet. "Is this who I think it is?"

"Hold on," a woman answers. She unrolls a piece of folded parchment to my left. "Oh gods. It is."

The crowd around us gasps.

"Now what?" I ask. "I can't see shit."

The man bends me over the hard edge of the box. Another pair of hands holds mine behind me and wraps rope around my wrists to bind them tight.

"Whoa! What did I do?" I wriggle. The splinters of the box dig into the soft flesh of my exposed stomach.

"In the name of Sarai, cease and desist," the man orders. "George of Kothos, you are hereby in possession of the Celestene guard."

"What?"

Hands grab my upper arms and drag me out of the box. It tips over and I stumble off of the wagon. My legs buckle after being cramped for so long. I dare to crack open an eye. In the bright light I can distinguish the outline of uniformed guards. A group of them surround me, two having hold of my arms. I'm limp as they drag me away.

The guards tighten their grip on my arms, "You thought you could sneak in here, did you?"

I don't respond. I keep my eyes closed and shake my head. I try to bring my legs up to walk. The strain pains my arms.

"She's trying to escape!"

"What? No!"

A woman helpfully throws powder in my face.

I'm unconscious. Again. *Bastards.*

15. Not Again

I'm positive an elephant stepped on my face while unconscious.

All I can concentrate on is the pain until it fades to a dull throb. We're indoors. I open my eyes and glance up to two guards in shiny metal armor carrying me by the arms. Helms cover their faces. When they look down at me, I see only their matching blue eyes. They're dragging me through a corridor face up, my heels sliding along polished marble floors. My ankles and wrists are bound in shackles, which hang heavy. A metal chain between my ankles drags the floor.

The guards stop and let go of me once they notice I'm awake. I slouch on the floor and rub the back of my neck. I moan, clutching my head.

"Can you walk?" the guard's voice is cold as he leans over to examine me.

I wriggle my toes and shift my weight.

"I asked you a question, prisoner," he bends over to grip me.

The other guard bars him, "Give her a minute."

I like that one.

"Yes," I say, "I think I can walk."

The nice guard stoops down and takes my hands to help me stand. He holds me steady while my head reels in pain. I suck in my breath and close my eyes. I open them and look around. Tapestries of bright colors and summer days in bloom line the narrow hallway with guards. Sconces with flickering candles cast shadows. At the end stands a closed wooden door. Several guards line the hall. There are no windows and the weak candlelight glints off of their polished armor. We're underground.

I nod at the door, "Is that where we're going?"

"Yes," the nice guard answers.

"It's the dungeon," the asshole guard volunteers.

"Everyone here is human..." I lean down to peer under their helms.

"We have not been corrupted by dark magic as you and your kind have," asshole replies.

I turn to the nice guard and give him my best puppy dog eyes, "What have I done? Why am I here?"

He sighs and shakes his head.

"Come on," he takes hold of the chain between my wrists.

I can't rip my gaze from the little door as we approach. Two guards stand in front of it and greet my captors. They unlock the door. It swings inward. They march me through and I can't believe how massive the room it opens up to is. A prison with levels of cages and walks and suspended bridges guards patrol.

Like back home. Well, at least like the ones in the movies.

I dig my heels in, "I didn't do anything!"

The nice guard yanks on my manacles.

"We'll have to put you out again if you don't come

quietly," he warns.

I moan and follow them down the narrow stone steps to the large bottom level of the cavernous room. I catch glimpses of other human and humanoid prisoners, but I focus on my shoes. We approach a new door of metal. It's large and six guards man it. The asshole guard pulls out a small parchment from beneath his metal plate and hands it to them. They unroll and study it, peering over the edge to me.

"George?" the guard holding the parchment asks.

I scowl and cross my arms.

He nods. The others step back with caution, raising their swords.

"I'm not going to bite," I lie. *I would totally bite their asses. Not their asses but—*

Keys turn in the lock of the door and they drag through to a wider set of spiral stone stairs, with additional guards and torches, which wind down. I sigh.

This is going to burn.

They prod me forward to walk down. Extra guards accompany us. Their armor clanks and their swords bump against their plated legs.

"Where am I?" I ask.

The nice guard, who still holds onto me, glances over his shoulder.

"You don't know?"

"She's lying," another answers for me.

They all look alike. I'm not sure who to glare at. I stay quiet.

My thighs are on fire. I'm in the middle of calculating how many calories I'm burning on the descent when the stairs come to an end. Steel double doors meet us with ten guards standing around. Most are at attention, but a couple are sharpening swords or polishing armor.

Well, if nothing else I can give some tips on how to hold the blade better. Thanks useless sword sharpening book! I'm sure they'll let me go after a few free pointers! Why didn't I read a book on martial arts or something?

The asshole guard hands off the same parchment to the one with keys. He holds it next to a sconce and his blue eyes scan it quickly.

"We weren't expecting her yet," he rolls it back up and returns it to asshole.

Yet? What? They're expecting me?

Asshole guard nods. The man with keys unlocks not one, but five locks. Two on each corner where the doors meet in the middle and one in the typical place next to the handle. My eyes widen.

I think I know how dictators feel when they're caught. Except for the evil brewing inside of me since birth condemning my soul to the eternal fires of hell. As far as I can tell at least.

The doors scrape along the stone floor worn with the track of their movement. Beyond them lies a torch lit corridor. Another closed door waits at the end.

A man's scream rips down the hall as we enter. We stop and stare, all of us. I shake my head.

"I don't wanna go in there," I plead to the nice guard.

His gaze fixes on the door before us and he pulls me down the hall. The spell of fear breaks and others follow.

"I'll never get used to it," one of them says behind me.

"It must be done," another replies.

"I know."

The rusty metal door at the end opens before us as

we draw close. A small greasy man with a black comb-over backs out, holding a metal tray. On it lays a sheet of white paper stained with blood and surgical tools. *Recently used surgical tools.* He turns and I yelp. A lump of flesh stains the paper red.

I sway and fight the urge to both vomit and run.

A pair of large muscular guards accompany the little man. The three of them move against the wall to let us pass. I swallow. Another set of narrow stairs lead down to a room dug out of the ground with a sloppy tilework floor. The walls are choppy and uneven. A person with a shovel and a mission dug the place out all on their own. A complex system of chains and pulleys hang from the high ceiling down the wall leading to a single figure in the far left corner. Braziers hang to light up the room with dim, warm light.

My face crumples as they push me in. A foot of mud and good covers the floor. It's not cold, but it sends a shiver down my spine when I glop down off of the stairs. The cell airs out from a crude duct in the ceiling as the guards nudge me to the opposite corner of the man, who curls up half buried in the mud, sobbing.

What's he done to justify this? What have I done to justify this? Are they going to cut something of mine off?

The guards attach my manacles to the system on the wall. Heavy chains pull me down. I plop into the warm mud and peer up. Only the nice guard lingers to ensure nothing pinches and everything's secure. The others are out the door, escaping the cell.

The nice guard gazes down at me, "I'm sorry."

"I understand," my voice breaks.

He nods and leaves me alone in the pit with the strange man.

I think hours pass. It's impossible to tell.

The man stops crying and shifts in his deep sleep.

Why am I always locked up here? I'm such a good, law-abiding citizen…Okay so I downloaded a few songs off the internet, but hardly worth the hard time I keep serving in Werdofium.

I sniff and stand up to stretch my limbs.

Is this where I die? I should have said…done so many things differently. The last thing I told Asrieth is the worst. I should have told him I loved him. I should have supported him.

I gaze at the glowing line of the brazier hanging above us.

I should have told my brother I loved him.

The last time I spoke with Anthony was a couple of months after Phillip disappeared. My little brother does love me, more than my parents ever have. I understand what they did or didn't do isn't his fault, but I hate him all the same. I can hold my tongue on the nasty things I want to say because I know he doesn't prod them to ignore me. He's innocent.

When he gave me advice on how to deal with Phillip's disappearance, he was callous as he tried to talk me into "normalcy." At the time I wondered if it drove him bonkers he wasn't the center of attention for once.

"You're going to have to get over it," he said.

I sat on my couch, gripping my phone like a vice. I could only sit as my insides boiled. He was effective in getting a reaction out of me besides depression and sadness. Anger isn't the best replacement. I know he tried to help, but it didn't stop me from retaliating. I ranted. I swore. I informed him he never had to deal with hardships. And who was he to give me advice on adversity? After I cursed and insulted and dealt him the lowest blows I could, he was quiet.

And then, "I'm sorry. I love you and only want you to be happy."

"Fuck you," I hung up on him.

I'm sorry. I'm sorry Anthony. I'm sorry Rachael. I'm sorry Phillip. I'm sorry…Asrieth.

I cry in the present.

The man shifts to the right of me. I drag my blurry gaze from the brazier to him. He's sitting up and studying me. He realizes I'm here.

If someone just cut off my body parts I wouldn't notice the new girl either.

His eyes glow a light gray in the dim shadow of the corner. He crawls forward into the light. His wild hair is cut haphazardly.

Probably with a sword.

Blonde, black, and bloody red locks are dull from dirt. He's pale.

Like Asrieth.

His upper body is clean with a few smudges of mud. Scars cover his ripped torso. Mud hides the lower half of his body. He scrutinizes me, eyes flickering up and down to study me.

I blush and look back to the brazier. I sit and hug my legs.

The man stops his approach with my movement and sits back in the mud. I glance at him and his expression changes from wide-eye surprise to curiosity.

I gasp as I notice the dark blood caked around his mouth and down his chin and neck. I curl my arms around my stomach.

The lump of flesh was his tongue. I should talk to him, but it might be in bad taste considering…No pun intended. I'm a horrible person.

He stares at me. A range of emotions convey over

his handsome face. He settles on mild amusement. He sits a few yards away. I turn to face him.

"Hi," I say.

He smiles, "Hi."

"I'm George," I smile back.

"I'm Naphtali."

Maybe they didn't cut out his tongue. I'm not going to ask.

"Are you real?" he asks.

"Yes. I think so at least."

"Why are *you* here?"

I clear my throat, "I don't know."

He cocks his head.

"Why are you here?" I ask.

"I can do things," he answers. "They're afraid of me."

I nod and find myself crawling away to bump against the wall.

"Are you going to hurt me?" I whisper.

He shakes his head, "Never."

"Did you hurt someone else?"

He frowns, "I've never hurt anyone."

I unfurl my legs and lean against the rough wall.

"Then why are they afraid of you?"

He bends his leg, resting his arm on his knee, "I'm not sure I should say."

"All right." I'm not going to push it. *I don't want to know if this guy is a baby eater or serial bunny rapist.* "How long have you been here?"

He stares up to the braziers. His eyes are quicksilver in the faint light.

"I don't know," he says.

"Oh." I can see how he doesn't know. *I'm not sure how long I've been down here myself.*

"Since I was a child," he offers.

I turn to him and inch closer, "What? Since you were a child?"

"Yes," he keeps his eyes on the brazier.

"How is it you're so…" I begin.

"So what?" his eyes flicker to me and back to the brazier.

I force myself to finish, "Clean and…in shape?"

He laughs and looks at me. His teeth are sharp and bloody, but none are missing. His tongue seems fine.

"What did they do to you?" I blurt, to my regret. "Why are you bloody?"

He grunts and inches closer to me. I want to back away, but I feel bad for him. I hold my ground.

He's probably starving for friendly attention.

"They cut out my tongue," he sticks it out.

"What?" I stare at him. "Why? How are you talking? How—"

"It grows back. Every day. And every day they cut it out."

I put my dirty hand to my lips. He chuckles as I spit. Mystery mud covers my hands. I forgot. I pout and cross my arms.

"Used to I would say I don't believe you," I spit again. "But there's a lot of things I didn't believe in months ago. So, why do they cut it out?"

He smiles and shrugs, "It has to do with my ability. It's a precaution. An effective one, but it doesn't last long enough."

"Don't take this the wrong way, but why don't they kill you?" I ask.

His smile dies, "I don't know. I've asked, begged them to many times. They never say. I think perhaps they hope to use me for their own goals someday."

It's difficult not to pity him, "Now the mystery deepens. What can you do?"

"How do I know you're not one of them? Trying to tempt me into giving up my secrets?"

I laugh, "I'm hardly a temptress."

"I think so. You are the most beautiful thing I can remember ever seeing. Why else send you, a woman who seems to possess no magic, to this dungeon? I've never had a fellow prisoner."

My brows furrow, "I think maybe you're not picky because you've only encountered tin cans for who knows how long. Believe me, I'm not the cream of the crop. As for the other, I don't know why I'm here. Last thing I knew I waited for Asrieth to come—"

"Asrieth?"

"Yes," I cock my brow. *This must be how it feels to date a celebrity.*

"How do you know him?" he crawls closer until his chains tighten and restrain him inches from me.

I back away.

"He's my...um, fiancé?" *I don't know what to call myself. May as well use the label he gave everyone else in Mythreale. No harm in that, right?*

"You're from Hori?" he asks.

I shake my head, "No. Earth."

He slouches and leans back until the chains slacken.

"Oh. We're not thinking of the same person then."

"Maybe not." I don't continue. *Maybe he's the spy. For...whoever the tin cans represent.*

Silence fills the room and I settle into my corner. I close my heavy lids and teeter on the edge of sleep.

"I pass the time by exercising," he startles me awake.

"What?"

"You asked how I stay in this physique," he says.

"Oh. I see," I close my eyes again.

"I don't pose a physical threat," he continues. "It's magical. They don't mind me mulling around the room so long as I don't go for the door. I never do. I learned that lesson young."

Pity motivates my eyes to open and I lean back to gaze at him.

I guess he's in the mood to talk now.

"Like this," he stands. He jumps to grip a bar stretched across the room above him to support the pulley system. He grunts as he does one handed pullups.

I cringe. *I've had enough practice watching people workout way too hard on late night television to feel guilt watching him sweat…and pant…and wowza.*

Instead I fantasize about how Asrieth keeps in shape with less guilt.

My stomach tries to cave in on itself with hunger as Naphtali finishes showing off. He smirks and sits down in the mud, panting, pushing his hair back with his muddy hand. Muck covers him after doing pushups and pullups and stretches and burpees.

He'd make a good personal trainer back home…I'm happy I'm not alone down here.

"So, do they feed you down here?" I clutch my stomach as it makes another protest to being empty.

"Yes," he leans back against the wall to catch his breath. His hair is dark and slicked back with mud, "They clean me too."

I stifle a laugh as I picture guards giving him a sponge bath, "Really?"

"Can you see that doorway?" he ticks his head to the far corner on the right.

I squint in the dim light, but find nothing. I shake my head.

"Back there is a little room for the purpose of bathing and..." he glances at me. "Other things."

"A bathroom?" I perk up. *I need to go so bad.*

He nods with a smile.

"Awesome," I jump up. "You couldn't mention this sooner?"

I launch myself towards the corner before my chains catch up with me and yank backward. Instead of letting me plop into the mud Naphtali catches me. I fall back against him as he braces the impact.

"There's one in your corner too," his voice rumbles in his chest behind me.

That's embarrassing.

I sigh, "Thanks."

He holds me just long enough for it to get awkward, but not for me to justify a protest. He smiles and walks back to the wall, sliding down and leaning back. I return it and approach my dark corner. The dim light of the braziers is in need of fuel and threaten to go out altogether.

I place my hands on the wall and feel around as the door at the top of the narrow stairs opens. Torchlight spills into the dungeon and a line of six guards stride down into the muck. The substance sticks to their shiny armor. Two of them carry torches, the one in front and back, while the other four approach Naphtali. He stands and lets them guide him to the dark corner.

The torch bearers remain at the door as two guards come down towards me with their own to light the way. I spot the doorway.

Slurping and sucking fills the room and I jump as the muck and goo inches down into a drain. My guard with the torch nudges me into the doorway, light bouncing around the small enclosure. A crude toilet carved out in the corner rises up off the floor. A hose hangs from the ceiling across from it over a drain.

"We'll take your clothes," a female voice beneath the dark helm offers. The guard holding the torch turns his back to us, taking up the doorway with his large frame.

"I'm going to get more, right?"

"Of course."

Cold water pours from the hose in a weak stream. I keep my back to the female guard who's watching me as I rub my hands over my chilly skin. I'm happy, regardless, to be clean. They offer me white heavy cotton pants and a simple white double-layered tunic. I'm not given any shoes or boots to replace the ones they take, but they drain and spray clean the floor during my shower. I braid my hair and the guard offers me a leather strip to tie it. I find momentary reprieve from the weight of my manacles as I dress. Then they strap me back into the pulley system.

The stone floor cools the bottom of my feet and the chill of the shower lingers as I walk back into the main room of the dungeon. Underneath the mud are primitive beds carved into the walls two feet off the ground. A thin sheet covers a thick layer of fresh hay. Small bits of hay poke through the fabric. A simple blanket is folded at the foot. Naphtali has the same as I on his side. He waves to me. He's also squeaky clean in fresh clothes. Including a shirt.

Moving up in the world!

Set in the middle between our two respective corners is a modest wooden table and two matching stools. The table has a spread of bread and cheese and water with mysterious meat. I don't bother to contain my excitement and dive for my seat. The guards chuckle and Naphtali sits across from me. A guard steps forward to pour water for us.

Good enough for me!

We have bowls of hot mystery stew set down before us. Naphtali and I don't speak, but the guards engage in idle chitchat while we eat.

I don't pay attention. It doesn't matter to me. They're speaking in a language my translators don't pick up.

"Why can't I understand them?" I ask Naphtali with a mouthful of bread.

"Celestene dialect," a guard answers for him.

"Oh."

The guards clear away everything and I shuffle to my makeshift bed. It isn't a Serta, but it's better than a stone floor drowning in mud. I dare hope for a good night's rest. Questions to ask Naphtali mull through my mind.

They can wait.

After the room clears the guards leave without a word. The braziers have been refueled and burn bright, illuminating the dungeon. The doorway in the corner is visible. Naphtali sits on the edge of his bed on the wall opposite of mine. He clasps his hands and rests his elbows on his knees. He appears deep in thought, and so I turn to my own bed and sit.

I moan and lay back onto the hay.

"Goodnight," I mumble closing my eyes. *Not that I'm sure it's nighttime.*

"Goodnight, my George."

The tickle of a droplet sliding down the curve of my cheek rouses me from sleep.

I close my mouth, which is always open during any unconscious state of mine, and wipe at my face. Then, breathing. Breathing close to me. My eyes shoot open and I stare up into a black shapeless mist with a face floating loosely around inches from my own. It's lipless and shows gruesome dark gums and flat broken yellow teeth of its oversized mouth. Its permanent grin is made worse by the large yellow eyes with tiny pupils boring into me. The teeth part to allow a misty tongue to lick around them. Spit dribbles onto me.

I can only stare with wide eyes.

"Gaap," Naphtali calls. "What are you doing?"

The misty thing takes its creepy gaze from me, "Inspecting."

"Come away. You frighten her."

Gaap continues to hover over me. I gasp as a cool moist touch creeps up and down my arms. His misty hands roam my flesh. His face floats closer and I squeeze my eyes shut.

"Gaap," Naphtali says.

"Yes. Yes."

The moist hands are gone, but heat leaves my body where they made contact. I curl up and hug myself, pulling my blanket up to my chin. I open my eyes and he crosses the room to Naphtali, who stands and watches me.

"There's nothing to inspect," he crosses his arms and glances to the misty form.

"No matter now."

"Have you news?" Naphtali asks.

As I listen to them I realize the mist's voice is far away and faint. Like he's shouting from a distance.

"I do my dark prince."

"What is it?"

"Your freedom is close at hand."

Naphtali's expression rests in stoicism.

Asrieth gives the same look when he tries not to show excitement or sadness.

"It is?" he sits down on the edge of his bed. "Are you sure?"

The mist bobs. *I think he's trying to nod. Kind of hard without a neck I guess.*

"Yes. They are on the move. Thanks to her," he points to me.

Naphtali peers past Gaap to me, "Her?"

"She delivered the rose right into your mother's hands."

My stomach turns.

Asrieth mentioned a son. I called him Lilith's sob story. He did say he was a child when he was put in the dungeon...Is this all for him? The huge war, the rose, trampling down the city is all to get him?

I sit up in bed, shivering from the linger of Gaap's touch, but excitement courses through me.

"He's right. I did," I draw up my knees to hug them. "You're Lilith's son, aren't you?"

16. Reunited and it feels so…awkward!

"Yes," he answers.

"That's why you're in here?" I ask.

Gaap hovers up the stairs to the door. His misty hands rest on the metal surface as he stares at it.

"No. I'm here because of my ability," Naphtali corrects.

I tear my eyes from the creepy mist man and watch Lilith's son. He remains sitting on his bed, his quick-silver eyes fixate on the mud seeping into the room.

"Oh yeah. Your mystery power."

"I can tell you, but I don't see the point," he leans back against the wall, casting him in a shadow beyond the brazier's reach. His eyes glow as he continues, "They know what I can do, but not when or how."

"It's fine," I'm losing interest. *I'm pretty sure he's here because Lilith is the dude's enemy. A powerful enemy.* "You look nothing like her," I add.

He smiles, "Yes. People would say that all the time."

"Sorry. That was rude," I bite my lip.

He laughs and leans forward, resting his elbows on his knees.

"Does it matter? She's my mother."

I nod. *He's right. Not many mothers involve so many lives and lay siege to a fortified city. Although they probably would if they could. If Lilith doesn't absolutely love him, she isn't the type to spend the money to go to war. Unless it's a front and excuse for her to go to war...* Thoughts race through my mind. I put my hand to my temple as if it will actually help.

I tick my head to Gaap, who continues to drool at the door, "And what about him?"

"A friend."

"That's all?"

"In a place like this it's all you can ever want."

My brows furrow. I can't imagine what he's been through. Despite my complaints of childhood, it's nothing compared to an eternity in a dungeon. I give the place another glance-over imagining decades inside.

"He keeps me up to date on what's going on outside," Naph continues.

My eyes snap back to him, "That's good."

He nods.

"So," I begin. "Did they dig this hole in the ground just for you?"

He shrugs.

"It's pretty crude compared to the rest of the place," I say.

"So Gaap has said. When they placed me here, there was only a farmhouse."

My eyes widen, "What? But the fortress up there is huge..." A thought strikes me. "It would take decades to build, if not centuries..." I gape. "How old are you?"

Gaap takes the liberty of answering, "On the 17th

Tide he'll be nine hundred and eighty-six."

"You're shitting me!"

"That's…I'm not sure what you mean," Naph stands. His chains clink with movement. He shuffles closer, "Are you all right?"

I laugh, "Sorry. It's an expression…just holy shit. Wow."

Gaap turns to hover down the steps, placing himself between Naphtali and me.

"Think Earthian. Time passes differently here than in your world."

"I didn't think of that," I huff and cross my arms. "That's still an impressive age."

Naph smiles, "When we get out, can I keep her?"

I laugh.

Gaap studies me in earnest and my laugh dies.

"Perhaps," he scrutinizes me. "We'll see what your mother says."

I suck in my breath to protest and choke on my own spit. After a violent coughing fit, I lean over to breathe. I close my eyes. I open them and sit up, hugging myself.

"You can't be serious," I say.

"Very," Naphtali's eyes glow in the dim light.

Gaap shushes us as I open my mouth to reply. He floats up to the door and lays his misty hands on the metal surface. A low rumble erupts from his far off voice.

"It's begun."

"Convenient," I glare at them. They're both too busy staring at the door to notice.

The room quiets save the crackling wood and coal burning in the braziers above us. I hold my breath to listen for the sounds of battle or bombs or magic missiles. Naph stands in a tense stance. I glance at him.

As excited as I am to get out, I can't imagine how he feels.

I remain on the bed and draw the blanket around my shoulders. My muscles ache from tension and sleeping on hay over hard rock. I blow slow, deep breaths out through pursed lips. I can't say how much time passes until a mute boom vibrates the dungeon. I can't identify what it is, like a gunshot in the distance. *Do they have guns? But with magic, guns aren't necessary right?* I clutch my head again. The damn quiet and dim light always has me thinking. *Thinking thinking thinking.* I'm not fond of thinking.

Boom.

Soft, but closer.

Gaap backs down the stairs, his yellow eyes fixed on the door, "My prince, I think I should go before they come for you. I fear my presence isn't welcome."

Naph nods, "I understand."

Gaap bobs in an awkward bow before poofing out of view.

I shiver and try not to think of Naph keeping me when this is all over. *No way would Asrieth let that happen.* My cheeks flush. *Although I can think of worse people to be stuck with I guess. I'm such a hussy.*

I sigh.

The braziers swing overhead before a deafening boom rumbles above us. I cover my ears. The stone cracks around us and chains of the pulley system loosen and crash down. My ears ring and I can't understand what Naphtali shouts at me. He strains against his bonds, reaching for me. Tears sting my eyes in the sudden violence of the walls and ceiling collapsing around us.

We're going to die in here. This is it. Crushed to death in the chaos of the battle above.

The earth shakes around us and the chains fall down with rocks and puffs of dust and dirt from the ceiling. The braziers clank against the debris and hold fast, swinging around, light moving with them. Shadows leap everywhere and misshapen figures dance around in the darkness. They laugh.

I don't mind going mad. If I die I won't know the difference!

The ringing in my ears dies down and booms and crackling electricity stifles the air, but distance and earth muffle them. Naph yanks on his chains and they give way, clanging down with falling debris. He dives for me and has me on my back, against the bed niche, seconds before a boulder falls behind him. It takes one of the braziers with it and we're cast in flickering darkness.

"Get up," he commands.

I shake my head. I can't think or act.

He grips my manacled wrist and tugs me to my feet. The cuts of tiny sharp rocks and debris sting the bottom of my soft feet as he pulls me along the wall to the carved out bathroom in the corner. We duck in, walls cracking and crumbling in the small space, but they hold. We crouch together, Naph covering me as best he can. The last brazier crashes and light sputters out as it hits the floor. I blink and only Naph's silver glowing eyes watch me.

"It'll be okay," he says.

I nod. I wrap my arms around his neck and squeeze him.

"I don't want to die," I blurt.

"You won't," he kisses my temple. "I promise."

I scream as rocks cave in and crumple into the

doorway, blocking our exit.

The crashing and chaos of the collapsing dungeon halts. The ground moans as it settles. Darkness drives me to near madness and I focus on Naphtali's glowing eyes to ensure I'm not blind. I panic with the small space and lack of air closing in on us. Naph rests his finger on my lips.

"Breathe. Slowly."

I nod. *This is a perfect fucking time to panic!* I close my eyes and breathe out through my mouth and in through my nose.

"Good," he says.

I relax and sit in his lap for lack of room in the confining space. His arms hang loose around me, fingers clasping in my lap. Naph leans back against the wall and I lean with him.

"Prince," Gaap's call carries from the darkness.

I start and slap at the thin air, "Don't do that!"

Two globes of glowing yellow with tiny pupils hover inches from my face. His drool falls onto my legs, seeping into the cotton pants. I lean back, pressing into Naph, who unclasps his hands to tighten his arms around me.

"Don't do that Gaap," he repeats.

"I apologize, but I thought you should know they're close. I have lead them to you without being seen."

"Excellent. You've done well," Naphtali says.

The eyes bob in the darkness, "I live to serve."

I doubt that.

He disappears and Naph loosens his grip. I want to ask him about keeping me. *Is he serious? What would become of such a demand? Can it be fulfilled?* I shake my head. *No way. It is me after all. Asrieth wouldn't let it*

happen. He'll take me home…do I still want to go home? I
miss the internet.

I slouch in Naph's loose grip.

"Are you feeling well?" he asks.

I start at the deafening silence broken by his voice, "Yeah. I'm fine. Ready to get out of here."

"You think you are," he chuckles.

I smile, "Yeah."

Metal crashes yards away and we both jump. I hit my head on the wall in front of me.

"George?" a muffled man calls out.

"Here!" I brace myself against the wall, my back to the crumbled ceiling. "Here! Here!"

"Okay. Okay. I hear you," he says. "Give us a minute."

I all but squeal in delight.

Naph unfurls his legs and remains sitting.

"I told you we would be all right."

I can't resist a grin. I chomp at the bits as rocks shift and dirt shovels close by. A lot of swearing and magical incantations later, pieces of rock fall from the doorway. A blue glow spills into our small pocket. Hands reach through the hole in the debris and pull rocks loose. They crumble down to reveal stronger blue light. When the opening is big enough, Naph puts his hands around my waist and steadies me as I walk on the shifting rubble and out into the dungeon. What remains is a small tunnel dug leading to the stairs. There are several blue orbs of light floating in place along the tunnel. I turn to my rescuer.

"Seneh?"

He helps Naph out of the opening. His bird is missing and he glances over his shoulder, "Yes?"

My heart flutters in disappointment. I fake a smile.

"Glad to see a familiar face."

I can't keep the smile long. *Where's Asrieth? He's supposed to rescue me. Like in a fucking fairytale.* I swallow and decide to save my questions for later, but the inevitable concern he isn't capable of rescuing me keeps shouting through the hollows of my mind.

I place my hands along the sides of the tunnel, ducking under globes of light, and work my way towards the stairs.

"Your majesty," Seneh says behind me. "It's an honor to meet you."

"I can honestly say the same...," Naph says.

"I'm Ambassador Seneh Qa'a of Jiptia."

"I can honestly say the same, ambassador."

I duck through the opening onto the stone stairs which are still mostly intact. Naph calls after me. I ignore him and climb. The ceiling is low to the steps and I crawl up. I try not to panic about Asrieth.

There has to be a reason he isn't here. He's fine. He's okay. I'm sure he is. But I want to know. I'm afraid to ask. I don't want to find out in this dark strange place.

As I make my way down through the crawlspace they dug out, I can't distinguish any of the halls I came through or where I am. I'm not following a set path, but a chaotic tunnel that is the quickest route. I don't recognize anything until I crawl out into the cavernous prison. All of the cages are open and vacant. I spot the narrow stairs leading up from the double metal doors blasted off of their hinges. The remains lay in pieces around the foot of the stairs. My feet bleed from cuts of the rock and chain and metal lying around in the aftermath of destruction, but I don't care. Naph calls after me, finding it difficult to navigate through the narrow openings with his large frame. Again I don't care.

I need to find Asrieth.

I climb up into the wide stairwell to find a group of familiar black-armored soldiers from Lilith's regime clearing rubble. I slip past them to the top. I don't slow until I reach the hall with tapestries, some of which are burnt and dark residue layers others. From here it's difficult to navigate. I reach the ajar doorway at the end of the hall and peer out. Lilith's soldiers are everywhere. One sprints past me down the hall, knocking me off balance on my cut feet.

I don't care. *I need to find Asrieth.*

I can't imagine the fortress before the attack, but white marble columns lay broken and others remain upright with deep cracks jagged along their otherwise smooth surface. It's open like a villa with the remains of a beautiful courtyard in the center. The sky isn't red like in Mythreale, but a brilliant light blue with a tinge of gold. The sun is hot and average save its large size, the second is out of sight. Water spews up from the remains of a fountain's ethereal design. Pieces of brush and trees and other flora are strewn like a hurricane ripped through. I look around, wishing I could have seen it before the battle.

I follow the side of the wall, which is clear of most debris, and avoid the worst of the damage. I stumble and catch myself, hand on the wall. I glance down behind me and a small dainty foot sticks out from beneath a pile of rubble.

I tripped on a foot.

My hand clamps over my mouth. Naph walks up and turns me away from the body. I fan my face.

"They're dead," I say. "I can't do this."

He points to the blood smearing around me, "Gods,

George, your feet."

He kneels in front of me and picks up my foot to examine it as I keep my balance.

The foot beneath the debris forever engraves my memory.

That's a person. Was a person. A living being. That could be my foot.

Naph hooks an arm behind my knees and shoulder blades to pick me up. I let him. I don't want to walk around and trip over feet. I don't want to know how many more feet there are to trip on. I shut my eyes and press my hands against my face.

"Where is he?" I whine.

Naphtali doesn't comment as he walks. I keep my face covered and ignore the rest of the decimated beauty that is the fortress of Celeste. I can't be bothered to deal with anything until I recognize Lilith's unmistakable commands.

"You! Yes, you idiot. Send thirteen more to the south gate," she barks.

"Yes, my Lady."

I perk up and slide my hands down, keeping my fingers around my mouth.

We're in a street, the fortress looming behind us in a ruin of marble and metal. Naphtali stops, staring at his mother. She's flawless and beautiful in the sunlight. The white limestone-cobbled streets at her feet contrast against her dark skin. Her pink hair flares bright in unfiltered sunlight. Smoke stacks rise in the city all around us. Entire walls of buildings are rubble or missing. Ulai, Lilith's large-and-in-charge general, stands next to her. He says all he needs to with his war hammer resting on his shoulder. Blood drips from its pointy tip, staining the white street at his feet.

Neither Naphtali nor I can bring ourselves to garner attention. I'm overcome with emotion myself and try to imagine how he feels.

"Naph," I'm sentimental. I want, need, something sweet in this war and death. "I'm glad I can be part of this moment with you."

His quicksilver eyes glance down to me.

He smiles and nods, "Me too."

I try to wriggle down from his grasp, but he holds me to him.

"Why don't you go see her?" I ask.

He peers over me to Lilith, "I'm afraid."

"She's your mother," I remind him.

He nods, "I know but…she's a stranger to me." He glances down to me, "What if…"

"She's not the way you remember?"

"Yes."

"She might not be. She won't be perfect, but she loves you. Give her a chance."

"All right, but I'm not letting you go."

He avoids my gaze and stares ahead as he resumes walking.

Lilith's back is to us, but Ulai doesn't miss a thing. The general's dark gaze follows us as we approach. Naph stops a few yards away, holding onto me. He clears his throat. Lilith can't be bothered to turn as she shouts orders. The street slopes downward before us and commotion erupts in the distance. Buildings of the avenue lead down into an open square. The straight row allows a line of sight to the busted-open gates of the city.

"My Lady," Ulai grunts.

She puts her hands on her hips watching the frenzy of activity in the square, "What?"

"Naphtalith," he says.

Her casual pose stiffens. She turns slowly until she faces us. Her face betrays joy a moment before her expression hardens into irritation.

The silence is awkward at best.

Naphtali continues to hold me. I'm his shield from her scrutinizing glare.

"Why are you holding *her*?" she asks.

"Her feet are tender."

"As are yours," she points downward. "Set her down."

His grip on me tightens, "No."

"Is that anyway way to speak to me?" she crosses her arms.

He doesn't have a chance to reply. A soldier huffs up from the street.

"My Lady, a pocket of infantry came out of hiding and attacked the forces in the square." He bends over to catch his breath.

"Very well," she turns. "Ulai, take eighty troops from unit twenty-three."

"Yes, my Lady," Ulai and the messenger say in unison.

Ulai keeps his war hammer resting on his shoulders as he points to a few of his troops standing nearby. He begins to gather a small force from the chaos.

Naphtali's face remains cautious. I want to comfort him.

I'm sure this isn't the meeting he imagined all this time, but I can't blame Lilith. I guess she's upholding her image and is in the middle of a battle. It's hardly the time or place for a teary family reunion with teddy bears and flowers.

The flicker of happiness is all Naph gets for the moment.

Lilith turns back to us, "Come." She begins her

saunter down to the square full of fighting figures.

Naphtali follows carrying me.

I don't know what to say to him so I say nothing. Soldiers clear out the houses around us and toss finery and valuables into piles on the street next to us. A woman screams from inside. I ignore it, plugging my ears and concentrating on Lilith's black leathery wings.

Shame blankets me in guilt.

Naph shifts me in his arms, rolling me towards him to shield me from the sight. He seems as uncomfortable as I.

We draw close to the square and I unplug my ears to the clank of metal clashing. There's an occasional blast of magic. Sonic booms fly with debris and bodies. The competition smashes an infantry of Celestene soldiers. A whip cracks the air and men cry out. A group rushes from the square, their swords dropping to the white cobblestone. They fall to their knees before Lilith and beg for their lives. She looks down on them with her white eyes.

Naphtali and I remain on the edge of battle. Lilith ignores those who plead for their lives as her men cut beneath their shining armor to pierce their hearts. She plows through the crowd without fear. The whip cracks again and black feather wings catch my eye.

There he is.

In his true form, Asrieth double wields his whip with a bastard sword, giving chase to those who remain. He ticks his wings to launch himself forward with speed to cut them down two and three at a time until they're a bloody mass. His white skin and hair are dark with blood and black residue. He flings out his sword; blood slings from the metal. He rubs his forearm to wipe his eyes.

How did I not notice him first?

He towers over the other soldiers.

I sit up in Naph's arms, wanting Asrieth to take notice of me.

Naphtali glances down at me, "Does this mean I don't get to keep you?"

"I'm afraid so," I can't take my eyes off of my demon man. I'm ecstatic he's alive. *Alive! I can be conflicted about why he's covered in blood later.*

"Too bad."

I smile up at Naph, "Is it?"

"Don't worry. I'll get you later," he mirrors me.

I laugh and turn towards the square.

Let me go.

The crowd of Lilith's' regime parts for Asrieth as he approaches her. He bows to his sovereign. She leans forward, whispering in his ear. As she does he straightens and searches the crowd, his dark gaze landing on Naphtali and me.

I squirm in my captor's grasp and he sets me down.

Asrieth pushes past Lilith and troops step aside. Their curious eyes follow him to me. I blush under the sudden attention of a thousand people. I ignore the pain of my feet and glance back to Naph, who smiles and ticks his head to Asrieth.

I don't know why I feel so shy.

Yes I do. That look he's giving me.

Asrieth masks his expression in his way, but a hint of happiness and desire stand on the edge of bursting from it. He can barely contain himself.

I, however, don't bother.

I beam at him and run.

It's the right dramatic thing to do.

I expect daisies to bloom and birds to sing as I draw

close, running through the new opening in the line of soldiers as he opens his arms. I jump up onto him, latching my limbs around his torso as his hands support my weight. The crowd erupts in cheer. He grins.

And looks ridiculously handsome in the bright sunlight.

Asrieth folds his large wings around us for privacy as he kisses me with more heat than I think humanly possible.

Well, he is only half human.

17. Ferrets of War

Everyone speculates about how they will die.

Me included. During my time in Werdofium I consider it. All the time.

It's the approach to that thought process that makes us unique. Most imagine being old and surrounded by loved ones to slip peacefully into eternal life. Unless they don't have loved ones and then it's different altogether.

I always wonder about people who die of stupidity. The winners of the Darwin Awards. It's funny to read about how people go out. A man will die from sucking too much helium and I have to wonder, *What did he say in his last moments? Was it funny? Even a death cry would sound like a shrilly squirrel.*

In a darker line of thought, I can't help but to imagine how it is for people who end in tragedy. *Are they suddenly religious if they aren't? Are they suddenly not religious feeling abandoned? Do they make promises to be good?* It's easier to think bad people don't exist. It's easier to pretend things like that don't happen. Until it happens to you or someone you know. Then it's all you can think about.

I wonder what Phillip thought about. I wonder what the people of Celeste thought.

Lilith cuts our reunion in the square short by ordering the masses of men back to the portal. The troops are chaotic at first, but fall into line under the watchful gaze of Ulai. It takes them mere minutes to form their units. In the mean time I attempt to observe a thousand things at once.

Asrieth stops a soldier and asks for his boots. The humanoid doesn't hesitate and unlaces them before yanking them off and offering them.

Poor guy.

He leads me inside of a ransacked house. I keep my eyes on my hands, wringing them. I can't handle another pair of feet sticking out. Asrieth finds a fancy chair covered in fresh dust in what must have been a parlor earlier this morning. The northern wall is missing and ceiling buckled down in the corner. The chair, other than the dirt and small rubble, remains untouched. Asrieth hits the cushion; a puff of dust rises. He waves it away and sits me down.

I don't know why he bothers. My white-cotton clothes are smudged with dirt. He kneels at my feet to examine them. I lean back in the chair and close my eyes.

"I'll be right back."

His heavy footsteps on the marble floor alert me to his location, debris crunching beneath his heels. He returns and I open my eyes to find him kneeling again with a white-cotton skirt and a bowl of clear water. I'm nauseous.

Such a small skirt.

He grips one end of the skirt and yanks to split it,

making bandages. He dips the strips of cloth into water and soaks them. Asrieth has difficulty separating a strip out with his claws, but he pinches one free and drains it. He takes my foot, careful not to add to my array of cuts, and drags it across to clean the wounds. I suck in my breath and he glances up, pausing. I nod for him to continue.

I can't say why, but his bandaging my feet is intimate.

When he's done he slips the boots on and tightens the buckles as far as they'll go. I stand up, placing my weight on my feet for a test run. They sear, but it's an improvement. I keep it to myself as I don't want to be carried around anymore. The lifeless feet sticking out from under the rubble in the fortress burns from my memory and it brings unexpected tears.

At least my feet can feel pain.

Asrieth stands and rests his hands on my biceps before drawing me to him.

"It's okay," he whispers. "I've got you."

I nod. *I know. Even Naph had me before that. But who had the feet? I'm alive. The feet aren't.*

I squeeze him, "I'm okay. Really."

"George, I'm so sorry," his brows furrow.

"It's fine."

"No, it's not—"

"We'll talk about it later."

He takes my hand.

Asrieth leads me out onto the street and we join the flowing river of Lilith's soldiers bottlenecking towards the gate. I tiptoe and catch a glimpse of the massive mirrored surface of a portal waving past the front gates. It's over ten stories tall and hundreds of yards wide.

I blink.

"You came through that?" I ask.

"Me? No, but they did."

"Where did you come from then?"

"Lilith has a summoner following her around and I'm considered part of her elite."

"Her elite?"

"After what happened to you, I insisted on being in the front lines," he smiles.

I return it, but can't shake the thought of him tearing through women and children like he did the soldiers in the square.

"What happened to me? I was unconscious for most of it."

"Sarai had you kidnapped."

"Sa....ra....?"

"Sarai. The sorcerer of Celeste."

"This place?"

"Yes."

I shake my head, "No. That can't be right. They said I tried to break in. If he arranged it they wouldn't have thought that."

"Hmm," he cocks his head. "Did you see your kidnapper?"

I nod, "Red and black hair, feathers. Kinda silly."

"Nobody says silly anymore."

I smile at the familiar argument, but it fades as he frowns.

"You know him, don't you?" I ask.

He nods, "Yes. I know who did it, but it doesn't matter now. What matters is we get you home." He grips my hand and tugs me alongside the uniformed troops. "C'mon."

Home? Which one?

I follow, trying not to limp with my injured feet. It's

261

like nails line the insoles of the boots.

"Are we going through gigantor portal?" I ask.

He scoffs, "Of course not."

"Then where—"

He pulls me down an alley off to the side.

Staring at the top of buildings he whispers incomprehensible words. We wind our way down the back streets where the finery laying around remains untouched. I know there are feet, but I won't look.

Maybe they aren't really there. I'm pretty sure they aren't.

We pop out of an alley and approach a white marble watchtower situated at an intersection of streets. I marvel at Asrieth's internal GPS. The tower remains intact with no holes or blasts of damage and at the top I recognize Lilith's winged form. Ulai stands next to her with Naphtali, and a small figure in a black robe. Grime and blood cover soldiers standing with their pikes at attention to guard the wooden door at the base. We pass and it opens up to a narrow staircase. We shimmy past soldiers lining the stairwell and Asrieth knocks them over with his wings. They're caught by their fellows and we continue without a hitch. He doesn't apologize.

I suppose with his reputation it isn't expected of him.

We reach the top room lined with windows for a three hundred and sixty degree view of the cityscape below. A balcony runs around the outside of the room. The glass door leading out is ajar. Asrieth pulls me by the hand outside. I stop to shut the door with care and he lets go of my hand to approach the entourage.

In his true form Asrieth towers over the group and stands behind them to observe the city below. The small robed figure sweeps a dainty hand to pull the hood back from her blue face. Her skin is the color of the deep ocean. Her black eyes are big with no whites and she's pretty with high cheek bones and little rosebud lips. Though petite in stature, her confidence is obvious in the condescending glare she manages at all times. Her blue hair twists into curled fluffy buns. Small purses hang from a thick black belt cinched in at her tiny waist.

I don't like her.

Hovering behind everyone, I sidle up to the balcony's edge and squint in the sunlight. The city gleams brilliant beneath a layer of destruction.

I can only imagine how bright this place is when it's clean.

Sunlight beats down and I watch my shadow dance around with my movement. I glance upward to the second sun rising to join its sibling.

Thunk!

I turn to the glass door to find an unfortunate man ran straight into it and recovers by rubbing his nose. I stifle a laugh and watch as he opens the door and pushes past me to Ulai. He bows.

Ulai grunts, "Speak."

The soldier points to the portal towering before the front gates, "Sir, Sarai and his troops are on their way. ETA is seventy minutes."

Lilith cocks a brow and I watch her profile as she turns to speak to Ulai, "That's quick. It should take him days to get here. Not hours."

Ulai nods to the soldier, "Go."

The soldier bows and retreats, careful of the door, and closes it behind him. I watch it for a moment and secretly hope to catch someone else running into it.

"How convenient. For him," Lilith continues. "It's fine. We got what we came for. We have plenty of time to retreat."

Everyone nods in agreement but me. I know they'll address this in Mythreale.

I'm not a military genius like they are and even I realize there's a spy or mole or some other rodent feeding the bad guys our information.

A violent gust of wind picks up and presses against Asrieth and Lilith's wings. The two of them catch themselves and tuck in. It forces us against the glass and we shield ourselves. Asrieth pulls me against him and keeps the worst of it from me. The summoner studies me with scrutiny, noticing my presence for the first time. She cuts a glare from me to Asrieth before a loud explosion shakes the foundation of the tower. I screech and cover my ears. The glass cracks, but remains intact.

The wind dies.

We straighten ourselves and Asrieth keeps his heavy arm draped over my shoulders. Ulai checks Lilith over. She bats him away. The summoner checks her purses and pouches and robes. Naphtali brushes his wild hair back and smirks at me raising his eyebrows.

I glance at the northern wall and admire the fertile landscape beyond the gate.

Why didn't I notice that forest before? I bet unicorns live in there or something…Wait.

"Oh shit!" I point. "The portal's gone."

Everyone looks up in unison and Asrieth curses under his breath behind me.

For the first time since I've known her Lilith conveys emotion. Fear.

Ulai states the obvious, "We can't make another. We must leave the remaining troops here."

"But…" Lilith raises her hand to her mouth. "My army. We can't leave them here and come back with a fraction of my forces. It's begging for civil war."

Well, maybe you shouldn't have pissed off so many people in Mythreale.

Ulai grabs Lilith's arm and nods to the summoner.

The petite robed figure of blue mystery bobs her head. She reaches her small hand into several of her pouches and flings dry components of herbs and powders into the air over the balcony. Her hands sweep around in a jerky motion as she recites a well known spell. As she does this the components swirl a few feet from the edge of the balcony and gain speed. The small bits of ingredients blur until they reach the middle and a light flashes. Silver liquid spills out from the center until the mirrored portal hovers before us. It's vertical and a two-yard jump from the balcony.

Handy for the people with wings.

I glance at Asrieth, "Can we go together?"

"Of course," he nods.

Ulai drags Lilith towards the stone railing and mutters a formal apology under his breath before tossing his sovereign over the edge. She yelps and disappears behind the reflective and rippling surface headfirst. Ulai picks up the summoner by her robes and throws her in next.

Good aim.

He turns to Naphtali who shakes his head.

"I can manage," he approaches the edge and peers down. He hops onto the railing with dexterity and launches himself forward, disappearing into the portal.

Ulai grunts and slides his war hammer from his shoulder to toss it in before him.

I cringe. *I hope everyone else was out of the way.*

He hoists his thick body onto the ledge and throws his weight forward into the portal.

Asrieth lets me go to hop up onto the railing. He

offers his hand and I take it. He helps me up next to him. My balance waivers and he holds me steady. We glance over the city of Celeste. I'm glad to leave.

Maybe in another time or under other circumstances I can come back and swoon at its beauty and fantasy qualities.

Asrieth picks me up. His grip holds me fast under my knees and back. I hold onto him as best I can.

Can't get a grip on tight leather. Although he does look good in it.

He crouches and launches forward. His wings spread out to glide us into the portal.

Before we disappear I can't help but to feel sorry for the masses of panicking soldiers left behind.

Asrieth holds onto me while we shoot through the portal, but once we're free he releases me to freefall into the water. I go under, preparing for once, and kick up for the surface. The warm water is pleasant. When I break the surface I notice we're not in the portal cavern I'm so familiar with.

Two rows of giant columns lead a straight path through, their height disappearing up into the darkness of the massive room. Blue globes cast light and hug the columns, forming a ring around them. Shiny floors and columns consist of black marble and intricate scenery carvings. I know this is Lilith's room, but the other side of the darkness that hides her door from view.

Asrieth breaks the surface next to me and grabs the back of my shirt to keep me afloat, ripping it with his claws.

I bat his hand away, "I'm fine."

He lets go and swims through the water to grasp the edge. I follow him and take hold myself and observe our surroundings. The pool we're in is dug out of the marble floor with silver lining. The edge is carved in scrollwork patterns for a grip. I turn in the water and blink. A massive heap of gold and jewels and treasures twinkle in the faint light. I turn back to find Lilith flapping her wings to shake them of excess water. The others squeeze their clothes. Water splashes on the marble floors. It sloshes in the confines of the pool as Asrieth hoists himself out. The muscles in his arms and chest flex under the strain. He flops onto the floor like a wet bird.

At least the blood washed off of him.

His breathing labors, but he turns to the pool and offers his hand to me. My own arms shake as I try to drag myself out of the water and he grips my wrist to assist. His claws break the skin on my forearm and blood mixes with droplets of water cascading onto the floor beneath us.

The portal flashes and Seneh's falcon swoops out and glides in a downward spiral. His master follows and splashes into the pool. The portal disappears behind him.

Seneh sputters and swims to the edge, wiping his eyes. The makeup lining them smears and he blinks slicking his hair back. He rests his head in his folded arms over the edge of the pool a moment, panting, before lifting out and staggering to his feet.

Our posse—*I've always wanted to say that*—straightens itself out. Lilith doesn't bother to hide how losing her soldiers upsets her. Swearing fills the silence of the room. We follow the straight lit path and app-roach the cloud of darkness. Lilith and Ulai disappear with Seneh and the summoner into the black curtain.

I glance up at Asrieth.

"It will feel like fog," he says.

I nod and take his hand. Naphtali stands next to us

Anne Coffer

as enthusiastic as I about going into the dark cloud. I reach for him. Asrieth squeezes my hand as Naph's fingers close around mine. Together we walk into the darkness. It's thick and suffocates for a moment. I hold my breath, but I release and Asrieth is right. A cool mist tickles my skin and smells like Glade. *Freshly laundered scent I think.*

We step out.

Lilith stands with her wings out and legs apart. Her hands rise before her as magic sputters from her fingertips while she holds back a spell. Ulai slings his war hammer across his broad shoulders with his feet apart and knees bent. Seneh's bird sits on his shoulder guard and the summoner hovers behind them, but Seneh's left hand slides a hidden dagger out from the back of his belt. It glints.

Between us and the doorway is Rinkai.

"Holy shit," I blurt.

I almost forgot about him.

He's as gruesome as I tried to forget. His long tongue hangs from his gaping mouth to the marble floor, smearing foul saliva around the shiny surface. His small torso bobs with his breathing. His long puppet like limbs shift.

No one says anything for a long while.

"I know you're not alone," Lilith breaks the silence.

Rinkai laughs; a soft voice in my head.

"Tell your lackeys to show themselves," she commands.

Rinkai bows, "As you wish." He raises a thin arm and flicks his long fingers at the darkness to our right.

I gasp.

Thecla steps into the light and behind her Jonah extends an arm reaching around her middle to hold a knife against her stomach.

"Jonah?" I gape.

I let go of the hands I grasp to lurch forward. Asrieth shoots out and grabs my torn tunic to yank me back.

Jonah's brown eyes fall on me and he nods his head.

"What is this?" I ask.

What's he doing here? With Thecla? She's an Earthian sympathizer.

"Yes," Lilith continues. "What *is* this?"

Rinkai smiles, "Your downfall."

"Naturally," she replies.

Rinkai's beady black eyes roll towards Jonah and Thecla, "He's one of mine." He curls the long tongue up into his mouth to moisten it. It slops back onto the floor at his feet.

"And if you want your servant back alive you will give me the girl," he points to me.

"What?" *What the actual fuck?* My eyes widen and my heart thuds against my chest. The same feeling I got when he talked to me in Lubbock. About me. *Anything to do with him and myself.*

I shake my head and shuffle back. Asrieth steps forward to place himself between us. Naph remains between him and I.

"Over my dead body," Asrieth unfurls his whip.

Rinkai chuckles, "Exactly. We all know she's the control panel for Mythreale's most lethal warrior." He slurps his tongue. "Especially now."

I hug myself.

"Too bad," Lilith lowers her wings and hands. The magic dissipates.

"You can kill Thecla instead," she says.

Thecla gapes, "What?"

"I thought you said she would go for it," Rinkai's toothy grin dies.

Lilith cocks her brow, "Go for what exactly?"

"But I'm your warden. I've been a loyal subject for years," Thecla says.

Lilith hisses, "And you can only dream of being as valuable as Asrieth."

"Fuck you," Thecla growls. "Have you any idea how many assassins I've killed and innocent people I watched tortured for you? You ungrateful bitch."

Lilith laughs, "Yes. And now I have an idea of how you betrayed me."

Thecla's face pales.

"How you paid off Larodin to take Asrieth's guard shift so Rinkai could escape. How convenient for Asrieth to be left abandoned in the Earthian realm so you may proceed with your plans. And you," she turns to Rinkai. "Do you truly think I can't smell out a rat who sits right beneath my nose? Why do you think I left her behind? I didn't want her ruining the mission."

"No matter," Rinkai flicks a hand to Jonah. "Let her go."

Thecla moves, but Jonah holds the blade against her flat stomach.

"Ah, well, about that," Jonah begins. "It seems I'm under obligation to hold the rat against my sovereign hostage." He smiles.

"What?"

"He's a Ferret," Ulai says.

Any other time I'd laugh my ass off. I refrain and watch as the complex web unravels.

Rinkai roars, specks of saliva flying from his open mouth.

"No matter," the puppet kind says. "Your army is dead. The city is ours. Give it up. Larieth is in shackles. You're alone."

Lilith pulls her shoulders back and sticks her chin up, "Very well."

That was easy.

"Mother," Naph steps forward. "You can't be serious."

She glances over her shoulder and silences him with a shake of her head.

"Take us to the square so I may see the glory of your army and bow before it," she smiles.

"I prefer you do it here," Rinkai says.

"No. I want to see this mighty army and my fallen city before I do such a thing."

Ulai nods to Jonah, who lowers the blade and backs away from Thecla. He keeps the blade before him and doesn't take his eyes off of her as she draws out a short sword until he's by Ulai's side.

Rinkai flicks his long arms and out of the darkness step uniformed soldiers. Not Lilith's. As opposed to fine black armor these are outfitted in mismatching leather and bronze. Though their armor is shabby their weapons are sharp and point at us.

"Your weapons," Thecla points to the ground.

I shake my head.

I thought better of her. Wait, what am I saying? How dare she not worship the woman who just massacred a city? Okay, in that context I don't think I can blame her.

Everyone pulls swords and knives and darts from hidden pockets. A small pile accumulates at Seneh's feet. Asrieth drops his whip and sword with a clang. The summoner unhooks her pouches and components at sword point. She curses as she removes her robes to reveal a dozen pouches inside. She unsheathes a set of daggers from beneath the simple black tunic, breeches and scuffed boots. Ulai sets down his crude weapon.

"Satisfied?" Lilith asks.

"For now," Rinkai grins.

I think it's a grin. With this guy's mouth I can never be sure what facial expression he's going for.

The puppet kind turns his back to us and slinks down into the stairwell. Thecla grunts for us to follow. Rinkai's men descend after him and we shuffle down like the defeated party we are.

I expected at least some kind of epic fight, but this is real life. Real life. Not a fantasy book.

We walk single file downward, guards now surrounding us on all sides. Asrieth walks sideways to accommodate his massive wings, as does Lilith. We progress through the palace halls scattered with bodies of servants and soldiers loyal to the Lady. I stare at the floor.

I don't want to see anymore feet, but God I know they're there.

Our procession follows Rinkai down familiar halls and out the front doors past the gates of the palace.

Copper blood hanging in the air finds its way into my mouth as I breathe through my nose. It sticks to my skin. The streets are clear and Rinkai's shabby guards keep a roaring crowd back on the boardwalk. They throw flowers and jump with excitement as Rinkai leads our sad posse towards a square. There are no signs of battle or resistance.

Maybe Lilith is the bad guy. At least in Celeste they put up a fight.

I study the populace and black twisted buildings of Mythreale clearly for the first time. Most of the people are like Asrieth and Thecla and Seneh. They're humanoid with distinguishing features that scream not human. Wings, fangs, claws, horns, skin an unnatural color. Dotting the crowd are mutated humans in a state of servitude to their celebrating masters.

The streets are wide and we spot Rinkai's army as we draw further from the palace. They're amongst the crowd, on top of buildings, and blocking the citizens from the roads. They part for Rinkai and allow us to pass after him. They fan us out into the square. On the other side, on their knees and gagged in chains, are the powder white woman from the war meeting and the man who kidnapped me. Both of their pale faces are cut and bruises well up around their beautiful features. The man's goggles are broken and hang around his neck. Close by the body of his lizard mount lays lifeless.

Lilith, Ulai, and Naphtali are in the center of our line. Asrieth and I are put on opposite ends. Seneh stands to the right of me and the summoner to the left of Asrieth as well as Jonah. The crowd quiets.

"Larieth," Lilith's lilt carries. "Are you all right?"

The pale woman nods, the black gag a stark contrast to her powdery skin.

Lilith ticks her head at my kidnapper, "Mahali?"

He nods.

I narrow my eyes and glare at Lilith's profile. *Again? Really? You? Ugh. I'll bring this up later. Assuming there's a later to bring up my kidnapping.*

Lilith folds her arms. The soldiers raise their weapons.

"Release us," she says.

Rinkai laughs, as does Thecla and then the crowd.

I glare at Thecla, *disappoint.*

"I'm giving you one, last, chance," she faces the

crowd.

The crowd and soldiers quiet. Fear blankets them in silence.

My heart thuds. *Maybe this is what I'm waiting for. I've yet to see Lilith work that badass magic everyone always talks about.*

"I will always love and serve my Lady," a male voice in the crowd carries. Another follows. Then another. Just as quickly the people of the capital cheer for the Witch as they did for the puppet monster moments ago.

"Fickle bunch," I say.

Seneh smirks and nods.

"That's what I thought," Lilith uncrosses her arms.

Rinkai raises his hand to silence Lilith's cheers.

"I don't understand," he begins. "You have nothing left. Your army is defeated and in Sarai's prison. Your death is at hand." He slurps his tongue, "Admirable adversary you are, you must be destroyed all the same."

Lilith bows, "You flatter me, but I cannot reciprocate. You were foolish enough to bring me out into the open."

"Excuse me?"

"Have you forgotten who I am? The reason for your little rabble army's name?" She places a jeweled hand on her hip.

I glance at Seneh.

He rolls his eyes and leans in to whisper, triggering the soldiers by us to raise their weapons, "They're called the Slayers."

I nod. *What does that have to do with anything?*

He shakes his head, straightening up.

"Please," Rinkai says. "We know you can't turn anymore. You've been in this form for too long."

"And who told you this?" Lilith asks. "Your spy?"

Thecla bristles.

"You're bluffing," he says.

Lilith ticks her head to the soldiers holding my kidnapper, Mahali, and the pale woman Larieth.

"Release them. I have many new openings in my army," Lilith turns to the soldiers. "You're welcome to those positions if you let them go. Now."

The soldiers exchange a glance.

"Stand down!" Rinkai huffs. "She's bluffing."

My hair whips around in a gust of wind, which I know to associate with strong magic. Seneh grabs my arm and pulls me away from Ulai before he backs into me. Lilith's brilliant pink hair flies around and loosens to snap around in the strong air flow. Her body grows; first the limbs get longer and her torso catches up. Her cool black skin shines with scales and her wings expand with the rest of her. Flapping pink hair solidifies into spikes running down the back of her head, spine, and tail. Claws protrude from gargantuan gnarly hands as she leans over to stand on all fours.

"Holy shit!" I back away from the massive form of a beautiful black dragon.

18. I'll never let go, Jack.

I've had a phenomenal relationship with books my entire life.

I was one of those kids reading at the dinner table because the sorcerer disintegrating the evil wombat was more important to me than mashed potatoes and green beans. I was scolded, forced to put away my precious handheld world, and ate and listened to how amazing everything my little brother did that day was...amazing.

As a teen, heroes of books and stories romanced me. What girl needed a gangly boy taking her to the movies when she could have a sexy thief stealing her into the long hours of the night page after page? *Me, apparently.* I let my younger years slip by me while I kept to myself and lived my life only in my active imagination. I preferred the sharp edge of pages to the soft warm embrace of a flesh and blood man. But even the men of books and adventure left me after "The End" and I had to start all over again. Fall in love and be heart broken all over again. I have always loved books. I always will. The better the story the harder I cry and hate those words. The End.

And Rinkai's end fast approaches.

A dragon. A dragon. Now this is a dragon! It's right up there on my list with unicorns and mermaids. I squeal and clasp my hands.

Lilith's nostrils flare and the scent of acid and flowers fills the air. Soldiers shake as they unchain their captives. Larieth limps to her sovereign, Mahali's arm around her waist to assist. They walk beneath the dragon's large frame. With her two servants out of harm's way, Lilith unleashes a bright pink electric breath weapon onto the mass of soldiers. The crowd shrieks behind them. Rinkai's mind-penetrating screams ring as pink lightening dances around his gangly form and shoots out of his eyes and mouth down to the tip of his tongue. Burnt flesh mixes with sulfur and flowers in the air.

Now that's a pair of feet I don't mind going down.

In a flurry our group runs to avoid Lilith's feet as she obliterates her enemies. Except Ulai.

As he pimp walks to safety.

The rest of us scramble. With a flap of his wings Asrieth shoots to me and takes hold of my waist. He glances over his shoulder and snaps his wings to jolt us away from the heat of action. The crowd of spectators flees in panic, trampling and shoving each other to get down alleys and side streets unnoticed.

Asrieth touches down with the rest of our group next to a tall shop of twisted black wood and stone. He holds me to him, my back to his torso and we watch Lilith massacre Rinkai's forces.

"Why didn't she do this in Celeste?" I ask.

Asrieth shrugs, "It wasn't necessary. And she's one of the last. It's been centuries since she last enjoyed her true form in public. Now she'll be hunted not only for her role as a leader, but for her blood and skin. Many thought it a rumor about her anyway."

I frown. *The woman can't win, but she does today. If bodies are points there's a lot of win for Lilith.*

No one proves a challenge. When none are left in sight, or alive, she turns and finds us with her milky eyes. Her nostrils flare as she twists and morphs back into her humanoid form. Lilith stretches and pops her limbs into place before sauntering up to us.

Larieth, with Mahali's assistance, limps up to Lilith and they embrace each other. They kiss on the lips and Lilith tucks Larieth's head against her neck, hands running through her white hair. Asrieth rests his chin on top of my head as we watch the reunion. Lilith reaches out and Mahali slips under her arm. He holds out his and the summoner patters up into his grip, dragging Ulai with her. Lilith offers her other arm, Larieth still clutching her, and Seneh shuffles in. Jonah walks up without invitation and smiles closing his eyes as he hugs Ulai, who doesn't seem pleased with the close contact.

Asrieth, Naphtali, and I stand outside of the hug circle in silence.

Larieth loosens her grip on Lilith, shifting the circle. With her pale arm she reaches out to us.

A warm surge wells up inside of me. It brews from the bottom of my stomach into my eyes. My vision blurs as I pull from Asrieth, taking his hand in mine. I glance over my shoulder to Naphtali and hold out my hand to him. He smiles and nods, taking it. We dart forward into the hug and they embrace us. I've never felt this warmth before. I searched for it my entire life. It's not love and success like I thought it would be.

I feel like I belong.

The moment doesn't last as long as I dare hope and we begin the trek back to the palace. Lilith walks hand in hand with her son and Larieth. I'm happy for Naph.

This is the greeting he expected.

Asrieth keeps my hand in his and I ponder what whirlwind adventure will happen next. The gates of the palace are shut behind us and we stand in the steam surrounding the volcanic palace.

Lilith turns to me, "You can go home now."

I start and glance up to Asrieth. His eyes are downcast.

"I can?"

She nods and turns to the summoner, "See to it she leaves. Now."

The summoner bows.

"Say your goodbyes before I change my mind," Lilith waves at me. She takes Larieth's hand and holds the other for Naph. His eyes dart between us.

"I want to say goodbye," he says.

Lilith drops her hand, "Be quick."

Naphtali nods and walks up to me. He leans down and kisses my cheek.

"I wish I could keep you," he whispers.

Asrieth rests his hand on my shoulder.

Naph lets me go and turns to his mother. He takes her hand, glancing back to me over his shoulder. With Mahali and Larieth they disappear into the steam holding onto Lilith.

Seneh claps his hand onto my other shoulder, "I'd like to say it was fun, but let's face it." He smiles, "Good luck."

I nod, "Yeah, every time I see you something bad happens."

He laughs and shakes his head, disappearing into the steam.

Jonah shoves his hands into the pockets of his white pants.

"I'll walk down with you," he says.

Asrieth nods and the three of us turn to the summoner, who waits crossing her arms.

"You done? I have other things to attend to," she says.

But I'm not done. I want this to last forever. My grand adventure can't come to an end yet.

I sigh. My hand sweats in Asrieth's. He doesn't say a word and neither does anyone else on our way down. My heart pounds with nausea rising from the pit of my stomach.

I don't want to say goodbye. Not to Asrieth. I just got him. But I need to go home. I don't want to mutate. I don't want to be like Katherine. Maybe it's for the best. Maybe it's better to sever the ties we have and be done with it. It's inevitable anyway, right?

My legs burn as we make our way down to the grand portal room. The summoner leaves us without a word and as we reach it she's back with her robes intact. Asrieth turns sideways to maneuver through the doorway. We step out into the cavern. We're its only occupants and I'm thankful for privacy.

Jonah turns to me.

"Jonah," I say, trying not to cry. "What was all that about?"

He smiles, "I know, right?"

"So you're a ferret?"

He laughs, "Yeah. Ulai's secret police."

"A ferret though? Really?"

"The general read about them once as a child. He thought it was a good name. Ferrets are smart and sneaky. Something like that."

"So you worked for him when you were with HSAER?"

He nods, "Yes. Rinkai too technically. They were both after the rose and then I stumbled upon you. Lilith told me to watch out for you, but I had no idea you were Asrieth's. When I found out I knew it was only a matter of time before he came." He shrugs, "Or so I thought. And I thought right."

"Wow. So why did you tell them about Asrieth? Did you know I'd be locked up like that?"

"Of course," he says.

I cross my arms and frown.

"Oh come on. It wasn't that bad," he smiles. "I needed to know where you were at all times. You know how many people were down there George? When things went down, and I knew they would, I wanted to find you fast and give you the rose without raising suspicion."

I quirk my lips, "Well, okay. I guess."

"I've never heard of you," Asrieth cocks his head. "I know most of the Ferrets."

"I posed as a new Earthian to get into HSAER," he shrugs. "So you wouldn't have. That was the idea."

"How long have you been here?" I ask.

"A few decades at least," he answers.

So he was at least telling the truth about that.

"I have a mutation. It's not obvious," Jonah winks

Asrieth nods, "One of the lucky ones."

"Yeah," Jonah clasps my hand. "George, I really like you. Just so you know."

I blush, "Really?"

Jonah smiles, "Really. Well, I'd say to tell my family hi, but they're long gone. Do me a favor though, next time you come bring me confectionary."

I nod, "Confectionary. Sure thing." *What the hell is confectionary?*

"Until next time," he glances from Asrieth to me with a smile. Jonah turns and ascends the stairwell.

The little summoner bustles around with another robed figure who emerges from the stairs, talking in a language neither I nor the translator can pick up. She barks high-pitch orders and the hooded man replies.

Asrieth places his hands on my shoulders and turns me to face him.

His black eyes stare into mine. He doesn't mask his face with neutrality. For once he lets his emotions show, and it's sadness.

"Don't look at me like that," I say. "I don't want to remember you sad."

He sighs, "You don't have to go back."

I bite my lip. Tears well up in my eyes.

"Please," he gets to his knees, spreading out his wings so they don't drag the ground. His head level with my stomach.

"Please don't go," he says.

I put my hands over my mouth. I shake my head.

"I can't," I blubber. "I don't want to mutate." *I don't want to give up everything I have at home to mutate and you abandon me, Asrieth. I don't know what will happen and neither do you. I can't stay here and be alone. I have a chance alone at home, but not here.*

He takes my hands, careful of his claws, "Please don't go." Black liquid rims his eyes and spills down his cheeks.

I throw my arms around his neck, "Come with me."

He squeezes me.

"I can't. My magic will fade over time and I will look like this always."

"I don't care!"

"I don't care if you mutate!"

"You say that now," I can't speak coherently for my crying, "But it's too good to be true."

He sighs, "I can't convince you. Can I?"

I shake my head, turning into him, inhaling his musk. I haven't taken the time until now to feel him. To get a sense of him physically. I burn it into my memory.

He pulls away to look me in the eyes, "Then I will find a cure. I will find a way to stop your mutation."

"Can you?" I ask.

"They've researched for years now. Maybe they're close."

I nod, "Really? How long?"

"A few centuries, but we can work with that."

I wail, "That's not funny!"

Asrieth wipes my tears with his thumb. The claw scrapes the surface of my wet skin.

"I love you. Isn't it reason enough?"

It should be, but I'm stupid.

The summoner flicks the ingredients into the air and waves her hands around. A portal spills out into existence accompanied by her murmuring chant.

"We doing this or what?" she asks. "My Lady will be pissed if I wasted good coin."

I glare at her. Asrieth rises to his feet and holds my hands in his before sweeping down to lift me in his arms. I wrap my limbs around him. His hands support me as he draws in for a kiss. Asrieth's soft lips reflect the gentle soul I know resides within his hard shell, behind the mask of careful neutrality and repressing emotion.

I can't say how long we embrace and hold onto each other, but it's not long enough. It never will be. Forever isn't long enough.

But forever we don't have.

We don't have a day or hour, but a few minutes to say goodbye. I know he won't come with me. It's impossible for me to stay. I have things back at home to answer to. Responsibilities. Mutation looms over my head. I forget about the hundreds of times heroines in novels frustrated me when they decided to go home.

When you're the one adventuring and enduring the hardship of shock and pain it's a little different. I'm homesick. If this was an adventure with singing birds and dancing bunnies it might be different.

I slide down Asrieth to stand on my own feet.

The summoner stands near the portal, arms crossed and tapping her foot.

Asrieth leans down to kiss me again. And again. And again.

He presses his forehead to mine, "It's not forever. Just for a little while."

"Of course," I lie.

"It's more like see you later."

"Yes," I say.

He won't let me go until the last moment. It's heart wrenching, holding onto his hand, knowing I have to burn his image and touch into my mind. Millions of times I wished for the chance to say goodbye to Phillip, but knowing you'll never see someone again is as painful—if not more so. I don't know what to say and so I say nothing until I stand before my own rippling reflection.

Asrieth's grip on me tightens. I dip my fingers into

the mirror surface. I glance at his reflection and turn to him, keeping my fingertips in the portal. Its other-worldly pull tugs.

"This isn't a dream is it? I won't wake up in a hospital? You're real?" I ask.

Asrieth smiles, "I'm real you silly thing." He wipes his cheeks, smearing black on his pale skin.

"Nobody says silly anymore," I smirk, fresh tears pouring down my face.

He nods.

I can't look away. I step back, the cool liquid of the portal enveloping my wrist and forearm. The portal's pull increases and my feet slide along the rocky ground. Asrieth lets me go. The portal engulfs my arm and I continue reaching out to him. His own hand hovers out towards me. The cool liquid startles the warm skin of my back.

In the stairwell a flicker of movement catches my eye.

Lucifer leans against the frame of the carved out door, his legs and arms crossing. Next to him hovers the misty form of Gaap. The Devil blows me a kiss and I open my mouth to warn Asrieth a moment too late.

The portal sucks me inward. I'm on my way home.

In the darkness I brace for impact into water, pressing my legs together and crossing my arms over my chest. A move I learned from watching movies. My braid whips around seconds before I penetrate the cold surface of a playa lake. Kicking my booted feet for the surface I break into the air, gasping. I tread, disoriented, and search the surrounding area to get a grip on my location.

I know where I am. A new sensation for me. The water is freezing and a thin layer of frost covers the brown grass of Maxey Park. The familiar bright lights of the hospital nearby reflect on the calm water of the lake. I swim for the bank close to the community center and sit on the grey mud. I rest my forehead on my knees. My body shivers and goes into shock after leaving the warm humid environment of Werdofium for Lubbock's cold, dry air.

Why is it so cold? I wasn't gone that long. It should still be summer.

I shrug it off. West Texas isn't known for its weather consistency. Hugging my knees and resting my face against them, I sit still and cry. A frigid wind blows the wet cotton tunic against my skin, drying it before I can bring myself to stand up and face reality. Face home.

What have I done? I search the air above the lake. The portal is gone. There's no sign such a thing existed. The only tangible proof of my adventure are the clothes on my back and translators. Clothes that could have been bought at any store in the summer and a metal band and cuffs picked up at any alternative jewelry shop.

Careful to lift my legs so the suction of the mud doesn't pull my boots off, I trudge to the small drop-off a few feet above the bank of the lake. I climb up onto the frost covered grass and look around. It's dark. Given the gray hue along the eastern horizon I know it to be early morning.

It's just as well unsuspecting park goers don't witness me shooting out of thin air into the lake.

I turn in circles. My feet are unsure of where to go or what to do. I know I need to get to shelter before the affects of hypothermia begin.

I should have stayed with him. I should have been happy with cat ears or laser hands and stayed with the man I love. I'm lucky enough to love twice. And stupid enough to lose it twice.

I press my cold hands against my cheeks and get my bearings. I begin to walk home. Keeping to the sidewalks on empty neighborhood streets I wonder what I'll say.

Will I tell them the truth? Probably not. They'll think I'm crazy. But what can I tell them? I have to say something.

When I find myself on my home street I come to a decision; fake amnesia. I study my modest rental house. Lights are on, blue cotton curtains in the picture window filter them. A different car than mine sits in the driveway. I approach the mailbox and find a name not mine printed on the side with the address. The little red flag is up. I smile.

It makes sense. If I've been gone long enough, Mrs. Morgan would rent out to someone else. She needs the extra income.

I chafe my arms. My eyes drag to Mrs. Morgan's ceramic mushrooms scattered in her front yard. They pop up out of the mulch and grass in the dim light of the streetlamp. I shuffle down her walk.

Should I knock? I have no phone, it's not like I can call ahead. I don't have any money either. What should I do?

I ring the doorbell.

Minutes pass. The house stirs in the dark. I dance as the cold seeps further into my core. Continuing to rub my hands up and down my arms I ring the doorbell again, many times in a row.

I should have stayed.

"Who is it?" I recognize Mrs. Morgan's quiet voice.

I don't doubt her loaded double barrel shotgun presses against the door. The porch light flashes on and I close my eyes against the sudden brightness.

"Mrs. Morgan?" my lips shiver. "It's me."

The muffled answer is inaudible. I remove my translators.

"Mrs. Morgan?" I repeat. "It's me."

"Who?" The locks of the door click out of place and she opens it. She tightens her blue fluffy robe around her small frame. Her teenage daughter holds the gun behind her.

They stare at me with wide eyes, like I'm a ghost. I look the part in thin white clothes, shivering, and pale as the moon. Recognition crosses their faces and Mrs. Morgan smiles. She pulls me into a tight hug.

"We thought you dead," she whispers against my hair as I embrace her.

I huddle against her, enjoying the gush of warmth from her house. Her daughter sets down the gun against the wall and throws her arms around us. We stand in the doorway. The three of us cry.

Relief.

All the time in Werdofium I pitied myself thinking no one cared. *She does. She tried to save me from the portal. I let myself forget what she tried to do for me. What they both tried to do. I can tell them the truth. They saw it.*

"Persephone, what happened?" she asks.

I smile hearing my real name.

Epilogue: Dun Dun DUNNNNNN!

It's October 26th, 2008.

I disappeared from Earth on June 11th, 2008. I returned October 16th' 2008.

One week, two days, and nineteen hours since I left Asrieth.

The hubbub of my return passed. I lay awake in the soft comfort of the twin bed in my brother's guest room. Weak moonlight shines through the thin layer of frost around the edges of the window. I draw the cover up to my cold nose and study the neutral pictures of wildlife scenery on powder blue walls. I still can't sleep and shift further beneath the heavy blankets to turn on my side and form a cocoon of warmth to battle the winter air.

After the news, family, friends, and people I didn't even know I knew, visited and well-wished me to death, I can relax. I have peace. I'm alone with my thoughts.

Finally.

I followed through with my decision to fake amnesia. In the comfort of her warm living room drinking hot cocoa, Mrs. Morgan and I devised that was the best plan. Originally she told the police she found the house destroyed and back gate open. I was simply missing. She feared if she told the truth she would be labeled unstable and her daughter taken away from her. I more than understand. *And I'm fine anyway.*

The doctors suspect I'm faking it, but they can't prove anything. I overheard them in a conversation with my brother over the phone. They believe I'm lying about the amnesia because I don't want to relive the horrors I endured or to identify my kidnapper, torturer, whoever, for fear of repercussion. They told him it's best to leave me alone until I come forward with what happened.

Come forward my ass. Only if I want to spend my life in a cell with padded walls. I don't want to hear them tell me Asrieth isn't real. Werdofium isn't real. It's a strange unfortunate place I fabricated to deal with the harshness of my reality. Although I might believe it myself if not for Mrs. Morgan and her daughter. They saw Rinkai and Asrieth both. They saw the portal. They know. And with them I know I'm not crazy.

I roll over and guilt wrenches my stomach. Phillip's parents reacted badly to my disappearance. Their outrage and anger towards the police surprises me. They brought into question whether or not Phillip's killer knew him personally. They think this attack on me is proof. It's too much of a coincidence for them. I keep my mouth shut and insist I can't remember anything. They look at the case with scrutiny. They bombard me with more questions. It's easier to say, "I don't remember."

Being home I struggle to hold onto the crisp memory of Werdofium. Reality two weeks ago is another fantasy mulling around in my brain. Despite this fuzzy memory, my feelings for Asrieth increase. I'm glad to have the internet back, glad for normal plumbing, and pizza. I packed my nightstand drawer with chapstick. My brother and Rachael give me coke anytime I ask for it.

But I miss him.

I'm alone despite the hoard of friends and relatives surrounding me. The same people I longed for years before. The people who didn't realize Asrieth stayed with me for weeks because we never talked. Every time I think of him I can only smile as regret yanks on my insides for leaving him behind.

I keep watching the news for any signs of the thousands of soldiers abandoned in the Sahara, but they say nothing. I can't help but to wonder if it was a cover up or if they all perished beneath the sifting sands of the desert.

Scratching at the edge of the window snaps my thoughts back to the present. I rub my eyes and sit up. A branch of the old pear tree in my brother's backyard waves around in the winter wind. I yawn and flip the covers. I swing my feet around and curl my toes when they contact the cold laminate flooring. I pull on fuzzy pajama pants, curtesy of Rachael, and stumble to the dresser filled with my few belongings. My last clothes from Werdofium and translator gear. The clothes had a distinct aroma of spices for the first few days. I still smell them every day.

Most of my things left behind in the rental were put into storage, but as a part of her grieving process Rachael kept a few of my trinkets in the house. She's ecstatic to return them to me.

I kneel and reach for the bottom drawer. Phillip's drawer. Tears well my eyes. *I don't have a drawer for Asrieth. I have nothing of his.* I swallow and open it. I dig past the clippings and clothes to the velvet box beneath.

I pull it out. I open the lid and the small diamond gleams in the light from the window. I shut the box and get to my feet. The pear tree scratches against the glass. I don't bother with a robe and navigate the house to the backdoor.

I'm silent as I open and close the door behind me. I walk to the back of the yard and kneel at the roots of an old oak. The wind bites through the thin cotton of my t-shirt. It blows my hair around and I tie it back with a rubber band I wear on my wrist always. I claw at the soft earth beneath the cover of the oak until I cup out a hole. I breathe in. Then out.

I place the velvet box into the hole and cover it with my hands. I cup them over the mound.

Goodbye, Phillip. I glance to the waning moon hanging in the night sky. *Hello, Asrieth.*

I stand and return to the warmth of the house. I wipe loose leaves and dirt from the bottom of my pajama pants and shut the door. I catch a splinter in the hallway and hover near the nightlight to dig it out. In the faint warm glow my brother's snore drifts into the hall. I rub my eyes and study the floor. Six lines mar the polished surface, scratched down to the foam layer beneath. I follow it to my room. The door shuts by an unseen force. My heart thuds in my ears.

I turn the handle, cold in my grasp, and the door swings open into the dark room. I fumble for the light switch. The blinding light reveals the trail leading to the now open window. I search the room and dive down to search beneath the bed. Nothing. In the closet. Nothing. Under the covers. Nothing.

I dart to the window. The pear tree branches wave around, but not close enough to reach the pane of glass. I panic. The wind blows inward. Arctic tendrils weave around me.

"As of someone gently rapping, rapping at my chamber door," a distant murmur calls through the window.

I shut it and turn the lock. I pant. Sweat runs down my cold skin.

Now I know.

It's not over.

ABOUT THE AUTHOR

Anne Coffer lives in West Texas where nothing grows but the imagination. Born in the 80s, and growing up in a small town in New Mexico, only the local library offered escape from the confines of reality and school.

Anne's fascination with science fiction and fantasy were inherited from her father, who sat down with Anne as a child weekly to catch the newest episodes of *Star Trek: The Next Generation* and *Xena: Warrior Princess*. A slew of other fantasy books and films would feed the inner muse monster that would eventually push Anne to write her first full-length novel at age 11 (after many, many unfinished attempts). It was about a girl exactly her age (and suspiciously looked exactly like her) going on whirlwind adventures.

She won her first writing contest in 7th grade, and has felt empowered to force her stories on people ever since.

She's sorry.

Anne Coffer

More From LeeLoo Publishing!
http://leeloopub.com/

Crowbar by Anne Coffer

Terrified, alone in the dark and caged like
an animal, she waits to die.
Not suitable for children.

Anne Coffer

Brick Wilson: Clueless by Marq Truong

Brick Wilson's adventure takes the reader crashing through universes, galaxies, circuits and alternate realities where anything can and does happen. On his search for the lost (or was it stolen?) Pesnort, Brick is continually challenged by dangers real and imagined as he skillfully avoids the Ultimate Galactic Headquarters Tax Authority, dodges the increasingly menacing plots for his demise by arch nemesis Terd Murchison, and is continually stalked and mocked by the color Red. Can he save the Pesnort, the Universe and himself with a psychotic android in tow?

Anne Coffer

Dragon Bloode: Covet by Mishka Williams

Dragons.

Once a mighty race of winged gods, they're reduced to three. No longer do they resemble the scaled flying marvels of their ancestry, but the humans who interbred with their forefathers.
The Bloode is thin and dying.

Mishka Williams's dark fantasy debut is nothing short of spellbinding. Dive into a realm rich with magic, Dragons, and lust. Set against a gothic backdrop in the world of Alperin, Williams takes you to the Draak Empire. Rife with division between the Emperor and his Dragon generals, the empire faces enemies on all fronts. From the Fae, the Elves, and from within.